SID
and
TEDDY

H.D. KNIGHTLEY

Over Our Heads Publishing

Other titles by H.D. Knightley

Bright: Book One of The Estelle Series
Beyond: Book Two of The Estelle Series
Belief: Book Three of The Estelle Series
Fly: The Light Princess Retold

Hdknightley.com

To the Moms, for sharing your dreams, hopes, and wishes
with me.
(You know who you are.)

PART ONE

ONE

SID

My chair was freaking cold and hard. How long had I been sitting here, staring at this bed, the machines, the steel table with two cards, a bouquet of flowers, and that sink — oh yeah and my mom. I tried not to look at her too often though because of what might happen. Collapse. But not in the good Lack-of-Feeling way. When I looked at her face, quiet, sleeping, unconscious, blood rushed to my head and the surge of pain that came with it was so awful, so frightening, I wanted to fall down and cower. To buckle under. Oh, and my ears hurt. Really badly.

I pulled a bottle of aspirin out of my bag's side pocket and took out two and swallowed them down. I shoved the bottle in my bag.

I was clutching my phone in my hand, had been for hours. I opened messenger and read Teddy's latest texts again:

What's happening Sid?
Do you know anything?
Call me

Did I know anything? Dad and I had been waiting for the doctor for hours. I knew nothing except the diagnosis: liver failure. When I Googled it, there was a chance of recovery. Also, a chance of non-recovery. Google was pretty vague with their predictions.

I kind of figured a lot of survival depended on mom wanting to survive, and that didn't seem —

I wrote a text:

> I don't know anything yet.
> Can you come?
> Please?
> I really
>
> . . .

He couldn't come. He wasn't family. He could only come during visiting hours and what time was it even? I deleted the text.

I wrote another:

> Can you come?
> To the waiting room?
> I need to talk to
>
> . . .

I deleted that one too.

I couldn't leave. Even if he came, even if he stood in the waiting room and held me while I cried, I couldn't leave long enough for that. Could I ask Teddy to drive to the hospital to hug me for two minutes? I couldn't. And my ears hurt. Trying to figure this out sucked.

I wrote:

> I need you.

And then I deleted it, pulled my chair to the foot of my mother's hospital bed and put my head down right beside the lump that was her feet and cried.

TWO

SID

Sid. That's what she named me, thinking it was cool to give me a boy's name (the runner-up was George) and I'm pretty sure the Sex Pistols were part of her reason. My mom was a lot punk rock. And she loved anything British. But not Australian, she took offense when people assumed I had been named after their city. She would say, "Not a shortened Sydney with a y, Sid with an i." Come to find out my name was French, anyway. But whatever. My mom's gone. I can't ask her what in the world she was thinking.

My mother died hard.

Really hard. The way most women die, laid low by the Ache of Tears Behind the Eyes. Not physical pain, but that emotional crap. The tears you stuff down, the fear, the anguish, the loss, the meanness of the world.

All that pressure and pain you stuff into that spot right behind the eyes, the place of suppression and oppression, the emotional dam. That hidden place that feels tight and heavy and threatens to burden you to the ground. That heavy place.

All women have it and if you don't care for the spot with tenderness and consideration that dam will break and once it does — oh man, you'll feel it — the Ache.

That burden, that heaviness, those stuffed feelings, that spot behind the eyes, it's all menacing is what it is. The Ache grows with stealth, patience, and a particular brutality, the kind that takes your breath, then your strength, then your life. With a crush. And a crash.

That's how my mother died. She was a spectacular, singular, independent and innovative force, and she died a very sad woman. Soul crushed. It would be heartbreaking if it wasn't so common, so expected. So damned woman-like.

And broken hearts are exactly the point, don't feel it dear friends, gulp it down, laugh it off, ignore it, lest the Ache comes.

But then and also, I hate to say it, but I must. You can't hide from it. So there. The sadness first then the Ache will come and after, everyone who ever loved you will have the tears to prove it.

And so it goes. The Ache runs in families. Because: love.

THREE

SID

Teddy was on his way to pick me up to go surfing. We had been living three miles from each other for years and years and three miles is close in Los Angeles, practically next door. To live that close to your best friend in LA was a miracle and Teddy had been my best friend since we were two. Earlier if babies in the same Mommy and Me playgroup can be friends. Teddy's mom liked to tell a story about how one day, I was screaming my head off in the back seat, in my turned around car seat, a literal baby, and Teddy, whose car seat had turned to the front already, put his hand out and held mine. While I cried. Apparently we had chubby little fingers and it was so cute that both our moms will never forget how cute it was.

It means something, how cute it was. Or so our moms said. All the time.

Our mothers were close, and Teddy and I had always been together. All the time.

Our interest in being friends hit a low point though, when he was seven years old. He learned to despise me because Lou Daniels predicted we would be married someday and Letitia Sanders sang a song about how much we loved each other. Teddy hated to have his romantic interest predicted and definitely not five years before puberty. He scowled. Sometimes he screamed. Once he cried. Then he got smart and played exclusively with the boys, shunning me, sometimes with name-calling.

My mom would ask, "Does it bother you?" No, it didn't. His interests in those days included Nerf guns, Lego, and Super Smash Brothers on his PlayStation, and don't get me wrong, those things were cool, but he had a serious obsession with them, culminating in costume wearing — All. The. Time. We barely tolerated being in the same room together

That period must have been a tough time for our moms. Teddy and I were homeschooled so getting us together was a priority. For socialization's sake, but mostly because the Moms wanted to socialize too.

So when we were nine years old, the Moms created a twice-a-week Project Club, gathering all the crafting supplies, wacky recipes, and games they found or invented and forcing us to comply. Urging us to enjoy. And soon we became friends again.

By the age of ten we were inseparable.

By twelve he was like my brother.

Around that time I became fascinated, kind of obsessed with Mary, Queen of Scots, and you know what Teddy did? He listened. He asked questions. Maybe he pretended, but he was interested enough.

Because we were so close I needed to show an interest in something he liked, and Teddy loved surfing. So I learned how to join him in the lineup. After that our moms met twice a week at the beach break near Teddy's house, El Porto. A lovely beach, with a consistent surf break and easy parking (sometimes), Southern California style, in the shadow of industrial towers and oil tanks.

Between the beach days and Projects Club we spent most of every week together. And any other chance we got.

No one joked us about dating or love or marriage anymore. It was clear to anyone who met us we were that better thing, best friends. We joked and laughed and teased and behaved in a way so familiar and comfortable that love was out of the question. It's hard to love someone you grew up with. Complicated.

So that's why, when I turned thirteen, I let Jason hold my hand. And when I turned fifteen, I let Marcus, in all his sweaty-palmed, nervous glory go to third base. And when I turned seventeen, I let Cameron go all the way. Because he was hot and made my heart go pitter-patter when he looked at me, and Mom and Dad let him sleep over. So we did stuff, lots of stuff, under the covers, fumbling and awkward, but it was fun.

Teddy had girlfriends too, some were mutual friends, others were Strange Girls that appeared and glommed on, like his scent said: available. He was handsome, in that athletic surfer way, wide shoulders, lean, tan, dark brown hair that was curly enough to tousle. His girlfriends probably ran their fingers through his hair, but I tried not to think about that, because they were ridiculous, too in love to get that this was My Teddy. The guy who had always been my best friend. Not their boyfriend only. Mine, mostly.

Teddy once asked, "Is it okay if I bring Sarah along surfing on Tuesday?"

And I screwed up my face. "Does she even like surfing?"

"She likes to boogie board, so it's kind of the same thing." Which was not true and the fact that he said it made me roll my eyes, because if he was willing to say that, to conflate boogie boarding with surfing, then he was in deep, and sorry, but no. He said, "Come on, you'll like her once you get to know her."

And so I tried. But here's the thing about me and Teddy, we would paddle out together into the lineup and giggle and talk and float and surf and dream, and there was no way someone boogie boarding in the beach break could compete.

My Marcus, or My Cameron never even came to the beach. They saw my friendship with Teddy and faded away without attempting to surf, without letting me push them into the waves. Their inability to compete with Teddy's ease on a board kept them from even trying.

Not that it was a competition. It was simply complicated and if our boyfriends and girlfriends couldn't wrap their minds around the spiral that was me and Teddy, our wrapped lives and conjoined orbit, they spun out and away. Leaving me and Teddy to our trajectory, and that's how our story begins.

FOUR

MARY, QUEEN OF SCOTS

So imagine this. You're a young girl in Scotland, not just any girl, a princess. Your father goes away to war and never returns. This changes your fortune drastically. You had castles and security and food and now your mother is worried, terrified, but also calculating and political. You are a queen. She bundles you away to live with southern relatives you've never met. They are richer. Their palaces are sprawling extravagant examples of their power. They plan to create in you the perfect match for their son. You are five years old and your whole life is decided.

You travel south by ship. Because, and you're still imagining, there are no cars or trains or definitely not phones. You'll write home, once you've learned to write. The letters of love and news will take weeks, or months even, then they'll be translated, because you're being educated in another language.

The people who accompany you are strangers and you arrive in a place that is foreign. To live forever. Imagine how scared you would be to live in a new home, among new people, in a new world? Stripped of everything and then new things piled on top. Would that pile crush you? Possibly.

Unless you learn to climb and grasp and balance. To make do. To adapt.

You remind yourself every day that the weather in France is nicer.

FIVE

TEDDY

Today was the day with Sid. I knew it. She knew it.

I rolled up in my car in front of her house and she bounded out, because that's how she moved, with leaps and bounces, leggy and wild. She shoved a cooler into the trunk and flipped her hair over her shoulder and let me rescue the board under her arm. I put it on the racks and strapped the front while she strapped down the back.

When she dropped into the passenger seat, she sprawled, every limb at an angle, her knee on the center console, a foot on the door. Then she sat up straight, excited, and drummed on the glove compartment, and as I started the car, proclaimed, "Mali-BU here we come!"

I said, "Headed to the Bu!"

She slumped in her seat, strapped her belt, and in one brisk movement wrapped her hair up in a bun. She shifted to face me, a long pale, sun-kissed lock swinging loose by her cheek, and counted on her fingers. "I brought tons of sandwiches: snack sandwiches, they have a smear of mustard and ham; lunch sandwiches, smear of mayo, mustard, cheese, ham, lettuce, and avocado; afternoon snacks; and dinner sandwiches. Those are roast beef." She grinned.

I was past knowing anything she said, because of the way the curve of her neck met her shoulder, and I only got glimpses from the corner of my eye over my driving arm. She might have said, "Liver and onions," and I would have answered the same, "Sounds delicious."

I rolled the car onto the highway. Sid fished a book out of her beach bag, pulled her bare feet up to the seat, and leaned on the door, the book open in front of her face.

From the corner of my eye I read the title, Bittersweet Within my Heart. "Let me guess, the poetry of the Queen of Scots?"

She said from behind the book, "I thought I'd read all the poems to you while you drive." Then she dropped the book to her lap with a grin. "I'm kidding." She giggled. "I've been planning that joke all morning."

I said, "Besides, you read the entire book out loud when we were twelve."

"Yep, I see you pay attention. Seriously though, I might be obsessed, but even I get she was more a personality than a poet. Now Willy, he's a poet." She pulled a thin copy of Macbeth out of her bag and held that up over her face.

I asked, "How far have you read?"

"Two pages. You?"

"Three pages, after lunch I'll read it to you while you nap, and then you can read it to me while I nap." I glanced at her, and for a tiny unsatisfying moment, our eyes locked.

She said, "Perfect."

This was how our plans had been made; how we both knew we had made plans: we had finished our morning surf, last Friday, wet, sand-covered, breeze-cooled, wrapped in towels, shoulder to shoulder, looking out at the waves, and I had asked, "What if we went to Malibu on Tuesday, just me and you, there's a good swell coming."

She smiled and looked at me from the corner of her eye, lashes catching the sun and shimmering there, and said, "I'd like that, what if we spent the day, um, just me and you."

I nodded. One of the locals caught a wave, my eyes followed him as he dropped in, sped down the line, and kicked out over the back. I turned to her. "All day — I'll bring my pop up tent."

She looked into my eyes. "I'll bring food for the day. Sandwiches okay?"

We were discussing our simple Surfing All Day plans but also talking about moving to the next level. Suddenly, after all these years of friendship, we were going to change everything about Sid and me.

Plus we needed to finish reading Macbeth by Wednesday. We had a deadline. So that was part of it.

Sid punched the buttons on my radio and found Oasis's Wonderwall, and we both sang along. It predated us, but it was her mother's favorite song, band, sound, and so it was familiar, much like each other. Me driving, Sid playing air-guitar. Like the olden days, listening, riding home in our car seats from those Mommy and Me playgroups, holding hands, Wonderwall streaming loud through the speakers. Sid's mom, Alicia, and my mom, Lori, singing at the top of their voices. Like that, familiar and also historic, like this now.

SIX

SID

The thing about surfing with Teddy was this — he's epic. He started surfing with his dad once he learned to swim, and seriously surfing, just after his Nerf Gun (I Despise Sid) phase. His dad surfed all the time, so Teddy had lots of practice. Like it was in his blood. Genetic.

Once I took surf lessons and got competent, our moms would sit in the sand and discuss Mom Things while Teddy and I surfed. And I got better and better, but still Teddy was always leagues above. He could have been on surf teams, surfed competitively, but he said once, while we floated on our boards, "It's not about that. It's about me and my dad and my board and the ocean. The other stuff just gets in the way."

I wasn't other stuff. I was flattered that he wanted me along.

SEVEN

TEDDY

Sid was fantastic at surfing. A strong paddler, fast down the line, beautiful turns, and she was learning aerials. Her only drawback was over-exuberance. I told her to sit, watch, count the waves, wait for the right one, be patient, and she would nod, say, "Absolutely Teddy," in total agreement, and paddle like crazy for the very next wave even though anyone watching could see it was a big crumbly mess. She'd tumble over the falls, head and feet flying, come up with a splash and a giant smile, and paddle, laughing, right back out to where I was sitting. She was almost always laughing.

We parked; loaded up our bags and cooler and books, boards under our arms; threaded through the surfers and cars; and hiked down the beach toward the point. Sid dropped her bags and screwed up her nose, facing the stagnant stretch of lagoon. "Explain this? How can a place so beautiful, so epically fun, have such a mucky cesspool butting up to it?"

"Don't know, I hear they're cleaning it." I dropped the tent to the sand, but Sid was still staring at the lagoon. "The bad helps us keep the good in perspective, maybe? Dad says never to look that way, keep your eyes on the waves."

She nodded and we set up my tent, loading our towels and cooler inside. This was a big production and we hadn't even paddled out yet. So we did. The conditions were good, the waves were good, and it was a weekday, the surf wasn't too crowded.

I looked out at the horizon, and she stared at the side of my face.

I pretended not to notice, but she did it deliberately, more intensely.

Without turning my head, I asked, "Yes?" Then added, "You'd be better if you'd watch the waves."

"Oh I would, would I?" She plowed her arm into the water, and with a forceful splash all over my face, turned and paddled for a wave. She rode down the line, the top of her head disappearing as the lip curled, spray emanating from the arc of her turns. I watched the area where her ride would end. She kicked out of the wave and flopped to her board, beautiful, smiling, awesome. I cheered as she paddled back to me.

"Did you see Teddy? Wave of the day!"

I did see. I really did.

EIGHT

SID

I returned to the beach first, exhausted, because of all those waves I kept taking, most of them not worth the effort, but don't tell Teddy I said that.

He stayed out for another hour. I loved watching him, scanning the horizon in stillness, then spinning his board, movement and energy, to drop down the face, carve along the top, catching air; finally, he paddled ashore. Then he did what he always does, walked backwards from the ocean. It was as if he couldn't drag his eyes away, only glancing toward me to correct his path, lingering on the waves; three more steps, then a surfer did a big air and Teddy whistled, took two more backwards steps, and stopped. His eyes swept the landscape, and then, at last, he turned and walked to me.

"Hi Sid." He gently placed his board on mine.

I squinted up at him as his shadow fell across me. He smiled, brightness haloing his head, leaned over and flung his hair, sprinkling me with saltwater.

"Hey, I'm dry!"

"Exactly! You came in too early, missed all the best waves. If you would just let the bad ones pass, wait for the great ones, you could stay out longer." He smiled because of course I knew that, he always said it, and yet I still took every wave that came. Just my way I supposed.

"You and all your crazy ideas. Patience? I'm a woman of action, reaction."

He dropped beside me on the towel, "Speaking of action, I'm hungry, can you hand me a sandwich, I'm wet."

I pulled the cooler over and rustled inside, pulling out the first layer of sandwiches, and passing him one.

He tore off the wrap and flipped up the edge of the bread to inspect the inside and took a big bite. Chewing, he said, "Epic day, huh? What were you thinking about up here on the beach?"

"I was thinking, why don't we come here more often?"

"Yeah, me too, but I don't believe you." He swallowed. "I think you were thinking, I wonder if Mary Queen of Scots would have liked surfing?"

I laughed, "It crossed my mind, but I already worked that issue out, like three years ago. The answer is, no. She would have hated it. She only went on the ocean when she was being transported from home to a place she barely knew."

He took another bite of sandwich and stared out at the horizon while he ate, then he said, "Have you got your passport Sid?"

"Not yet, you have one?"

"My mom got me one last year, when she and Dad started planning our trip to Indo next Spring. You should get one. We should go to Scotland."

He fiddled with his sandwich, eyes cast down. We had talked about going to Scotland together, but in a Friends-Want-to-go-Explore-Castles kind of way, not this, this seemed big, important, today, on this day, Teddy said he wanted to go with me to Scotland. Me and Teddy. He leaned on his shoulder, looking up at me from under his brow. His eyes squinted and intense.

I said, "I'll ask Mom to get one tomorrow."

NINE

MARY

(Explained to Teddy, when he and Sid were 12)

Sid was sitting on a swing at their favorite park, dangling and spinning, feet twisting in the sand. "Teddy, did you know Mary was a teenager in France?"

Teddy was sitting sideways on the other swing, swaying side to side. "I didn't realize that."

"She was, she played music, wrote poetry, danced and had a bunch of friends. Imagine that — she was a baby in Scotland and then was shipped off to France. The weather was probably so much better. She lived in a palace surrounded by exquisite gardens, fancy dresses, riches."

"That was probably cool."

"She was promised to the Dauphin of France, that's a prince, at five years old, Teddy, can you believe it? Marriage plans — at five. He was a year younger, and then she married him and at sixteen, she was the Queen Consort of France and the Queen of Scots."

"That's a lot of power."

"And contrast that with before, contrast it with what comes next."

"What does come next — it must have sucked, because she isn't known as the Queen of France or anything."

"Because all that ended a year later, Teddy, one year. The prince died of an ear infection. I'm serious, an ear infection."

"That's totally tragic."

Sid looked at Teddy for a long pause and then said, "Thank you."

Teddy asked, "For what?"

"For getting the tragedy of it all."

TEN

TEDDY

Why today? Why now, why not five years ago, why not three years from now, next week? How come we both decided to spend this day, full of locking eyes and long pauses, together. I didn't know, I couldn't explain it, but we were leading up to something big.

That's what kept running through my mind, but now, after we finished our sandwiches, lying half in and out of my pop-up tent, I thought, why here, in a tent in Malibu, why not at home? If I had ever said, "Hey Sid, let me spend the night." All of our parents would have swooned with delight.

The Moms would have rejoiced, "We get all of our Thanksgivings together!"

My parents would probably give Sid a key to the house and book every Christmas with her, mark it on the calendar, with ink. This was a lot of pressure. Maybe that's why we were here, now. Spontaneous. (Can a lifetime relationship be spontaneous?)

Sid gathered up our trash and deposited it in the cooler and then fluffed up the sand into a pile to lean against. She was half under the tent's shadow, her legs jutting out into the sun. "Naptime!"

I pretended to be incredulous, "Naptime? We have the entire Scottish Play to get through!" She groaned.

"Now now, the Moms said we have to read the play before we go see it, and I'll remind you, the Griffith Park Shakespeare Festival starts tomorrow."

"Didn't they graduate us already? You're going to college, you've been accepted, I didn't think we'd have to do anything educational. Ever again." Sid grinned. Then she added, "And aren't Willy's plays supposed to be seen? Why do we have to read it first? But man, I love opening night."

"Never missed one yet. I argued all of this with Mom, and she said, and I quote, 'Teddy, when you were homeschooling high school,' she put air quotes around high school, 'you surfed every day, all day, and hung out with your friends, and I literally,' she stressed literally, 'am asking you to do one thing that acts educational. Read Macbeth, then go see the play. We'll call that the English class that I already gave you a grade for.'"

Sid cocked her arm under her head. "So this is going down on your permanent record?"

"And yours, the Moms have spoken. Or if they haven't spoken, they've mind-melded over it."

Sid asked, "So you're reading to me?"

"I'll start, sure." I fished the book from the bag and plowed sand to make a berm to lean against, but Sid patted her stomach, inviting me to use her as a pillow. So I did.

Saying it like that belies the moment though, makes it sound casual and easy, comfortable. Getting my head down to Sid's belly and relaxing enough to bring the book up to my eyes and calming enough to read the words on the page was fraught with difficulties. Somehow though I read aloud, head nestled on her soft skin, and maybe I could continue, but then she entwined her fingers through my hair. Twirling. I tried to concentrate. I read to the bottom of the page and halfway down the next before I dropped my arm holding the book to the sand.

She continued to twirl, indifferent to my reading or not.

I turned my head, rested my ear on her belly, then I turned over and kissed her stomach, under the bellybutton, in the soft skin just above her bright pink, bikini bottom.

There.

I kissed it again.

I have to admit this was a baller move: to go straight from Shakespeare's Macbeth, page four, to kissing her between the bellybutton and the panties, and whoa, here's me and Sid, can't do things the same as everyone else.

I fell in love with her when I still wore a cape safety-pinned to my shoulders, in public. Had been best friends with her for all these years, and our first kiss? It was on her stomach. First kiss.

I put my ear back to her stomach and looked up at her face again; her eyes were closed. Her lips curled up in a half-smile. An unmistakable bedroom smile, the kind of smile that happens in the dark, eyes closed, not to be shared, just because what you're feeling makes you happy — that kind of smile. Sid was Bedroom Smiling for me.

I rose onto my hands and knees and crawled up her body, aiming for her lips — her bag emitted Jack Johnson, crooning Banana Pancakes. Sid giggled. "Perfect timing for a phone call."

I dropped to the side and laughed too.

She said, "Wait, that's Dad, why would Dad be calling?"

She sat up, rifled through her bag, and fished out the phone. "Hi?" Then "Umhmm," and "oh," and, "uh yes, okay, um," She looked away from me, at a seashell near her foot, madly twirling the end of a strand of hair. "Yeah, about an hour, I'll call when I'm close. Okay, room 148. Okay Dad. She's okay, right? Um hmmm. Okay."

She hung up the phone and covered her face with her hands.

"Sid, is everything okay?"

"Mom's in the hospital. It sounds bad." She ran her hands up her face and through her hair and looked around at the stuff, the tent, our boards. "I have to go." Her voice sounded like an explanation, but I was already packing our bags.

ELEVEN

SID

Mothers aren't supposed to fall down. We all know that. So when they do — causing the gasp to run the opposite way — when it's the children with panic in their hearts, asking, "Mommy, are you okay?" It's a tragedy. If every moment of mother panic causes another grey hair, what does panic in children cause? Shortness of breath? Despair? Lack of ease — it might not show on the outside, but inside you've gained a bit of something bad, dislodged something important, like your center's gone askew.

And that's when Mom falls down.

What happens when Mom falls down dead? What if she acquires a Falling Down Dead Disease, or a Can't Stand Up Anymore Syndrome? Something that knocks the knees out from under her and causes her children not just to gasp but to stumble over themselves trying to pick her back up. And what if mom can't be picked back up? What then?

TWELVE

SID

Mom was asleep on the bed. Mouth open, small snores, pale thin skin, dark circles under her eyes. Her hair was stringy. I tried to remember what she looked like last time I saw her. It wasn't this morning, she had slept in while I packed sandwiches. Had I seen her last night? I passed her in the kitchen to eat dinner in my room. When was the last time I sat and talked to her, looked her in the eyes, three days ago? Jeez. That sucked.

There were two chairs in the room beside Mom's hospital bed. Dad sat in one, staring at the side of Mom's face, "We're waiting for the Doctor to come during his rounds."

I slumped in a chair beside him. "What did he say when you saw him this morning?"

"It's liver failure and that's a lot to deal with. But luckily she'll just be here for a few days."

It took two more hours before mom woke up and looked around, surprised to be in the room. Her eyes fell on me. "Oh, Sid, when did you come in? I wish you would have woken me." She acted as if she'd just taken a small nap on the comfortable blue couch in our living room, instead of sleeping for hours in a hospital bed.

I said, "Just a little bit ago."

She gestured for me to come to the bed, so I perched on the side. Her hand had wires and tubes sticking out and looked veiny and dry and fragile. She placed it on my knee, so light, like it might float away. "How was the beach?"

"Good, or I mean, great, Teddy kissed me."

She said, "Well, it's about time."

I giggled, "Actually it wasn't an official kiss, it was right here," I pointed where Teddy's lips had been just hours before, "and then we were interrupted."

Mom said, "Well shit, I always did have terrible timing. Sorry about that. Is he here?"

"I don't — probably, outside somewhere, he can't come in because he's not family."

The Doctor walked in.

He told us he "didn't know anything," that we were, "waiting to see," that we, "would know more tomorrow," that they were, "doing all they could." And then he was gone, and Mom drifted away to sleep.

THIRTEEN

MARY (SID, A YEAR EARLIER)

Teddy (After walking backwards up the beach and splashing Sid with a flick of his hair): What ya reading?

Sid: I'm rereading this book about Mary's time in France and wondering if she loved the Dauphin. Sometimes I think no, sometimes yes. I'm pondering it.

Teddy (after dropping to the towel): She lived with him for how long?

Sid: About eleven years.

Teddy: He was friend-zoned then, too much like a sibling. Poor Dauphin.

Sid: Poor Dauphin is right, he was short and she was like, five foot eleven.

Teddy: I change my answer. He loved her for sure. He probably climbed her like a flagpole and she carried him around in her pocket.

(Once their laughter died down) Teddy: Have you asked Cameron what he thinks?

Sid: Kind of, Cameron's eyes glaze over, and he 'ums' a lot whenever I bring Mary Stuart up.

Teddy: Ah, of course.

(After a pause) Teddy: I think the Dauphin loved Mary desperately. She was the older woman, and he had loved her since forever. But she thought of him as a pawn in her political theater.

Sid: You think she was that calculating and cruel?

Teddy: No, more like just indifferent.

FOURTEEN
TEDDY

I waited for hours. Other people came and went. Sometimes the waiting room was crowded, a few times I was by myself, sitting, staring at my hands. My phone died and I wanted to go charge it inside my car. I also needed to go to the bathroom, but I didn't want to leave the waiting room in case I missed her. Finally a voice came over the loudspeaker, "Visiting hours are over, clear the waiting room." I kept my seat, determined not to go. They, someone, the hospital strongmen, would have to kick me out.

At last Sid pushed through the doors.

"Is everything okay?"

"No, not really, but they'll know more tomorrow."

"Aw, Sid." I wrapped her up in my arms and we hugged for a long time, her face buried in my shoulder.

The loudspeaker reminded me, "All visitors must clear the public areas."

I asked, "Do you need a ride home?"

"I think I better ride home with Dad." She pulled away and lifted her bag to her shoulder and said, distracted, "Yeah. Okay."

"I'll come tomorrow?"

She ran her hands down her face then up and her fingers through her hair. "No, um, no, I need to . . . I'll call tomorrow when I know anything."

I walked out of the hospital to my car, surfboards on the roof. Wet towels on the seats.

The next day she didn't call.

FIFTEEN

SID

The thing about mothers is this — they have plenty of hands. I think it's a forgotten or unnoticed part of pregnancy, the growing of extra appendages. Like multi-armed goddesses, mothers need that many arms to keep the children from running into the street. Mothers evolved.

But those of us who aren't mothers yet, we simply have two. Two arms, two hands.

And when your mom is pulling away, you need both those hands to grasp, to hold on. Because mothers are pulling away with eight arms, full strength.

You need your hands for that.

And you don't have them for anything else.

You have to drop everything.

And no one can blame you because you're literally doing the best you can, a mere non-mom mortal with not enough arms.

SIXTEEN

HOSPITAL DIARY

Day two: Today sucked. When Dad and I got to the hospital, the Doctor had already done his rounds for the day. Oh well, maybe I would catch him tonight, that's the tone the nurses took with me. Oh well.

Mom slept all day. She woke and a nurse spoon-fed her. She stared up at the nurse like a baby bird looking up at her mother bird. She said something to the effect of, "The election of the moon, necessible?" And then she slept again.

The doctor came in just before visiting hours were over. He seemed confused when he flipped the charts, his brow furrowed. Was that protocol, to express your inner confusion when looking at charts in front of the patient's family? It seemed like a rookie move, like I wanted to call a time out, and ask for a different Doctor, but also, what did I know? In a hospital it seemed like you got what you were given. He asked, "Did she wake up today?"

Dad said, "Yes, sort of —"

And the Doctor said, "Good good," like that was his diagnosis. He said he'd see us tomorrow and that we'd, "Know more."

Dad and I picked up pizza and drove it home and ate it in silence.

I didn't text Teddy. Because I couldn't.

Day three: Dad and I arrived early, but were told that today the Doctor had afternoon rounds. Great. We sat in the room while Mom slept. Kindly nurses came in, checked her vitals, smiled at us, and said, "We have to ask the doctor," whenever we asked direct questions.

Dad left for lunch and that was when the Doctor appeared in the room to flip through Mom's chart. This is what I learned: Because of confidentiality agreements, the underage daughter of the patient doesn't get to hear shit.

Mom woke up twice.

Once about 10:30 a.m. — she stared at me and then looked the other way.

Once about 5:00 p.m. — she said, "Foo . . ." And the nurse spoon-fed her again.

I got the distinct impression that Mom didn't even recognize me.

And then to make matters worse, I developed an earache, because I forgot the other day to use the drying drops in my ears. Now my whole head hurt with unspeakably painful radiating pain. Painful pain. Can't be eloquent because so much pain. You might think, hey, I was at a hospital, that a hospital would be a perfect place to ask someone about a terrible pain spreading around eating into my temples, but all I could think was, Don't distract them. They clearly needed to focus.

SEVENTEEN

TEDDY

Sid wasn't answering my texts or my calls. Wasn't there an unspoken agreement that when someone is in the hospital, the people not allowed to visit the hospital get news? Then I thought, Who would pass along the news? The mom. Sid's mom was the one in the hospital.

I tried to relax about it and give her time. Let her be with her mom, get her mom better. Then she'll call. What did she say?

"Three days."

Right, I would give her a couple of days. That made sense. It was the best way to help.

EIGHTEEN
HOSPITAL DIARY

Day 4: Dad accidentally slept in, so I accidentally slept in. I stuffed cotton balls in my ears and downed as many aspirins as I thought I could take, should take. (Mom would know how many aspirins were safe.) And we missed the Doctor.

But he had left a new order. The unhelpful nurse at the front admissions desk, informed us of it with a look that was all, "Can't believe you missed him; his rounds are random and unpredictable, but obviously you don't care enough."

The order was that, unless something changed by 5:00, Mom would be moved to a special unit at another hospital across Los Angeles. The current hospital was about fifteen minutes away from home. The new one would take over an hour, longer in traffic.

Mom didn't wake up all day, so around 3:00, nurses began bustling. They burst in to check Mom's vitals and then to administer potions and also to make notations. At 6:55, five minutes before visiting hours ended, a team of men entered and rolled her with great fuss and carelessness onto a gurney and wheeled the gurney down the hall and away. To some place new. Mom never even woke up.

Dad was informed that we should return home and meet Mom at the new hospital in the morning. Visiting hours were over, and Mom needed to get settled in. As if Mom would unpack her bags and brush her teeth in her new digs.

NINETEEN

SID

Dad and I went home and ate cold leftover Chinese food.

I went to bed at 7:00, the pain so bad it took three aspirin, some homeopathic remedies, mullein drops in my ear canals, and two hot water bottles, one on each side, just to lie down. I cried. A lot. Because you know who puts drops in my ear? Mom.

Have you ever had an earache? It has three levels. The first is the physical pain, like pain inside the canal, inflamed skin, sore cartilage, even the bone. Then there's the vague pain, the throbbing headache that makes thinking impossible. Lastly there are the twangs and twinges. A good earache takes all that other pain and says, "Wait, that's not all!" And will send shooting pains, even more painful pains, into and around the ear. These shooting pains were in my temples. That did not seem good.

Or healthy.

Or something that should go unmentioned —

"Sid?" A knock on my door.

I squeaked out, "Teddy?"

"Yeah." The door to my room opened. I could tell he was standing there, but I was deep inside a nest of my bedding clutching hot water bottles to my ears.

He asked again, "Sid?"

"I'm in here."

The edge of the bed jostled as he kneeled beside it. "Your dad said your mom didn't come home?"

"She . . . No, she's going to another one."

"Sid, I'm so sorry."

"Yeah." My insides felt tight, like I was chilled, shaking.

"How's your dad doing?"

"I don't know, we aren't talking much."

"He's playing Guns and Roses, loud."

"Yeah, he's been doing that."

"Can you come out of the covers, so we can talk?"

"Nah. I'm — tired."

"Do you want me to stay?"

A twinge hit. I grimaced and gripped the hot water bottles, waiting for the pain to subside. "No, I can't, I need to . . ."

I couldn't finish. I couldn't think. I couldn't want.

The room was quiet for a long time. I felt the slight movement of his head dropping to the mattress and after a few minutes he said, "I'll go, I'll call tomorrow."

He was quiet again for a few minutes more and then the bed jostled as he got up. There was a soft click as my bedroom door closed behind him.

TWENTY
HOSPITAL DIARY

Day 5: We arrived as soon as the hospital opened for business. It looked the same as the old hospital, same doors, same colors, same nurses. Bigger, but still, hospital. I looked in on Mom then descended to the cafeteria for breakfast and while we ate, we missed the Doctor. I kid you not. And bigger hospital meant he only did rounds once a day, but we could, "Make an appointment for later in the week." Or perhaps, tomorrow, never, ever, ever leave. Dad said he would bring a stadium potty and just piss in the room. The nurse did not consider this funny.

Neither did we.

He and I sat in the room and watched Mom sleep. She looked terrible. Am I supposed to say that? I wanted to wash her hair, pluck her chin, put a smear of Chapstick on her lips, lotion on her hands, but also she was unconscious; it didn't seem right, but when she became un-unconscious would she be angry? Was I the Worst-Daughter-Ever for not plucking the hairs? But also girl-power, looks aren't everything, and what a sexist thought, plucking chin hairs during a hospital stay. That's literally the one time you get to heal and not worry about beauty standards, right?

Mom woke up three times. We talked to her, but she only said, "Uh huh," in response. The nurse spoon-fed her. We watched.

TWENTY-ONE

SID

I wrung my hands. Come to find out that's a thing, massaging your hands distractedly at bed sides. Seems archaic, sounds like something you'd do in some other century, like the nineteenth. Mom is sick, uh oh, better wring my hands. Now we're more advanced, aren't we? But here I sat wringing. Or checking Facebook. Same thing, really.

The news of the world was shit today. Literal shit. Like stuff was going on out there that made me think we weren't advanced at all. Stuff that made me scared and made me not want to read anymore. The world goes on, of course, but does it need to go on so stupidly?

Mom woke up and a nurse bustled in. She was young, not much older than me. She carried a bowl of mushy stuff and a spoon. She sidled right up to mom and said, "Hello, Mrs. Dalton, how are you today?"

Mom said, "Uh huh."

The nurse stuffed a spoon of mush in Mom's mouth and brusquely wiped her chin.

I wasn't sure if it was protocol, or Out Of Line, because the nurses barely acknowledged me and Dad in the room, but I asked, "Is she going to be okay, I mean, I know you don't really know, but I mean, in your experience, being around this kind of thing?"

The nurse looked at me as if she had only just noticed I stood there, "Oh, well, what did the Doctor say about your grandmother?"

"That's my mother."

Her hand faltered mid-spoon-feed. "Oh, yes, I'm sorry, my mistake. I don't know the case, and I'm not her doctor, but we get this all the time, and there's usually a full recovery."

My heart raced. "Really — even from this?"

The nurse looked down at my mother, who looked up with her lips parted, waiting for another spoonful of mush, oblivious to the conversation. The nurse faltered again, then said, "Yes, of course, all the time."

My heart soared.

Dad asked, "What time tomorrow will the Doctor be on his rounds?"

"Um, I believe in the morning. What's the day, oh yeah, morning rounds. Just get here early, in case."

Dad said, "Thank you so much."

And I agreed, "Yes, thank you. That is fantastic, thank you."

The nurse left the room and we beamed down at Mom as she slipped into sleep.

Dad and I went out for our favorite tacos. We sat across from each other and smiled and even laughed a few times. The music was loud. It had been so many days since we had been in a loud, full of activity, real world, normal events, kind of place.

It was shocking, how everything around me kept happening, oblivious to the earthquake trashing my home. Shouldn't an earthquake this intense be felt by everyone? Chairs falling over, drinks spilt — something?

TWENTY-TWO
TEXTS

Speaking of everyone, I needed to let Teddy know:

> Sorry I disappeared.
> Hospital said Mom
> will be okay.
> Dad and I are eating out
> celebrating

That's awesome.
Woo-hoo!

I'm telling Mom.
Right now.

She says so wonderful
Can she call your mom?

I stared off across the restaurant, thinking about mom saying, uh huh, being spoon-fed, staring through me.

> Not yet.

> Soon though.

> I have to go, our food

just got delivered.

Let me guess,
you're at Wahoos?

Okay, letting you go
thanks for texting.

Good night

Good night, Sid.

TWENTY-THREE
HOSPITAL DIARY

Day 6: Dad and I sat in the car outside the hospital watching the sun rise. We had Starbucks drinks and pastries. As soon as the clock struck seven, we entered the front doors.

TWENTY-FOUR

SID

It took four hours for the Doctor to arrive in Mom's room. We stood and she said hello, but didn't introduce herself. She picked up Mom's chart, flipped pages, and huffed. Then she woke Mom up with a brisk, "Mrs Dalton, wake up."

Mom said, "Uh huh."

The doctor shined a tiny penlight in Mom's eyes, checked Mom's pulse, and wrote something on the chart. She asked, "Have you got any questions?"

Dad and I looked at each other.

Yes, I have questions, starting with, What the hell? But I asked, "When will she get better?"

The Doctor looked at me with squinted eyes. "She's not."

Dad asked, "What do you mean?"

The Doctor looked down at the chart. "She won't get better. We've done all we can." She flipped the pages on the chart and spoke directly to Dad. "The ammonia buildup, the fluids, the confusion. It's time to consider Hospice for End of Life care."

"Oh," he said, then he fell quiet, as if that was all the explanation he needed.

I looked from Dad to the Doctor and back again. "Wait, what?"

The Doctor glanced at me and returned to speaking to Dad, "The admitting nurses will provide you with some contacts for local Hospice care. I'll sign the release forms for tomorrow morning."

I said, "I don't understand."

She turned to the bed, "Mrs Dalton? Mrs Dalton?"

Mom struggled her eyes open and looked up at the Doctor.

"Mrs Dalton, I'm Dr Patel."

Mom said, "Uh huh."

"Mrs Dalton, do you know these people?"

Mom followed her eyes to me and Dad at the end of the bed. She looked at us, her eyes unfocused. Then she looked up into the Doctor's face.

"Mrs Dalton, do you know what year it is?"

Mom said, "Uh huh."

The Doctor asked again, "Do you know where you are?"

Mom said something that sounded like, "Shoneslaw."

The Doctor looked at us as if that explained everything.

TWENTY-FIVE

MARY

As I stepped down to the dock, gloved hands offered to help, to steady me. The fog was so thick I could barely see. I stepped cautiously. The dock rocked. It seemed inauspicious to stumble. Not today. Not in front of all these people. I had to queen this thing. Royal and all that.

What was happening in France at the palace? Better weather, definitely. Had anyone ever in the history of the world seen such a deep thick air as this? Grey and awful, in your lungs fog. Was that the way Scotland was, grey and awful, all the time? I took a deep breath and remembered the palace gardens and the sunshine.

Beside me well-wishers pressed, out of focus, their hands jutting, their faces leering. Maybe they were attempting to welcome me, but through the fog their smiles emerged cold and frightening. Strange. Strangers.

A hand gesture beckoned me toward land. Voices cheered, celebrating my arrival. I was led to the end of the dock. It shifted under me, water flowing, the sounds of the marina echoing, and me, all I could see was nothing. Alone in gray fog, floating free. Queen of all I could see.

TWENTY-SIX

TEDDY

I sat in the backseat of the car holding a casserole dish in my lap. When was the last time I rode anywhere with my parents? Not since I learned to drive. Not all three of us.

Mom was talking nervously, over-planning, over-explaining. "We'll go in, drop off the food. Maybe straighten up if it looks like they need it. Unless that's too obtrusive." Her voice broke and Dad reached across to hold her hand.

She looked out the side window and began again, "She definitely needs us to clean up, she would want us to. I'll straighten up and you can talk to Mike. Teddy will make sure Sid is . . ."

I looked down at the foil-covered cheesy, tomato, pasta bake. one of the few dishes my mom excelled at, and I was sure it wasn't good enough. A casserole? Because your mom got moved into Hospice?

Two days ago Sid told me her mom was okay.

Then yesterday Mike called Mom and said that was it, the end.

The two different things in two different days was enough to make your head spin. To make you dizzy. Was Sid okay?

I felt shocked. Ashamed. Like listening to my mom talk was a betrayal. Like delivering food that my mom cooked was rubbing Sid's face in it. Sorry your mom is dying, my alive mom made you a casserole.

All the Moms were making casseroles. One every night. For days and days Sid would go to Hospice and then eat casseroles made by other mothers.

I hoped Sid was too distracted to notice.

We pulled up in front of their house.

I climbed out of the car and straightened my shoulders. My dad stopped and stared at the house as if he didn't want to go in. He asked, "Is Mike always playing Guns and Roses this loud?"

I said, "It's how he deals, apparently."

Mom said, "You can hear it all over the neighborhood."

Mike opened the door. He seemed bowed over from the last time I saw him, earlier in the week, smaller. He led us to the kitchen and sent me up to see Sid.

I knocked on her door.

"Come in."

I pushed the door open and she lay spread-eagled on the bed. Staring at the ceiling.

"Hi Sid."

Without moving she said, "Hi."

I stood awkwardly for a second, then pulled her desk chair up to the side of the bed and sat. "Are you okay?"

"Not really. Not at all."

"I was thinking — the waves will be epic tomorrow — I could pick you up, early, we could go to El Porto, easy, and then I'll drive you to see your mom. I'll get you there first thing."

Sid looked at the ceiling, her eyes darting between the light fixture and a cobweb that stretched to the corner. "Nah. I can't."

I pressed on, "It will be good for you. You haven't done anything but hospitals for over a week."

Sid lifted her head. "Good for me? I haven't done anything but sit at the bedside of my dying mother for over a week. That's literally all one person can do. I'm not going surfing — while my mother is dying."

"God, Sid, that didn't come out the way I meant it at all. I'm sorry, I just thought you might want to — I don't know, get in the water, relax for just a minute, I'm offering to help. Just tell me what I can do to help."

"Every second I'm not there she could die. Imagine it Teddy, she dies when I'm not there."

I stared at my hands.

She said, "I'm beyond help. Tell your mother thank you for the casserole." She curled into a ball, facing away.

Yep, she noticed.

"Sid, my family is coming to Hospice tomorrow. Okay? Do you need anything, want me to bring anything?"

"No. I don't need anything."

"If you think of something . . ."

Her shoulders shook like she was crying.

I walked to the bed and perched on the side and placed my hand on her shoulder.

She said with a sniffle, "I think I need to be alone."

I said, "I don't know Sid, you might need some —"

She said, "What do you know? You don't know. You don't."

I sat for a minute more, wishing I could argue, but she was right. I didn't know.

I got up and returned downstairs.

TWENTY-SEVEN

SID

Come to find out, wrapped up inside a mother's body (All bodies?) was some magical essence that fluffed them up. That made them seem full and thick and substantial.

And as a mother's essence disappeared, as she lingered, before dying, she became smaller, diminishing in size. It was all one big fade away.

And that just seemed so unfair. That this giant presence, the person that created me — was always the big to my little, would have to get small first. In front of me. How is that fair?

TWENTY-EIGHT
TEDDY

Mom and I went to the Hospice; I couldn't believe how Sid's mother looked — shrunken and pale and dry. Then I couldn't believe I thought that. I hoped that my face didn't betray my thoughts.

We brought Chipotle, but as soon as I carried it in the front door I knew it was all wrong: too spicy, too smelly. Food that demanded to be noticed. That's the thing about Hospice — everyone is concentrating on the dying, and trying to be quiet, unobtrusive, unnoticed.

Poor Sid was hunched over, tear-stained and rumpled, and doing this thing — distracted, but also intensely focused. Like her mind wandered from our conversation, to stare at her mom, brow furrowed, thinking things through.

Like she would on the beach.

On the beach though, she would tell me.

Here, the problem was, I couldn't even ask.

I could only say, "Hi," and ask how she was and accept her answer, "Fine."

My mom fussed about the room, straightening the flowers and the sheets, talking to Sid's father, asking questions, and being, as Dad put it later, to comfort her, "A welcome distraction."

Then we took our leave.

Promised to come back.

Mom cried all the way home.

TWENTY-NINE
TEXTS

Sid, are you there?

You weren't in your mom's room today
When we visited.
Missed you.

Do you need anything?
Can I bring you anything?

Coming tomorrow,
let me know when
would be a good time.

Anytime

Hi Sid. We're coming just before lunch.
In-n-Out Burger
want your usual?

Sid?

I'll see you tomorrow.

THIRTY

TEDDY

Sid's Dad was listening to Guns and Roses, loud. He answered the front door, yelled that Sid was in her room, and returned to the couch staring at the wall.

"Mike, should I put this in the kitchen?"

"Yeah, sure. We're only home for a couple of hours, we'll eat it later, before we go back."

I put the casserole on the counter, with Mom's handwritten explanation for how to cook it propped in front and climbed the stairs.

Her door was cracked, "Sid?"

Her desk had been cleared to the floor and the downstairs television now sat there, wired up to a Xbox system. Sid was on the floor with a controller, leaned on the bed staring up at the tv.

I asked, "Downstairs too Axl-full-blast for Xboxing?"

Without looking up, her thumbs working, she said, "Definitely. I wish Mom dying had thrown him into an Oasis mood, but then I'd hate him spoiling Oasis. I guess there's worse music, wait, here's the guitar riff, and now his voice with an, 'Ooooooooowieooo, patience.' I hear it in my sleep."

"You only have two hours before you go back?"

Sid checked the phone on the floor right beside her. "We go back at seven. Nurse said they'd call if something . . ."

Her fingers clicked and flicked on the controller. She concentrated on the screen.

Without asking I grabbed a second controller. "Let's play Nuketown."

She nodded and we started a new game.

I dropped beside her on the floor, shoulder to shoulder. She barely said a word. We sat in silence playing side by side. Finally, I checked the time. "It's 6:40, you'll need to get going."

She dropped her head back to the mattress, "Yeah."

"You hungry? I could throw some of the casserole in the microwave on my way out?"

She nodded. "Thank you."

"No problem. I can't come tomorrow, but day after I'll come by, and we can do this again. Okay?"

She answered, "Maybe."

THIRTY-ONE
INSTAGRAM

Photo of Teddy, his mom, Zoe, Zoe's mom, Phineas, and Jude on a picnic blanket in Griffith Park, Old Zoo area.

Underneath it read:

Maybe the best performance so far! Thanks ISC!
#griffithparkshakespearefest @indyshakes
#macbethdinnerparty #outdamnedspot

THIRTY-TWO

SID

It was the eleventh day of hospice. I tried to concentrate on my mom. On our life together. On the things she said, did, was. But when I was at her bedside everything was just blankness and grief. And to be honest a lot of a big giant Pity Party for myself.

I stared at random things until my concentration would break, intermittent crying, staring. Sleeping. Occasionally I checked Instagram and Facebook and Snapchat, but as soon as I did, I had to turn it off. Something would freak me out.

You know the phrase, Life Goes On? It does. And it sucks that it does. That everyone else I knew, woke up and ate breakfast and planned their day. Anticipated fun. Did things with friends. Like Teddy, going to Macbeth without me.

I mean, I understood. I got why. Because Griffith Park Shakespeare Festival was the best. Because we never missed it. Because it was a great play and his only chance to see it. He had to take the chance. Because Life Goes On.

Me, on the other hand, I was dead stopped in Life Ending. And I didn't get to go see Macbeth. I never had the chance. And I understood. I got it.

But still.

Teddy went without me.

I stared some more, with intermittent crying.

THIRTY-THREE

SID

Three months earlier, at El Porto, I paddled up beside Teddy and sat up, 'accidentally' splashing him like always. The waves were big and rough. I had caught three waves and was wiped from paddling back out. "The next one is my last one."

Teddy spun his board around with a grin, a big wave standing up behind him. He called over his shoulder as he paddled away, "Make sure it's a good one!" He dropped into the wave, his head visible for a moment, and then he tucked and rode away.

I would be out here for a while, alone. I paddled for the next wave, but it sucked, both truly and physically. It hollowed out, sending me over the falls and crashing on top of me, shoving me under, salt water rushing up my nose. I scratched for the surface, coming up just before the next big wave. I grabbed a big breath and ducked under the surface again. Tumbling and rolling and losing where top and bottom were supposed to be.

Okay, fine, I was done anyway.

I tugged on my leash, pulled my board under me, and paddled for shore, where Teddy stood knee-deep watching for me, checking I was okay.

I waved with a grimace.

When I made it near shore, I let the last tiny wave beach me and laid there on my board, groaning, half in and out of the water.

Teddy said, "Well, that was epic."

I smiled, cheek pressed against my board. "For a while I wasn't sure if I was riding the wave or the wave was riding me."

"Generally speaking, if you're under the water, you're not surfing right." He grinned and offered me a hand to stand up.

We carried our boards to our towels. And stood watching the waves for a minute.

He said, "Well that was a short session. The Moms are having coffee; we have about two hours to kill."

I unzipped my wetsuit and dropped to the sand and tugged the bottom off over my ankles and feet.

Teddy watched the water for a few more minutes, his back to me, towel draped around his shoulders. Then he turned, stepped closer, and flicked his wet hair at me. "Jeez Teddy, every time?"

He grinned. "I got news."

"Really?" I stopped rustling through my bag. "The school?"

"Yep. I'm accepted."

"Teddy, that's awesome." I paused staring at him. Thinking. This news was awesome. It was what he had wanted for two years or more. For me this news sucked. This meant Teddy, my Teddy, was leaving for school. Santa Barbara, only two-ish hours away, but I didn't drive yet, because I hadn't worried about learning. I was too comfortable riding with other people, mostly Teddy. Crap. Santa Barbara might as well be the moon.

He was looking at me in a way that made me uncomfortable, like he could read my selfish thoughts, so I went back to searching my bag for a protein bar.

He said, "Yeah." He looked back out over the water. "I was thinking you might want to go to school there too."

"Oh? Um . . . you know me, I haven't decided what I want to do . . ."

"Bullshit Sid, you've known what you wanted to do since you were eleven."

I said, "Enlighten me," though I knew what he would say.

"You'll write screenplays, specifically the one about Queen Mary. You've been on about it for years. Come to Santa Barbara, you could go to the city college. Transfer in."

"Do they even have a writing department? I thought you were going for surfing?"

Teddy unzipped the back of his wetsuit. "I'll have you know I'm going for surfing and Marine Biology, and yes, they have a Film and Media department. Screenplays and whatnots."

"You researched this?" I squinted my eyes at him. What was Teddy up to? We had always discussed our plans, together, but they were our separate plans, this was the first time Teddy's plans spilled over onto mine and we weren't there, were we? Him and me. We were friends, right?

I said, "I planned to go local. Take a class or two. And frankly, this is way, way, way, too far in the future, right?"

He dropped to his towel and his jaw clenched for a second. He seemed irritated. "Five months."

I said, "Whoa, I prefer thinking of it as a long way off."

He unwrapped his own protein bar, "All I'm saying is think about it. You could take a couple of classes there as well as here."

I said, "Oh. Okay, I'll think about it. I suppose you need a surf buddy, right? Afraid you'll be stuck surfing with some kook that drops in on every wave, blows-it, and beaches himself?" I nudged him on the shoulder.

He said, "Yeah, that would be the worst."

We ate in silence, watching the big waves pound on the shore, small surfers scaling their fronts and dropping into them, sometimes successfully.

I said, "I guess I do need to figure out what I want to do now. If you're in Santa Barbara who will drive me to the beach?"

"My point exactly. You need to consider your future Sid, the time is now."

"And I need to get started on that screenplay. Someone else will make a movie about her life and then where will I be? Career over before it even starts."

"It doesn't matter, yours will be the best. Because you know all the reasons why she's awesome."

"Oh I do, do I, and what would those be?"

Teddy laid all the way back, arms behind his head. "Let's see, the reasons Mary is so awesome, how many reasons are there?"

I threw my napkin at him. He laughed. "I'm kidding, there are two reasons . . ." He looked at me questioningly. I raised my thumb, up, up, up. He said, "Three, four, I mean, everyone knows there's at least ten reasons Mary is so compelling. Starting with . . ." He looked stumped.

"Teddy, I have been telling you all the reasons for almost six years now."

"I know, I know, but I'm bored and you're entertaining when you're outraged. The ten reasons are: widow, murder, murder again, a super gory execution, conspiracy, explosions, lots of dark stuff."

"I see I need to write it down for you so you remember."

Teddy took a bite of bar and chewing said, "I learn a lot better with visuals, I need someone to make a movie about it. You know where's a good place to learn how to write movies? Santa Barbara." He grinned ear to ear.

THIRTY-FOUR

MARY

Ten cool things:

•She was a widow at 17.

•She was Queen of Scotland and Queen consort of France.

•She was Catholic, her country had turned Protestant, and she was like, whatevs, let's agree to disagree. (That was cool of her, but also her downfall.)

•Her second husband plotted with a bunch of folks and they murdered Mary's friend, right in front of her, during a dinner party.

•Then someone murdered her second husband. First his murderers tried with an explosion, but he was actually found dead, smothered in the garden. Who did it was a mystery, but many people suspected a man named Bothwell.

•Next, Bothwell abducted Mary, took her back to his castle, and probably raped her. Then he married her. (Nobody liked this.)

•Mary and Bothwell had to battle a bunch of Lords, but lost. Bothwell was given safe passage. (Because he was a guy? Probably.) Mary was taken to Edinburgh where crowds called her an adulteress and a murderer.

•She was imprisoned. Miscarried twins. Forced to abdicate her throne to her one-year-old son, James (by her second husband.)

•She escaped and fled to England and begged Elizabeth I for help, but was instead imprisoned. She was 26. She was beheaded when she was 44.

•The execution took three whacks. Seriously. Then the executioner, named Bull, raised her head up and said, "God Save the Queen." Also, her beloved pet dog hid under her skirts and came out after all covered in blood. Ew.

THIRTY-FIVE

TEDDY

I went to Sid's to play Xbox again. I wanted to talk to her about Macbeth. I had a whole plan — I would walk into her room and tell her about it — describe the costumes, tell her about the dinner party scene. Talking about something outside of Hospice would distract her and that would be good. I'd tell her how much I missed her and how I would take her to another show later. I would promise.

When I entered the room was dark, depressed, Sid staring at the screen. She chewed her lip and barely acknowledged me. I asked, "How are you?"

"Okay."

"Can I play?"

"Sure."

I picked up a controller and began to play.

Then she asked, without taking her eyes from the screen, without looking at me or anything, "Do you know what happens to men when their wives die?" Without waiting for an answer she said, "They die. They die too, because they can't bear it, to be alone. Or they remarry. They have two things, death or remarriage. That's a fact. It's what happens. There's no hiding from it."

My mind searched for something, anything, to say and then I said, "I hadn't heard that."

"Well, It's a fact, ask anyone."

She continued to play.

After that day Sid was just gone. She wouldn't answer the phone, texts, anything. Her entire extended family descended on the hospice room, and Sid seemed indifferent to any of us being there, so Mom decided I should skip going. Because I took up space. Clearly my presence wasn't helping. I wasn't helping. She visited without me. I asked her to tell Sid that I was thinking about her.

Now that seemed like a stupid thing to say.

I hoped she would send a message back, anything, but how would Sid respond to, I'm thinking about you?

"Uh, thanks, stalker boy. My mom's in Hospice, give it a rest," seemed like the only fair response.

THIRTY-SIX

HOSPICE DIARY

It took nineteen days for my mom to die. That's all. That's everything.

THIRTY-SEVEN

SID

After your mom dies you get to go home. Maybe alone. Maybe in a crowd of people. But those walls, that roof, the carpets and knickknacks she ordered and decorated and chose and dusted, you get to go back to that. You might think the house will seem empty without her. And it does, terribly empty. But also and how in the hell do these two things exist at the same time — it's also full. Your home is so chock full of her stuff that you can't even breathe. You become hyperaware of every fucking bit of it. You might suffocate from the lack of air because your mom has filled that home with herself so much.

You've been warned. Take an oxygen tank. Leave bread crumbs. Keep your phone in your hand, 911 on speed dial. Trust me.

THIRTY-EIGHT

SID

Dad and I drove home. We were silent, because we had been doing this together, just the two of us for three weeks. We had said it all, felt it all, cried it all, yet here we were at the beginning. Starting, again, all the saying and crying and feeling. Except now we didn't need to drive to visit someone anymore. That part was over.

Dad raised the garage door and you know what was the first thing I noticed? My surfboard leaned up against the wall. I stared at it for a long time. Just standing and staring. I supposed Teddy had put it there at some point over the last three weeks. And I never noticed, but now, coming home after Mom died, I noticed. It stopped me dead in my tracks. I don't know how to describe it, but that day on the beach, in Malibu with Teddy, that day had been interrupted. I had been interrupted. Mom had been interrupted. The whole freaking world. But now my board was back. I wasn't able to go back to that day and finish it. That day was done. It was all done. We were all done. It was suddenly final.

I burst into tears, sobbing, standing in the garage beside Dad's car, facing my surfboard. Teddy had waxed it. Cleaned it up. He was trying to be nice but instead he had stopped the —

Dad returned from the house, "Sid? I'm putting a casserole in, your Aunts and Uncles will be here in ten minutes."

I nodded and said, "I'm coming in a minute Dad thanks."

Guns and Roses played extra loud through the door over his shoulder.

————————————————

We fed everyone with casseroles that Teddy and others had been shoving into our refrigerator for three weeks. I got napkins and filled water glasses and spooned casseroles and set timers and busied myself in the kitchen while my heart screamed — didn't you people notice that my mom died and that Teddy returned my surfboard and the world stopped turning and I'll probably die of the Ache because there are so many tears welled up in my head that I might drown from the inside?

But nobody noticed. They ate. They held our hands and patted us on the shoulder and left at the end, oblivious to all but their own pain. Because that's what happens, come to find out, grief is isolating. Who would have guessed with so many people around to share it?

Dad and I watched them drive away and then we each disappeared. Dad turned the music, that our guests had forced him to turn down, back up. Guns and Roses, a live album. The applause made our house and yard sound like an amphitheater. I climbed the stairs and sat on Mom and Dad's bed. I didn't touch anything; I just stared at it all. I wished I was doing something amazing — like memorizing everything's location so that fifty years later I'd have a photographic memory of what her room was like. But no, I was blank-stare looking. After a while I went into Mom's bathroom and stared at her stuff there. I opened her dressing table drawer and stared down into that. I opened the linen closet and looked at all of that. Two hours passed of me looking at stuff.

I went downstairs, Dad was standing in the living room looking at the bookcase. Arms crossed resting his mouth on his thumb.

"Dad, it's eleven-thirty, I'm going to bed." I startled him because he had the blank-stare too.

"Oh, yeah," he looked around like he couldn't believe where the time went while he stared at the bookshelf. "I still have some things to do."

"Sure Dad." I went to bed, but he took another hour before he finally turned the Guns and Roses off.

THIRTY-NINE

TEDDY

I woke up the day before the funeral with a terrible cold. Like the worst. My mom, red-rimmed eyes and deep sighs, said, "It's just a summer cold, you'll be fine."

I got worse. Snot poured from my nose, my throat was killing me, I was chilled and then hot, and even worse — my chest rattled. It started with a dry hacking cough and progressed into the wet hard and loud kind of cough that racked my body and should not be heard out in public. It was the Get Out Of The Way kind of cough. I'm not telling you this because I know you enjoy thinking about mucus and phlegm, but to set the scene for the most tragic of moments.

I mean, that came out all wrong, the funeral was the most tragic of moments — the loss of Sid's mom. In comparison my tragedy was minuscule, but also giant.

This is what happened:

"Mom! I need medicine and all you've got is this bullshit homeopathic stuff." I walked into the kitchen carrying our remedy bin. It was full of little bottles of pills and oils and nothing to make a cough miraculously disappear. I punctuated my complaint with a coughing fit that doubled me over.

Mom stopped wiping the counter, and said, "Your body can heal itself." She appraised me. "You look like poop."

"I feel like poop. C'mon, I need the 'Beyoncé needs to sing tonight' medicine, this is Sid's mom. I can't go looking like this."

"I'll run out and get you something but let me get ready —" Another coughing fit folded me over. "Okay, I'll go now."

Somehow I managed to get ready. Suit. Tie. Clean shirt. Combed hair. I even had on shoes with socks. I usually tried not to do that on principle, but I did it. I carried the Robitussin cough syrup in one pocket, a wad of tissues in the other. I put on sunglasses to cover my bloodshot eyes.

I rode to the funeral suffering in the backseat. Blowing my nose, coughing, snuffling and moaning. The cough syrup wasn't working. Beyoncé would have been pissed.

Over a hundred people were there. Many friends that Sid and I knew. Many people that I assumed belonged to Alicia's family and friends from her past.

Mom and Dad and I stepped into the receiving line to pass into the chapel.

Sid was tiny at the end of the line. My heart dropped. She was looking into the face of an elderly woman who spoke to her holding both of her hands. Sid was nodding. She looked so small and weak and broken and I wanted to rush to her and shove everyone away and — I don't know — take her away from this. She shouldn't have to do this. She had to though. Because.

Mom said, "There's a big turnout. Alicia would have been so happy to know she . . ." She sobbed into a Kleenex. We passed a box and I grabbed another handful for my pocket.

It took a while to get to Sid and Mike. I smiled, the best I could, forgetting to take off my sunglasses. Then a cough climbed up from my deep inner core, a doozy. I held my breath, tried to hold it down and tried to be present in the chapel, as my mom held both of Mike's hands and told him how much she — but I couldn't control it. I coughed. Spasms folded me over, with croup and gunk and loud hacks. I directed my mouth into my sleeve and managed an, "I'm sorry," to Sid as I rushed back outside.

That was it.

Sid was going through the Worst Thing Ever, and I was her best friend, and had I done anything right so far? Nope.

I returned after the services began. I sat in the back row and lurched out whenever my coughing fits started. I was concentrating so hard on Not Interrupting that I didn't hear anything being said. I missed the first half of Mike's words. Then Sid got up to speak, and I tried to stay, but a doozy of a coughing fit forced me to leave.

I missed everything that mattered, and then I couldn't bear it anymore — I had failed so epically that I stayed alone outside on the steps, coughing, waiting for Sid's Mom's funeral to end so I could go home and go to bed.

FORTY

SID

All of this was new, so I didn't understand what to expect. I had never been to a funeral before. Or a church. Or a service of any kind. This was what I knew: I was expected to stand and greet everyone, personally. Also, that I needed to say a few words. I also had to wear black, so my aunt took me shopping, and I failed miserably because my heart wasn't in it. I bought a too-tight skirt and a too-big top. The effect made me look ill-prepared, but maybe, probably, that part was the truth.

I was ill-prepared. But then Teddy appeared at the end of the line. He was tall and handsome. Wearing sunglasses. A suit. He looked prepared. He worked his way down the line, and I tried to focus on the friends and family parading by. Each one said a variation of, "I loved your mother," and, "She was an amazing woman," and, "If there's anything I can do for you," but what I really wanted was this:

Teddy to sidle up and say, "Hey Sid."

And for him to stand right beside me, a little back from the line.

And for him to not say anything, to just be. Kind of like with the Xbox — shoulder to shoulder.

It was a weird want, for someone to stand to the side, caddy corner, a little back. What was that position even called? But then I realized it was called: I've Got Your Back. That's what it was. I wanted, truly needed, Teddy to have my back.

His family was right there. His mom talking to my dad. Teddy leaned in about to say something then he started coughing. He stepped behind his mom, gasped, "I'm sorry," and then he left.

Tears welled up in my eyes as his mom grabbed my hands, leaned in, and said, "Sorry about Teddy, he has a summer cold."

I nodded.

She said, "I loved your mom. If there's anything I can do for you . . ."

Tears streamed down my cheeks.

FORTY-ONE

TEXTS

Hey Sid, you there?

I'm sorry about that
I'm really sick.
Wanted to be there.
Feel really bad about it.

It's okay.

I'm going to bed now.

Okay.
I'll talk to you tomorrow.
* * *
Sid u there?

Sid?

?

Sid, it's been three days.
Is your phone broken?
I guess if it was
you wouldn't be able
to answer this.

Sid I called your dad
he says your phone is fine.

I'm so sorry.

Sid.

                              I'm here.
                    I'm just super tired.
            I think I need to go to bed.

It's 730.

            People go to bed at 730 sometimes

Baby people ;o)
I need to talk to you.
I'm calling.

* * *

Okay, here's the thing
I know what's happening
what happened
it's awful and terrible and
The only person you need to
worry about is yourself
but when you don't answer
my texts or the phone
I feel totally panicked
Maybe it's Zombies
or Ebola

or suicide
that's where my brain goes

I know you don't have to talk to me
but I need to talk to you

I'm calling you again

Please

"Hi."

"Hi."

"You really thought zombies were attacking my house?"

"Worse."

"Sorry about that."

"No Sid, I'm sorry. Can you tell me it's okay? I was sick and I . . ."

"Yeah, it's okay. These things happen and . . . What did you need to talk about?"

"I hadn't thought past getting you to answer. No wait, that's not true. I've been planning what I would say for weeks now."

Sid said, "Okay."

"I just — I don't know what to do. I don't know what to say. None of this makes any sense and you deserve better and I want to help. I'm no good at this."

"Me neither."

"So I need you to tell me what I can do to help."

"I don't know."

A long pause.

"What if I listed some things and you told me yes or no?"

Another long pause.

"Do you need more casseroles? My mom wants to know."

"No, not really, there's lots left and . . ."

"That was a trick question; I already told her to lay off the casseroles. How about a Starbucks delivery every morning until you beg me to stop."

"Nah. Thank you but I had a lot of Starbucks in the last three weeks."

"I'll pick you up and we'll go surfing, tomorrow."

"Nah, I can't, not . . ."

"Xbox."

"Maybe."

"Okay, I'll come play Call of Duty, give me a minute."

"You're outside?"

"Parked outside. Told you I was panicked about the zombies. I can hear your dad's music from my car. Guns and Roses still?"

"Yeah, it's all that's keeping him here."

"I'm at your front door."

FORTY-TWO

SID

A week later there was a knock on my bedroom door and Dad walked into my room. He took a look around — probably noticing the clothes all over the floor, the overflowing trashcan, and the lamp knocked over — pulled up a chair, and sat on it backwards. I was facing the screen, box of cookies open on the floor, half-eaten.

"I see you're having dinner?"

"Yeah, I'm hungry. Did you already eat? Need me to heat up some casserole?"

"God no, do you think those women will ever stop bringing them?"

I smiled, "We could order pizza."

"I just got off the phone with Lori. She's concerned about you and wanted me to check in, which I'm sorry to say I haven't done in a few days."

"Dad, I'm okay, and you're doing fine, you check in enough."

He smiled. "Let's agree to disagree. Lori pointed out that tomorrow is Beach Day and everyone would love to see you and —"

"I can't go Dad, I can't."

"Well, here's the thing, it's fresh air, friends, sunshine. It would be good for you." I sneered. He held up his hands and barged on, "Here's the other thing, grief makes us only think about ourselves and what we've lost. We become lost. That's a real thing, lost in our grief, it can be hard to find our way out."

"Says the man who has been listening to Guns and Roses for weeks. Full blast."

"True, but I also went back to work, had to concentrate on something else. You've had nothing else to do."

"Teddy came over."

"Last week. Lori says he's frantic about you, you won't answer his texts, you barely speak, and when he comes you just play Xbox. Teddy asked her to call me."

"Oh."

"Yeah, oh. When your best friend is worried about you, you might need to listen."

"But don't I get to be sad right now?"

"But you can't stay lost. Sometimes the best way to stop being lost is to think about someone else. If you went to the beach tomorrow Teddy would stop worrying about you, Lori would feel better about you, everyone would breathe better. Then possibly you would start to feel better too."

"This is a lot of fricking pressure."

"Yep. Sucks to go on living. But you must. Will you consider going?"

"Yeah, I'll think about it. I want Hawaiian, pizza."

"Pineapple, seriously?" He sighed, "Okay, fine, but only because being selfless confirms the pep talk I just gave you." He got up to leave and I spent the rest of the evening deciding which bathing suit to wear.

FORTY-THREE

SID

I had no idea how to navigate this stuff. You know who would have known? My mom. She could walk into a room of strangers and strike up conversations. She could make you feel better about your current situation. Was it the woman in her? Gender specific? In the receiving line at her funeral it had been mostly women that held my hand and told me that if I needed anything to call. Rarely the men. But then again, I was a young girl. Maybe the women handled grieving girls and the men handled grieving boys. Gendered grief and all that. Maybe.

Why did everyone tell me to ask if I needed help? To call them? Did I even have their phone number? What a weird thing to say. The thing about moms is they anticipate your needs. When you lose your mom your needs stop being anticipated, and now I was supposed to know what I need? To call people I've never spoken to before and tell them what I need?

I needed my mom back.

I assumed that was impossible.

Also, and let's be real, a lot of this stuff was the fancy magical remembering of a broken heart. Because leading up to the end there was barely any anticipating or navigating at all. Because some moms can't or won't. And the Ache that kills them in the end? It's too tragic to be spoken about. Their Death's Reason too awful to be mentioned.

The one thing I learned: We never speak ill of the dead.

FORTY-FOUR

SID

It took forever to get dressed for the beach because I was out of practice. Dad had been right, I needed to get out of the house. This would all do me good, but it would also stop him from worrying, keep the Moms happy, calm Teddy down. To accomplish all of that I should look great — legs shaved, eyes clear, hair washed. I put on my cutest bathing suit, then couldn't decide whether to wear shorts, a loose cotton cardigan, and a pair of Converse lo-tops; or a beachy sundress with flops. I pulled on the shorts, figuring it made me look older, more in control, less vulnerable. Long hair or a messy bun? Bun. Makeup definitely. My eyes had been red and swollen for so long that only brow pencil, eyeliner, mascara, toner and flesh-colored powder made them look passable. I glossed my lips, packed a bag with a beach towel, bottle of water, and sunscreen, and called for an Uber. I arrived at the Avenues fashionably late.

I stood at the top of the cliff. Down on the beach was my group: the Moms lounging on towels, under umbrellas, wearing sun hats, coolers at arm's reach. The kids were to their left, their towels crumpled, wadded wetsuits dotting the sand, Boogie Boards and surfboards in a pile. I counted about eight moms, seven teens, and twenty-two billion little kids. About normal, except me and Mom weren't there. We used to be.

I took a deep breath and descended the long staircase, reached the bottom, and set off across the sand. I scanned for Teddy. Our friends, Zoe, Erica, and Katy, were sunbathing in bikinis. Zoe's looked new and reminded me that her birthday had just passed. Note to self: mention it.

A few other friends tossed a ball farther down the beach. I got closer, thirty feet away, or something, and there was Teddy walking backwards up the sand to the towels from the ocean. Watching the waves. Hot in his wetsuit. Like really hot, gorgeous hot. Scoping to the right and left, eyes never leaving the waves.

I had a great mental image of running up behind him and putting my hands over his eyes. He would say, "Sid!" And fold me up in his arms, kissing —

But that's the trouble with mental images and expectations, other humans can rarely live up to them. They can't because they don't know. It's not fair to expect them to jibe with your imagination, but yet we do, expect. And my imagination was superb. My expectations, in retrospect, too high. And so I was twenty feet away when Teddy looked down at Zoe, smiled, and with a laugh, flicked his hair, sprinkling her with water.

I stopped dead in my tracks.

The sun was glistening. The day was beautiful, and this is what I knew: The world was a glorious orb of love and laughter and light, full of moms and not for me.

Life goes on of course.

But also, no.

No smiles.

No splash and flirt and

no.

I spun in the sand

and ran.

Behind me Teddy yelled, "Sid!" But I was in a full sprint for the stairs.

He yelled, "Sid!" again, running behind, "Sid! Wait up!"

I hit the stairs taking them two at a time, my breath rasping and ragged. Down on the beach, over my left shoulder, Teddy had his hands around his mouth, yelling,

"Come back!" The mothers and the other teens were standing, chasing, up, worried. Lori was running after Teddy, her phone to her ear. Probably calling my dad, telling on me. That I was — what was this?

Running away.

This was not something that would be easy to explain later.

But I didn't have time to worry about that now, I had to get away.

Teddy called from the bottom of the stairs, "Sid! Come back! Please!"

But I hit the sidewalk at the top and fled down the street. Two blocks over I called an Uber to take me home.

FORTY-FIVE
TEXTS

Sid why did you leave?

?

?

Sid are you okay?

Sid?

I'm going all Liam
Hemsworth in Frantic over here.

I don't think that's right.

Holy shit Sid.
Are you okay?

I just can't.
It's too much.
I'm okay.

My mom is calling your dad.

I guessed.

I'm okay.
I'm going home.
I just need

. . .

What do you need?
Tell me.
Xbox?

Liam or Chris?

Why Hemsworth brothers?

Only way you'll answer.

I need some alone time.

84

FORTY-SIX

SID

Dad, as soon as he came home from work, came up to my room as expected.

"Sid?"

I was looking through my friends's Snapchat stories. They all had a good day, sunny and bright and a lovely good time, and no one mentioned me. Which was a relief, mostly. Because that there was a sad turn of events. My whole self was a sad turn. Sid, bringing every scene down. Want to ruin a party? Invite Sid.

"What happened today?"

"I couldn't do it Dad. It's like so wrong to show up and be all . . ."

He squinted his eyes. "These people are your friends. Your mother's friends. This is the life she wanted you to have, the activities she wanted you to be apart of. You need to try."

"Do I Dad? I have to show up without a mom and sit with the teens and cry in the middle of their good time?"

"Your mom would have wanted you to."

"You know, she doesn't get a say anymore."

"Sid."

"You don't get to give up and die and then still direct my activities from the other side."

Dad looked down at his hands. "I suppose that's true. But here's what's happening. I'm a dad. The Moms are suspecting that I may be in over my head. It's all pity and worry whenever they're around, when they call. I need you to buck up and do something beyond all-day-alone-Xboxing so I don't look like such a failure."

"When did you worry about what everyone else thinks? I'd like to point out that the whole neighborhood knows you have terrible taste in too loud music. That doesn't bother you."

"These are the Moms. Alicia's friends, there's a lot of pressure."

"We need a unified front of awesome, huh?"

"Yep, back East where your mom and I grew up it was called Not Letting the Cracks Show."

"That's kind of what killed her."

"We don't get to make the rules, we just gotta play."

"I can't be a part of the group anymore, it's all moms and teens. It's the past. It hurts too much."

"Lori said Teddy asked you to go to Santa Barbara to school. She seemed to think it was a great idea."

"I think I'll just take a class or two here."

"Even Teddy?"

"I don't know about Teddy."

We sat in silence for a little.

"Promise you don't need expert help or something, promise you've got this?"

"I don't know Dad, but I'll tell you if it gets worse."

"That's all I can ask. Need some cookie dough? I bought a tube and my plan was to eat it with a spoon."

"We could binge watch something?"

"Sounds good, but we have to liberate the tv from your clutches and move it back down."

"It's only here because it couldn't take another moment of Guns and Roses."

"Ah, my Guns and Roses therapy, I think I may have reached saturation." He smiled and hefted the television off my desk.

FORTY-SEVEN

TEDDY

I walked into the kitchen as Mom said to Dad, "It's got to be hard on her especially since it was so terrible the last years — "

"What? Who?" I opened the freezer looking for something sweet.

Nobody answered.

I looked over my arm, "Who ya talking about?"

Mom said, "Um, Sid — you know, forget I said anything." A look passed between her and Dad.

"No, what did you mean, the last year, terrible?" I peeled the wrapper off an ice cream sandwich.

She didn't answer.

"Mom, what?"

Mom sighed. "Well, I'm sure Sid talked to you about it."

"About what, I have no idea what you're talking about."

"About why Alicia died."

"Liver failure, because of something, Mom, you need to tell me what you're saying."

Another look passed between them. Dad grabbed an ice cream sandwich and sat down to eat.

"She drank heavily Teddy, and it's no secret."

I gaped at her and Dad. Dad concentrated on his dessert, Mom looked at me steadily.

"Well, it was a secret, because Sid never mentioned it."

"It's why we didn't hang out much in the last couple of years, why Sid was alone. You really didn't know?"

"Jeez Mom, no."

I stared off into space chewing, considering, remembering, looking for clues. We were always with the moms, but also, alone, and also, frankly, not paying attention. "You said it wasn't a secret, does everyone know?"

"Most of us, yes."

I threw my wrapper in the trash. Ran my hand down my face. "Are people talking about it? Do you think people talked about it in front of Sid, did someone say something to Sid?"

"Oh, I hope not. Poor Sid."

"Mom you have to stop it, stop saying it, tell people to stop talking about it."

FORTY-EIGHT

TEDDY (ABOUT A YEAR EARLIER)

"Teddy, I've caught four waves to your one."

"That you have, but mine were epic." She smiled and splashed me. Then she turned fast, and paddled for a wave I wouldn't have even considered a wave. She caught it, dropped in, and surfed down the line.

I only had to duck dive two waves before catching the biggest of the set, dropping in, and weaving by her with a spray of water, as Sid paddled back out. Then I kicked-out, landed on my board, and returned to my spot beside her in the lineup.

I was glad she came surfing today; she had been dating Cameron and her commitment to our surf days had been spotty. I had even complained about it, but dropped it because I sounded like an ass. I knew Cameron wasn't the guy for Sid. She would see it eventually.

It had taken about nine months. Nine months of Cameron on the beach glowering at us, or worse, Sid saying, "I don't feel like surfing today Teddy, I'm just going to sunbathe." Which meant I was in the ocean glowering at them.

I was glad they were through. On a whole lot of levels.

I was beginning to think we might be good together, like deep good together.

We waited in the line up, Sid swishing her hands out and back and around through the water. She asked, "Did you know Paul Rudd helped write the Ant Man screenplay?"

I said, "No, but that would explain how funny it was. Did you watch it last night?"

She said, "Mom was in a Paul Rudd mood, we're working our way through his oeuvre. I don't know if I'm using that word right."

I said, "Sounds close enough. Is Paul Rudd still on her lockscreen?"

"Chris Pine, I mean how old is he? He has to be too young for her. She is such a Trekkie. I stayed up late though, reading about screenplays. It's so fascinating, how someone takes a story and turns it into a movie. How they write the words and it becomes pictures."

I enjoyed her languid movements, her hands twisting and splashing. If I stayed quiet she would keep going, filling in the details.

"I guess I should look for a screenwriting class, for next year, so I can start the Mary script. Did I tell you I had an idea?"

"No, we haven't talked about it in a while."

"Oh, yeah, well . . ." A wave came, she turned, paddled, and surfed away. I watched her over my shoulder as her head raced down the wave, then she kicked out, directed her board, and paddled back, appearing at my side again. "Where was I? Oh — I had an idea, the opening scene would be embroidery, being embroidered, an animation, you know what I mean? A needle running through fabric creating a scene, flowers and gardens and her motto: In the end is my beginning. But in the background, behind the music, hammers are banging. Carpenters are building the scaffold for her execution. She can hear it, Teddy. Then the camera draws back, it's revealed that Mary is old, hunched over, sewing, but the embroidery animation continues to create the floral scene off to the side and becomes a young girl running through the gardens of France. It's probably hard to imagine . . ."

"No, I think I have it."

She held up her hands creating a rectangle. "At the end of the movie, and in between scenes, embroidery trails off. I also want to mess with time, to take her back to the gardens of France at the end. Truly carefree."

I said, "That sounds good. Like a happy ending."

"And the soundtrack would be modern."

"When the executioner holds her head up and says, God Save the Queen, the Sex Pistols play in the background?"

Sid said, "You get a prize for paying attention."

I teased, "The prizes are the only reason I do."

Sid splashed me. "Not the Sex Pistols though, like what would Arctic Monkeys do with that song? Or maybe the Lumineers or Mumford and Sons, what would they do? Or better yet, Twenty One Pilots."

I said, "I missed this."

She cocked her eyebrow, incredulous, "You missed me telling you long boring stories about Mary Queen of Scots? I'm going to tell Lori you need more activities."

"Empty threat. The Moms would give you more stuff, too. You won't risk it, you like to surf too much."

"True. I do. And I missed this too. It's nice to be out of the house."

I said, "Our moms aren't hanging out much lately."

"Oh yeah. It's . . . I guess I hadn't noticed."

She rolled onto her back on the board, spread-eagle, and looked up at the sky. "The wind switched, now the waves suck." Her hands swished around and through the water. "I want to get across Mary's tragedy, but not go too dark. Her's was the commonplace tragedy of life taking you places you aren't prepared for. How fate holds your hand and drags you through, and there's no way you survive it."

"That sounds really dark."

She sat up on her board and looked right at me. "Teddy I have news, no one survives. Ever. And it's dark and tragic and fate has your hand, dragging you to the end. You might as well grab a wave."

She splashed away, paddling for a mushy lump that wouldn't take her far.

Leaving me wondering, how to keep her here, ask her to stop paddling away.

FORTY-NINE

TEDDY

"So how's Sid?"

I spooned a large helping of rice and forked a slab of steak onto my plate. "I don't know, she keeps turning me away."

"Oh." A look passed between my mom and dad, but then nothing. I was glad Mom brought it up, but also surprised she didn't have something to add.

"Got any advice?"

Mom sighed. "No. I hoped you could keep her involved, be her friend. I'm worried about her all alone."

"Me too. I text her, I go by. She barely answers, or says she's in bed, tired. I'm stuck."

Dad said, "Keep trying. She needs you, her friends, she just doesn't know it."

"I don't know, I feel like I'm hounding her, unwanted."

"Take her surfing."

"I'm trying. Mom?"

"Well, when I lost your grandma four years ago I was turned upside down for a long time. And we didn't even live in the same state. I barely saw her. I don't know how Sid will deal with it, the sadness. She needs friends, family, support. The trouble is, she might not know what she needs — what would help, what she wants. You have to be there for her, listen. Ask what you can do to help. If she asks for something, do it. That's all you can do."

FIFTY

TEXTS

Hey.
Wanna surf?

        . . .

Tomorrow?
Break wall?

I'll pick you up at 7?

       Not sure . . .

Surf report says big, good.
Heard Liam Hemsworth might be there.

      Oh in that case ;o)

Really? You will?

I'm kidding about Liam.

    Yes, and I know you are.
       He surfs the Bu.
    Not the lowly break wall.

Plus he's too old for me.
I'll see you at seven.

Are you busy now?
Can I come over?

I'm headed to bed.

Okay
goodnight.

FIFTY-ONE

SID

Dad smiled widely when he came home from work. "I had the most amazing thing happen last night!"

"Did you win the lotto?" I was opening a can of marinara for pasta, the only thing I was presently capable of cooking and interested in eating.

"Better. You know how people are always talking about the dead visiting the living? I mean, I generally think it's total bullshit, but Sid, it happened last night."

I poured the sauce in a pot and placed it on the stove. "What happened last night?"

"Your mom — she visited me. Oh man, it was amazing."

I turned and stared at him slack-jawed.

"I know, I know, it sounds crazy, but here's what I know. The people who leave this plane aren't leaving for good, they're simply living on a different plane, inside us, around us, above us and sometimes all at once." He sliced butter squares and smeared them on a loaf of French bread and down in between slices. "So they're here, and they have answers, news, things they want to tell us, but we have to be open to listening. We have to listen with all our heart, because they're talking, Sid, all the time."

I filled the pasta pot with water, slammed it on the back of the stove, and cranked the flame up high.

He continued, "Last night I was in my room and your mom appeared at the end of the bed. She held me and told me everything would be all right. And that she was glad I was starting to feel better. And you know what? It was like she took this burden off my shoulders. I do feel better. So much better."

Tears welled up. I tried to hide it by rinsing utensils in the sink with my back to him. I managed, "That's good Dad, I'm thrilled for you."

"Yeah, it was great." He hummed to himself for a moment as he wrapped the bread in tinfoil. "Has she visited you?"

I shook my head and because we weren't facing each other, added, "No."

"Keep an open heart and mind. You have to listen." He tossed the bread into the oven and left the room to go change out of his work clothes for dinner.

I stood at the sink, crying. And this is what I kept thinking — the reason why mom hadn't visited me? Because she knew I'd want her to explain herself.

FIFTY-TWO
MARY

Here's the thing about fate. You can't argue with it. You can't control it. You can't stop its ceaseless pull. You can only read the signs, try to understand which direction you should move, but you don't have to worry about it too much. Reading the signs is only necessary if you wanted to get a head start, be there before the push.

Think of life like this: You're a prisoner, and you can resist and struggle and be dragged kicking and screaming along, or you can stand firm, resolute, and be pushed from behind, or, and this is the hardest of them all, you can read the signs, understand, and take fate by the hand and follow.

This was Mary, following her fate when she had to govern a country that had embraced a different religion. She didn't fight, she didn't attempt to control, to suppress the people.

This was Mary when she married the Dauphin. When she fell in love with Darnley. When she accepted her union with Bothwell. She made the best of her available options.

This was Mary when she was imprisoned for being an heir to the throne. She sat and embroidered.

And this was Mary when she walked up the steps to her execution. Step by step by step. Wigged head held high, dogs under her skirts.

She was following where fate took her.

No sense struggling.

Follow the signs.

FIFTY-THREE

SID

Usually when Teddy picked me up to go surfing, he stayed on his side of the car. I would run out, load my stuff in the back and he would stand on the other side of the car while I strapped my board on the roof. I would pass the straps to him, he would pass them under the racks and back and I would secure them. We had a system. This time though, Teddy jogged up to my door, rang the bell, offered to help carry my things, carried my board to the car, and basically did the whole thing.

I watched him, separate from the scene. He buzzed around and merrily talked. While I stood watching. An empty shell.

We drove to the beach making small talk.

He asked if I had watched the latest Fear of the Walking Dead, and I told him I couldn't anymore.

He changed the subject, quickly, deftly, to music, and asked, "Your dad still listening to nothing but Guns and Roses?"

I chuckled, "I had a long talk with him. He's letting me turn him onto music. I started with Foo Fighters."

"It's hard to go wrong with them. Queens of the Stone Age might be good too."

"Oh that's right, I had forgotten them. His music education continues. My mission is to get his musical taste into the twenty-first century, even if it kills me. Either that or the volume needs to come way, way down."

"Your neighbors will thank you."

We pulled into a parking spot, and I put money in the meter while Teddy unstrapped our boards. Then I slung my bag over my shoulder and we picked up the boards and towels and walked down to the beach.

I said, "Thank you for cleaning and waxing my board."

"No problem, Sid."

I pulled my spring suit up and zipped it, while Teddy struggled his on, and then I zipped his for him, and we paddled out, side by side. It was big and crowded. Teddy paddled ahead. He moved faster, and it had been a while since I had surfed. Or done cardio. Or really done anything besides sit at bedsides.

I watched him, strong and sure and capable, paddling up the wave face and then dipping down out of sight.

When he reached the lineup, he sat up on his board, and planted his hands on his thighs, his elbows out, scanning the horizon, counting the waves. I paddled up behind him and he turned — his face wide open and happy, his smile wide.

It hit me like a tsunami — Teddy loved me.

He loved me.

And you might think that would be a good thing. Because I loved him too. But it wasn't. Because I didn't deserve him. I was a broken wretch of a sad thing of limp nothingness and despair. Seriously.

I cried because one of mom's tissues had been left behind on the nightstand.

I spiraled when I found, inside an old dusty shoe box, a pressed rose she kept from some long-ago boyfriend.

I curled up in a fetal position every time I remembered the last thing I yelled at her.

I didn't deserve him. And I loved him.

I wanted Teddy to curl up beside me every night and hold me in his arms while I cried. But how cruel was that? To want handsome, happy Teddy to hold while I cried, for how long? How long before he walked away and broke my heart?

Because he would leave.

The lesson I learned this summer was this: loving someone isn't enough to keep them there.

So that's what slammed into me when Teddy turned around with his smile, the sun glinting off the water drops on his hair, drips sliding down his jawbone, that his perfect happiness wasn't mine to have. I couldn't share it.

That tsunami I mentioned, the one that slammed this knowledge into my gut? It filled me and broke free with a sob. Tears streamed down my face. Teddy's wide smile turned to worry, "Sid?"

I turned my board and paddled for shore. But guess what? Tear-filled eyes made me miss the big wave bearing down. It picked me up, sent me over the falls, and slammed me down, the full weight of the lip shoving me deep. My shoulder smashed into sand. It felt like the entire ocean held me down, sea water filled my nose, and when I scratched to the surface I was rolling and roiling in whitewater.

"Sid!"

From the shore two red-shorted lifeguards raced toward me in the sea.

I was pulled sopping, covered in sand, to the water's edge, with pain on my foot's instep, a looseness that didn't feel normal. I pulled up my head. Blood spilled out in a bloom.

One guard told the other, "Get the kit."

I dropped my head back, suddenly lightheaded.

Teddy appeared. "Will she need stitches?" Someone was wrapping a bandage around my foot.

A guard said, "Probably, take her to urgent care."

Teddy said, "Sid, I'm running the boards up to the car. I'll be back to help you across the sand."

He darted away. If I twisted to look up the beach, I could see him jogging — a board under each arm, my bag thrown over his shoulder, towels under his arm — a goddamned superhero. I would have cried if I hadn't felt so much like passing out.

Teddy drove me to urgent care and sat in the waiting room while a Doctor stitched me up, and then he drove me home.

The details are murky, because drama and fear, and oh no, yet somehow we pulled in front of my house.

Teddy turned off his car. "Sid, I . . ."

"Teddy there's something I need to say."

He looked surprised that I interrupted. What had he been about to say? I'd never know because I barged into the middle of it and without thinking plowed on.

"I have to tell you thank you, for being there, for being so supportive — "

"Of course."

"But I need you to stop. I need you to go away."

His eyebrows drew together. "What?"

"I'm too big of a mess, and so I don't want you to keep coming around anymore."

His face changed to incredulous. "What are you even talking about?"

"You and me and how we're over."

"I'll remind you we never started, and you can't just break up with me, we've been friends since we were babies."

"We can't be anymore. I feel too sad. Whenever I see you I feel worse and guilty and awful and it's not fair to you. You deserve someone so — "

Now he looked pissed. "I think I know what I want, what I deserve, Sid. Don't break up with me and try to spin it like it's what I want." He mimicked me, "It's not fair? To me? I deserve better than that bullshit."

Tears spilled down my face. "I'm so sad, and you're not helping!"

His hands gripped the top of the steering wheel, his jaw clenched. "I'm trying to help."

"Your very nature, our circumstances, makes me so sad when we're together. I can't be with you and be happy."

"So I want to help, and you want me to stop?"

"Yes," I sniveled.

His hands flattened and gripped again on the steering wheel.

He turned and looked at me sidelong, eyes squinted. "You're not even going to friend-zone me?"

"I can't, I love you too much."

"Jeez, Sid, that's probably the meanest lie you've ever told." He drew his hands slowly down the steering wheel. "Your mom would be really sad if she knew — "

"My mom was already the saddest person in the world; she just hid it well. Also, that's exactly what killed her, being sad and hiding it."

"So that's your plan, to wallow in it?"

"No, my plan is to not be sad. Anymore. That's why."

Teddy sighed. He blew air up at one curl hanging on his forehead. "I don't understand. At all."

We sat for a long moment. He stared out the side window over his arm.

It was a long terrible moment. I wanted him to say something, anything, to tell me it was okay, that this was fine. That it made sense.

But instead he asked, "You want me to stop?"

I nodded.

"Okay, consider me stopped."

———————————

And that, exactly that, is how someone in the middle of a crisis of grief can blow apart their life.

———————————

Okay, maybe not anyone — me. How Sid blew apart her life. Like a bomb. My heart was so full of grief and tears that I took the best part of my life and drowned it in my tsunami.

Because, dumb ass. Probably.

Also, doing the best I could. Considering.

From my room I watched as Teddy unstrapped my board, carried it up the driveway, and propped it against the wall in the garage. He carried my bag up to the porch, and then he returned to his car and drove away.

What I had just done, there wasn't any take back. I had been ignoring him, evading him, for weeks, and this time I could see it in his eyes. He understood. He got that there was nothing to say because with me there was nothing left.

Sparkly fun Sid, laying on the sand in Malibu. Gone.

Sad Sid, looking through old photo albums, dreaming of ghosts?

Present.

Teddy?

Sent away.

PART 2

FIFTY-FOUR

SID

This was what happened next: a whole lot of nothing. Without Teddy, what did I have? No one to talk to. No one to plan things with. No ride to the beach. This might sound callous, all about me, what I had lost — but I couldn't think about Teddy and what he might be feeling. It was too much — also; he was probably fine. He had that easy smile on the beach at Zoe. He would get over me. Faster if he didn't see me. Which was easy, I didn't go to beach day. Didn't surf anymore. I stayed home, cleaned the house and watched tv.

But I only had to hide away for about three weeks before Teddy left for school in Santa Barbara. I marked the day by cleaning out my closet, deep, down to the carpet, and vacuuming there, but then putting everything back because I didn't want to deal. Halfway through I got sidetracked by a drawer in the bathroom full of old junk jewelry (mine). I cleaned that too. Trashing a third of the contents. I kept wondering where did the time go — I missed lunch, also mom only died one month ago, and also, Teddy was leaving already? How did this happen, everything in my life just sliding on by.

Then I curled up and watched Ten Things I Hate About You and cried through the end because it was my mom's favorite movie too.

Dad came home and staged an intervention. With Thai food. "Teddy is in Santa Barbara, huh?"

"Yep."

"Did you see him before he left?"

"Nah." I picked a spicy pepper out of my Tom Yung Gung soup and separated it into the middle of a napkin. "I told you we just don't want to hang out anymore." He looked at me intently so I added, "just moved past that part of my life I guess."

"Usually when someone moves on it's toward something better. Whatcha got on the horizon?" He said it casually, but I could tell that question had been stewing for a while.

"Did Lori call you again?"

"Yep, she was pretty sad. Teddy's leaving her, Alicia isn't around to talk to. She thought you'd be there to see him off. I got to explain that you two weren't friends anymore. Apparently Teddy is being quiet about the whole thing."

I said, "Oh."

"So it would help me if you'd have a plan. Anything. A reason you are withdrawing from your friends."

"It's been a month since Mom died."

"Yep. It doesn't have to be big or awesome or even thought-through. I need to have a way to explain it in my head and to Lori and everyone else who will ask."

I pushed my food away with a huff. "Fine. I saw there's a screenwriting class. Local. On Tuesday and Thursday nights. It costs about $475 for eight weeks."

Dad raised his eyebrows. "That's more thought-through than I expected. Let me try it out." He put on a falsetto voice, "Mike, why doesn't Sid come to Beach Day anymore, we're so worried about her. And I answer, Oh, she's very busy, she's taking a local screenwriting class." He smiled, "I think that works."

"I'll sign up for it tomorrow. I'm assuming you're offering to pay for it?"

"It's cheap for how much it will help me."

We looked at each other for a moment, then he asked, "How will you go surfing now?"

"Not sure. Not sure I want to."

He said, "Yeah, I feel that way about a lot of things too. I also feel like the most un-fun person in the world. And that sucks. I want to have fun again, someday."

"Yeah, me too."

He dramatically sighed. "But until then I have Axl Rose." He grinned.

I rolled my eyes, "You only gave Foo Fighters two days. You might be hopeless."

"And old."

"You said it not me."

"You want to watch a movie? Something new, something funny? Hopefully something neither of us will cry through and that I can quote tomorrow so my work friends won't think I'm as depressed as I actually am."

"I love you Dad."

"Love you too." We cleared away our bags and trash and went to the living room to pick a movie to stream.

FIFTY-FIVE

SID

For the next month that's what I did, a lot of the same, hanging out by myself in the house, watching movies with Dad, going to a class that met for a few hours a week. Dad and I called me busy, but we were mostly joking. I went to a coffee shop to write. I made a deal with myself that I would do more things soon. Next month. Six months tops.

FIFTY-SIX

SID

Then there was Gavin. I didn't fall for him, he slammed into me. Like an untimed wave that I forgot to look for. Trust me, Teddy might have said, time them, look for the good ones, be patient. But Teddy wasn't here and it had been a long time since he had advised me on things that mattered.

Cameron had called me with a favor. His band wanted to open for a bigger band called Broken Blasters. (I googled them, they were a hot and upcoming band out of England) The lead singer, the guitarist, and the drummer of Broken Blasters would drop in to see Cameron's band rehearse.

Cameron figured it would look good to have a small audience while they played. But his point was, basically, that it might sell them to have pretty girls watching them adoringly in the rehearsal studio where they practiced. I was a little flattered that he asked me. I was also a little irritated when he asked if I had any friends, and when I said I didn't, not really, he said, "What about Zoe?"

I answered that Zoe and I didn't hang out any more, and he huffed and said, "But you'll come, right?"

And I said I would because I was bored.

Man, it had been a long time since I had anything interesting to do. Also, Dad had just reminded me I was supposed to be trying to be the kind of person who had fun.

When I got to the rehearsal, I perched on the arm of a ratty old couch while Cameron's band, The Strange

Monikers, tuned their instruments and pretended not to be nervous.

Then they walked in.

By they I mean — Gavin. And two guys who were impossible to notice because of Gavin.

He was hot. Wicked hot. Pale pasty white, like he might need an intro to the sun, dark wavy hair, a jaw that looked like you wanted to kiss it. Anyone would want to. Guy or girl, it only made sense.

Living in LA you get kind of used to people who are celebrities, the famous, or the On The Cusp Of Famous, walking around in your normal world. By used to, I mean, able to spot them, capable of maintaining your cool, knowing to ignore them, but also track them, in case.

Gavin had that famous person aura. He wasn't a celebrity, but he walked into that room and every set of eyes landed on him. I caught my breath. The two young men with him, deferred to his decisions — where would he go, what should they do?

He swept the room with his eyes and then his eyes landed on me and he did this — I kid you not — he put his hand over his heart and took a step back. He literally said, "Whoa," under his breath.

I looked down at my Mexican Coke bottle trying to figure out what might be wrong that this gorgeous stranger lost his step at the sight of me. Probably spinach in my teeth. I brushed, but still.

Gavin beelined for me. I stood up and we almost collided which caused him to laugh. He swiped his hand through his hair, and looked into my eyes, as if we had known each other for a long, long time, like he was trying to get me to remember. Positioning himself right there. Close.

Then he spoke in a sexy, sexy British accent. Jeez, could he get any better? "What's your name then?"

"Sid."

"Sid? I never knew a 'Sid' to be quite so feminine."
Heat crawled up my cheeks. "My name is Gavin." I stared
down at my feet, one shoe on top of the other. He asked,
"What brings you here?"

I said, "My friend invited me to listen to them play
tonight."

"Ah, but see, you strike me as above decorating-the-
furniture-for-a-mediocre-rock-band."

I chuckled and said, "You haven't heard them yet."
And then I said, "You also just met me, this might be
exactly what I'm suited for."

He raised his eyebrows and smiled, head cocked back.
"Are you from around here Sid?"

"I'm from the Southbay, actually."

"Ah, Sid from the Southbay, makes perfect sense."

I knew I should also ask questions, but I was having a
hard time keeping up with his cocky assuredness. I took
another sip of my Mexican Coke.

He watched me, like he couldn't take his eyes off my
face. I nervously glanced at an old ratty Green Day
poster.

He put his hand over his heart and leaned in. "So Sid
of the Southbay, what do you do, your day job, when
you're not decorating concert halls?"

One of his band mates thrust a drink into Gavin's
hand and he took it without looking and drank. How
would that be? To have total trust that your needs will be
fulfilled because you're just that cool?

I said, "I'm a writer."

"Oh, really? See, I was right. What do you write?"

"I'm working on a screenplay, about Mary Queen of
Scots."

His eyebrows knit together and he looked at me from
the corner of his eye, "Mary? Our Mary? The Scottish
Strumpet?" He laughed loudly.

Heat burned up my ears.

He said, "Will you tell about how she murdered that one Brit and then tried to overthrow the Crown?"

I glared, "No, I'm going more for the tragedy of her life, how she was carried along by a course of events she couldn't control. That she was young, and basically good, but fate intervened."

"Ah, a retelling. I see." He ran his fingers through his hair. Then he smiled and his hand went back to his heart. "You see, us Brits, we're divided into two camps, either we're anti-royalists, like my father, or we believe Elizabeth the first was correct in all things, like my Mum. You won't find many Brits that will embrace a retelling of the Adulteress of Edinburgh to make her look like she was treated unfairly. It will be a hard sell." He looked deep into my eyes again, "That being said, a young American, like yourself, might be just the person to try."

One of his band mates whispered in his ear. Gavin took a deep swig from his glass. "I have to get to work deciding the fate of this band. You best resume your seat so your beauty can distract me from their imperfections."

He turned and stood with his band mates as Cameron's band started to play.

What the hell was I supposed to do now? I couldn't go sit on the couch. Not after being told to. But then again, he was just pointing out that Cameron had asked me to sit on the couch. Cameron was the problem, right? I also couldn't stand here on the back wall of the room, by myself, while a band played. I looked ridiculous.

So I did the only thing I could think of — I walked to the couch and perched on the arm and tried to look beautiful. Like I had been told. But here's the thing, you might think I had lost my power, but Gavin couldn't take his eyes off me. Barely ever. He listened to the band, but he watched me, the whole time.

After Cameron's set, Gavin came back. He sat on the couch leaned back, looking up at me still perched dutifully on the arm of the couch.

"I can see why you got this gig, you performed your part perfectly. Will you come to the show?"

Cameron was looking over at us. He was probably watching Gavin for signs of whether the Strange Monikers had been picked or not. Maybe he was a little jealous too.

I said, "I'm sure the band will invite me."

He said, "No, I mean, will you come with me, to the show."

"Oh, um, yes."

He nodded and ran his hand through his hair. He shifted his weight and grabbed his phone out of his back pocket and said, "Sid of the Southbay, might I have your number, please?"

I called out the digits and he worked for two seconds until my phone vibrated in my pocket. "Sid, it has been a pleasure. I'm greatly looking forward to spending more time in your company, as you take my breath away."

Seriously? This was real? He stood and cocked his head again. "It will also be fun to tell my parents I'm falling for a California girl named after Sid Vicious who happens to be a royalist and a believer in the goodness of the Harlot of Scots."

He smiled and gave a small shake of his head, not in a bad way, in an I Can't Believe The Way She Makes Me Feel kind of way. A way that made me get all hot inside. And then he said, "We have another band to see, will you be up later? If I text?"

I said, "Yes," because who could sleep after all of that?

FIFTY-SEVEN

TEXTS

Sid of the Southbay are you up?

                                          Yes.

You're beautiful when you say yes.

                              You can't even see me.

I remember.
Can I see you tomorrow?

                              It's my 19th birthday.

Good, I have a present.

                    Are you always like this, so smooth?

Usually not quite so.
You caught me on a work night.
I have to be all 'rock star'
You'll see when you invite
me over to eat cake tomorrow.

                    If I see you on my birthday you have
                              to share me with my dad.

I share.

I'm good at sharing.

                    Okay, you can come to dinner
                       and have some cake.
                              6 o'clock.
                    Presents aren't necessary.

Too late
I already got you something.

                                              :o)

Good night Sid.

                              Good night.

FIFTY-EIGHT

SID

Gavin showed up.

I hadn't even believed it was possible.

He was charming, shook my dad's hand, said, "Anyone who names their daughter after Sid Vicious is all right in my book," and was generally cool. I expected him to be sticky with rock-and-roll sweat, or inappropriately dressed, or maybe cursing too much, but no, he seemed like normal guy, but with fully intact famous guy aura too.

Hot. Wearing a plain tee, tight jeans, boots, and a few too many bracelets. He talked to my dad about music and then cut his eyes to me and smiled like we were together on some kind of secret. Like we had known each other for a long time, but here we were first time together (by choice) and it was my birthday and he was wooing me. Wooing me hard. And my dad. Dad actually got flustered a few times talking to Gavin. That aura was hard to resist.

We ate dinner. We had birthday cake. Dad had remembered to buy one from Becker's Bakery our family's favorite. Mom had always ordered it before. I was impressed and a little teary. Dad went to the kitchen to light the candles, and Gavin asked "You look sad on your birthday, Sid of the Southbay."

I said, "My mother only recently passed away, it's still a little raw."

He leaned his arm out long across the table for my hand. I placed my hand in his, and he enclosed his fingers around.

Dad returned carrying the cake, all nineteen candles blazing, and turned the lights off with his elbow. He sang

Happy Birthday while Gavin harmonized, causing me to become breathless and very incapable of blowing out my candles. Three tries.

When I looked up at him, shifted back in his chair, he raised his brows and smiled.

———————

After cake Gavin went to his car and returned with a cardboard tube.

I pulled the cap off the end and fingered inside for its rolled-up contents — a poster. I pulled it out and unfurled it on the table. It was a concert poster for Oasis from 1994. The year my parents got married. My mother's favorite band. Best part? It was signed by Noel and Liam Gallagher.

"What? Wow?" I said, speechless.

"You like?"

"Yes, oh, wow, yes!"

My dad leaned in. "This is a Los Angeles show. How did you get this?"

He said to my dad, "My old man's a record producer, he has connections."

To me, he said, "I'm glad you like, I suspected."

———————

And that my friends is fate.

There wasn't a doubt in my mind that this was destiny coming true.

A sign that this was meant to be.

And possibly a visit from my mom. Definitely maybe.

———————

Dad put the poster back in the tube and rushed it away to await the frame he would buy the next day, and I stood facing Gavin, suddenly awkward. What do you do next with the hot stranger that just celebrated your birthday, won over your dad, held your hand through your grief, harmonized your birthday song, and gave you the perfect gift?

Whatever he wants.

And what did Gavin want?

He leaned in and entwined his fingers in my hand and said, "Will you come stay the night, Sid of the Southbay?"

Oh yes.

FIFTY-NINE

TEXTS

I know this is against the rules,
but I'm sure this day was
hard without your Mom.
I hope you're making it through
and that your dad
Bought you a Becker's cake
and I just wanted to say
Happy birthday.

Thank you Teddy.
My birthday was good.

School going well?

Yes. When I go,
the waves have been

Can I call?

Can we talk?

I'm actually in bed right now.

Good night.

SIXTY

SID

Gavin drove up La Brea Boulevard to Sunset Boulevard and pulled up to his apartment in Silver Lake. It was small, but nice, and all his own. No roommates — which at his age, in this economic climate, in this city, was unheard of. Note to all of you paying attention, this was not only my first boyfriend since Cameron. (Teddy doesn't count.) This was my first night in a man's apartment. He pointed to the living room, gestured toward the bathroom, and offered me a drink.

I said soda which seemed a little young of me to say, but I said it. He asked, "Want anything mixed in your soda? Birthday and all?"

"No thanks."

He returned with Sprite in a glass and what smelled like a rum and Coke in his. He sat down on the couch and patted the seat beside him. I sat down, and then he jumped up to fiddle with a laptop. "Trying to decide if I should play Oasis, which would be safe, or something different, like — hmmm." He put on something I didn't know. "One of Dad's new bands."

He placed his drink on the coffee table and jumped his whole body lengthwise onto the couch, landing with a thud beside me, and then gently laying his head in my lap. "Thank you for coming."

"Thank you for celebrating my birthday, for the present."

"My pleasure, Sid."

Then with one motion he was up, kissing me, hand on the back of my head, pressing up on my mouth. Hot —

breathless — awesome. And yes, I kissed that jawline, and yes, he kissed my neck to my shoulder, and then he stood and pulled me by the hand to his bedroom — we both undressed by his bed and kissed and caressed before dropping down. He wrapped me up in his arms and legs with his chin on my breast. "I haven't been able to get you out of my head."

I stroked my fingers through his hair and said, "Me too."

He kissed my chest. "I could live like this, here." Then he crawled up and kissed me deeply and we spent a while there — I would give you details, but it was all a little wow, and oh, and oh my god, and lots of other stuff that was awesome. I'm a huge fan.

Maybe his number one fan.

I hoped.

But what are you going to do? The signs were all there. This.

———————

I spent the night. You know how in the movies the characters have all kinds of issues with people spending the night? Not Gavin. He curled in and wrapped up and woke kissing and then he got up and made breakfast: bacon and eggs. And kissed me and asked me to spend the day.

Yes. Oh yes.

———————

I spent three days actually. In the evenings I went home for dinner with Dad, but caught an Uber back to spend the night at Gavin's, kissing and whatnot, holed up in his apartment, stepping out to walk down the street for more food or coffee or a candy bar or just a walk around the block, my arm wrapped in his.

On the fourth day I woke up, and Gavin was standing in the kitchen talking on the phone. He said, "I know, I've got it. Yes. It's getting done. Yes, sir. Your office, yes."

He hung up the phone, tossed it on the counter, and stood leaned on his hands, head down.

"Gavin, is everything okay?"

"My father is coming to town, gather the troops, sound the alarm."

I tried for a joke, "He sounds lovely?"

Gavin stood and tossed a paper towel at the trashcan and missed. "He's not. He didn't get where he is by being lovely as you naively put it. He got there by beating everyone to the point of insanity."

"Oh, I'm sorry, I didn't mean . . ."

He looked straight ahead at the far wall. "I have a lot to do after my little hiatus here, so I'll be out of the picture for a while."

"Oh. Um, sure. I —"

"Can you get an Uber home?" He picked up his phone and swiped the screen.

Heat crawled up my cheeks. "Of course." I spun on my heels and gathered my things to go. Tears threatened to spill over, but I held them back until I got through the front door with barely a look from Gavin and not a kiss, because: dick, apparently.

And like a lost little girl I cried in the backseat of a stranger's car.

SIXTY-ONE

MARY

There was nothing anyone could say to dissuade Mary from marrying Darnley. She loved him. He was tall. Handsome.

Everyone warned her he was an ass, that he was using her for the crown of Scotland. She understood this, but still. She carried on. And then it was nothing but war and conspiracy and murder. Because that's what happens when you lose your mind in love. All out war.

SIXTY-TWO

SID

This was what I wondered, would Mary's mother have advised Mary against marrying her first cousin with the asinine attitude?

My guess was probably, but guess what? Dead.

If she hadn't been dead though, would Mary have listened?

Do daughters ever listen? I tried to think back on my Mom's advice through the years. She was watching me from a unique position — the ultimate, full-life, armchair quarterback. She dated. She had lovers. She had a big big love. We talked about it. She advised me, and her advice was blunt, funny, and usually good. I did listen. But the stakes weren't very high.

And now that I had big questions, she wasn't around.

What would her advice be?

I had a friend whose mom married the first man she dated, others, like mine, who played the field, learned the rules, rigged the game, and scored (to use way too many sports cliches) a lot.

Both types of mother were in a unique position to give advice. The Long Loyal Mom might describe the qualities that made a man a Long Loving Husband, how to secure their loyalty, how to make it through the tough times and enter old age after a whole life with one person. That would be good advice.

The other type of mom could show a daughter how to size them up, try them on, enjoy the ride, and gracefully move on. More good advice.

But now that mom wasn't here to advise, I realized that I never really listened. Here's what sucks about daughters, they don't want to know.

I suppose each generation wants to learn it all over differently.

But with each generation it's the same.

Piles of broken hearts and the Ache dropping us to the ground.

And so the Moms watched, or the Moms complained. Or in the case of Teddy and me, they urged. They prompted. They planned. And what did it get them?

Nothing good.

SIXTY-THREE

SID (TWO YEARS EARLIER)

"Mom, did you have a lot of lovers before you met Dad?"

She dropped her dish towel. "Why?"

"Because Zoe told me her parents met in high school. Young high school. And that they had only been with each other. Her parents would freak if she was sleeping with someone. You and Dad let Cameron stay over, so I assumed . . ."

She said, "You said you loved Cameron, and that was good enough for me. I told your father that as a young woman you get to pick who you love, and that we needed to trust your choices. You're welcome for that, by the way."

I giggled and said, "Thank you."

"As for my lovers, I had enough. Enough to have fun and enough to know when I met your dad that he was right for me."

"That's not really a number."

"I'm not giving you a number because you'll either think I've made too many conquests or too few, and when you compare them to your own, you might think I'm lacking or you're lacking. Counting lovers is like counting the years, you can keep it to yourself."

I smiled. Mom was always blunt and to the point.

I asked, "So you recommend lying?"

"Not what I'm saying at all. You don't list your life. Definitely don't list your loves. Sleeping with someone you love is fun and amazing and when it's no longer fun and amazing find someone else and love them even better. It doesn't matter how many or how few. It matters is your heart in it, is it the big kind of love, and if you can say yes, that's great. Do that. Do it a lot. Do it every chance you get."

You might wonder why a woman with such good advice would just go and die. I agree, I wonder it too.

SIXTY-FOUR
TEXTS

Sid of the Southbay are you there?

                                              yes.

I'm sorry about today.
My father makes me crazy.
Will you forgive a bloke?

Let me make it up to you?

                                    Not sure.
                        That was super uncool.

I've been in meetings and rehearsals all day
I could use some Sid time.
I miss you.
I have to do it all over tomorrow.

Come over.
I really will make it up to you.

                                         Okay.

I'll pick you up in half an hour.

SIXTY-FIVE

SID

I spent the night again. Gavin was smooth and attentive and the next morning he kissed me when I left to Uber home. He had to work again, with his father. He didn't text for three more days.

SIXTY-SIX
MARY

Every death in her life caused a major life calamity.

Her father died — she became a baby Queen.

Her future father-in-law died — she was married young to a child King.

He died.

Her mother died.

She had to move back to Scotland.

Her closest advisor was murdered in front of her (probably by her husband).

Her husband was murdered — she was blamed.

She never got to see her baby again.

Imagine that. To be young, twenty something, and you never get to see your child again. For your whole life.

It can be a cruel world sometimes to have those you love taken away.

SIXTY-SEVEN

TEDDY

I missed Sid. Terribly. I missed her smile and her laugh and the way she folded into my car and took over the radio and sang along loudly. When she sang she was always off key, but she loved singing. The words were the best part, she said.

I went to school. I met people. I made friends and my roommate was passable. We surfed all the time. Even when we should have been in class. It's what surfers do in Santa Barbara. They surf. I'd figure the whole thing out once the waves calmed down.

My friends had a group of girls that hawked them and one was circling me, which was fine. I was free. It was okay to be caught, but I played aloof. I made sure there was someone in between us on the couch. Made sure no plans sounded too date-like. I went back to my apartment alone. I didn't plan to become a saint, don't get me wrong, but not that much time had passed. I was only two months into the school year.

I went home for the weekend.

Mom said, "Zoe's mom said Cameron and the band are having a show. They're opening for some band that's on the cusp of greatness. She says it's Cameron's big break. Your dad and I wanted to go, but now we have this thing tonight. You should go."

I was nuking meatloaf for dinner and asked, trying to sound casual, "You think Sid will go?"

"I don't know. It would be nice to see her though, huh? You could text her and ask?"

"Nah, I'll go. It will be good to see everyone."

I ate dinner with Mom and Dad and then dressed and drove to Hollywood alone.

I passed my car to the valet. I paid the entrance fee for the show and stepped into the dark Fonda Theater. People were packed to the doors. I shoved through the crowd toward the stage where Cameron's band, the Strange Monikers, were already playing. From the looks of their sweat-covered skin, messed hair, and the cheering of the crowd, I figured they were deep into their set. They sounded epic.

They had been one of the local bands that had been meant for greatness. Cameron's family was musical, he devoted all his time to writing songs and practicing, and they performed well. This all pained me to say, because this was Cameron. He dated Sid. Had kissed Sid. Had spent the night at Sid's house. He and I barely tolerated each other's existence.

I scanned the room, but it was dark. Strobing lights, a crush of people, and when I stood on my toes, the room was a sea of bopping heads, swinging arms, and gleaming phone screens.

I needed to get higher. Along the back wall was a second level balcony, a better vantage place, but climbing up the stairs took an entire song's length, and I was trying to rush. I figured if Sid was here, she might not stay long after Cameron's set ended.

My plan was to sidle up and begin a conversation. I had some planned topics, but also felt sure I could come up with something in the moment. This was Sid, I had never ever had a problem talking to Sid. The casual sidle-up was crucial. This was my one chance to see her without asking to see her, something I knew she would refuse.

Why? I still couldn't explain what had happened.

Just thinking about her face the day she told me to go away — why the hell did she do that?

The Strange Monikers began their traditional last song, a cover of The Pixies, Gigantic. Usually Sid and I sang along with it at the top of our lungs because it was one of my dad's favorites. Tonight I was singing it to myself. I threaded my way to the center of the balcony and leaned. I concentrated, trying to discern individual people, but there was no way to tell who was who down there. The irony was that I was now too far away. The band was about to stop playing, and I hadn't found Sid. Once the lights came up, it would take forever to get to the floor to look row by row — casually.

Cameron put down his guitar and waved to the audience, "Next up, Broken Blasters!" Applause and cheering filled the hall. They had done really well.

The lights came up. Every head in the room seemed to look up and around. I searched and searched for her, but she just wasn't there. I took out my phone and considered texting her; I could probably say something like, "I'm at the show, Cameron's show. Are you here?" Just make the text sound casual. Or something.

The next band took the stage and started a song that was the best parts of rock meets punk; the lead singer strutted the stage, all full of rage and showmanship. Two girls to my left screamed and pretended to swoon when he climbed onto an amp and backflipped off. I whistled, he was putting on an epic show. After the first song he said, "Hullo, LA! We are Broken Blasters, it's pleasure to meet you —" The guitar and drums dropped into the next song.

The two girls squealed, "Oh my god, did you hear his accent!"

Cameron used to joke that his career would be made if he had been born in London, and now here he was opening for a Brit. Figured.

Speaking of Cameron, he appeared through the crowd, so I went over. "Great show, man, really great."

"Thanks." He took a swig from a bottle.

"Is Sid here?"

Cameron said, "Yeah, she was backstage earlier." Some girls rushed up and pulled his attention away and I returned to the railing and my search, but not for long because there she was, down in front of the stage, alone. I spun for the stairs, jostled my way down, shoved a path across the expanse of the floor to the front of the stage, aiming where I had seen her last. "Hi Sid."

She looked startled, "Oh, um . . . Hi, Teddy," and beautiful. Her blond curls spiraled down. We were both wearing the same color shirt, blue. It seemed important that we were wearing the same color. Like this was meant to happen.

I leaned close to her ear and said, "I hoped you would be here."

She yelled something back I couldn't quite hear, except, ". . . you in school?"

"It's only a two hour drive," I yelled, because the music amped up and for a few minutes there was no way she could hear me. So I stood beside her, shoulder to matching shoulder, watching the band which I was thinking was, by the way, awesome. My head bounced along, the singer jumped to the top of the speakers and then did another backflip off and didn't miss a step or a beat, and the lyrics were good too. I was impressed that this was the league Cameron was in now; the kind of music you'd hear on the radio, and me and Sid, were watching, together.

I moved past wanting to start a conversation and formed a bigger plan.

I missed her too much to accept her verdict anymore. I needed to talk to her and I would, tonight. She was out. She looked great, clear-eyed, almost bouncing. I would ask her to give me or this or us a second chance. For a reset. Like her mother used to say, "It's time for a do-over. Everyone can use one sometimes." I figured if anyone needed a do-over it was Sid.

The song ended and in the space between I asked, "Surfing much?"

"No, I haven't gotten in the water, you?"

"Too much." Another song cranked up, fast, loud, the lead singer had endless energy. I offered to go to the bar and buy Sid a drink, she said, "No thank you." So I asked, "Will you be here, when I get back?" She nodded, so I raced to the bar, bought two bottles of water, and headed back to the stage.

Finally after a long set, the band announced their last song. It was a rock anthem and sounded great, loud and fun and destined to end up on the radio. It was just a matter of time. That was one of the coolest parts about shows in LA, you might be listening to the Next Big Thing. People in the audience sang along. I repeated the chorus so I would remember it and look it up tomorrow. When the show was over, I whistled and clapped and smiled at Sid and then I leaned in to her ear and said up close, "You look great by the way."

She glanced down and blushed and then this happened —

I'm like two inches away from her face when the lead singer jumped from the stage landing in a crouch directly in front of us. He stood with a cocky eyebrow up and an incredulous smile. Then he swaggered up, hooked an arm around Sid's neck, pulled her forehead to his lips and kissed her there, on the spot between her eyebrows and hairline. Like he owned it. He asked, "Who's this bloke then?"

Sid's cheeks bloomed red spots, she was freaking out. "This is Teddy, Teddy this is Gavin."

Gavin smiled widely, "Teddy? Your nursery school friend? How'd you like the show, Teddy?"

I looked from Sid, the guy's arm cocked around her neck, almost like a headlock, to Gavin, his face tilted back, leering down his nose. He swigged from a beer.

I said, "It was good."

Gavin held his bottle up. "Thanks mate, we'll get along just fine, me and you."

He turned away from me to Sid and pulled her by the sides of her face up to his, and kissed her, roughly. Then, still holding both sides of her face, looking right into her eyes, he asked, "You liked?"

She nodded. Her eyes cut to me, standing, speechless.

He said, "Wait for me, I'll finish up in a few minutes. Okay?"

She nodded again. It made me want to go ballistic the way she looked into his face nodding.

The rockstar dude stepped back. "Teddy, a real pleasure meeting you," and he pushed away through the crowd.

Sid said, "Teddy I . . ."

I said, "Who is — no wait, don't say anything." Then incredulous I said, "Seriously?"

Her mouth opened and then closed, the bottom rim of her eyes filled with tears.

"Jeez Sid, that sucks." I turned and shoved my way through the crowd, wanting nothing more than getting out of there, fast.

I stormed to the street corner out front. It was dark, late, but bustling on the street. All lit up and traffic everywhere. I would get my car, go home, but what about her face just then? She was crying, I left Sid crying in a bar.

I stalked back to the club and showed the doorman the stamp on my hand and stepped inside the concert hall. Thinking, Sid wasn't alone, that guy was probably standing all up against her with his rockstar sneer. Who the hell was he, and how was he with Sid?

I spun and went back to the street corner and jabbed at the crosswalk button. Sid was dating? Dating British rock stars? How did that happen?

I missed the light staring blindly as cars whizzed by in the street.

SIXTY-EIGHT
THIS IS WHAT I KNEW

Two months ago Sid sent me away.
She had seemed sad and broken but . . .

Now she was with a guy,
Like really with.
Like his arm cocked around her neck with,
like he owned her.

The guy was in a band
Cameron had been in a band.

Sid and band guys.

Standing on that street corner I decided that Sid was
fine.
She liked guys who were edgy.
She liked musicians.

She didn't like me.
Not at all.

I had been wasting my time dwelling on her.

It was time to move on.

Still there was something about that guy.

That's why I went back into the club.

SIXTY-NINE

SID

Watching Teddy's eyes as he went from confused to understanding was the worst. Worse than a couple of months ago, in the car, when I told him to go away. That was bad, but this was way, way bad. For days now I had been thinking about him. Wanting to see him. Wishing for a time machine because Gavin was so confusing; I didn't know where I stood much less what I felt.

And then there Teddy was. Hot. I know I keep saying it, but he was, just in the opposite way from Gavin. Like night and day.

One was edgy and dark, the other open and smiling.

One was up on the stage, all bravado and strut and awesome public sexy. Girls were screaming and staring and panting, but I was standing front and center, 83% sure I would go home with him tonight.

The other? He matched my color and walked straight up with eyes only for me — leaning in, whispering in my ear.

His face flashed in my mind, Jeez Sid, and oh god, the pain that was there. And beneath the pain, disdain. I hadn't liked that one bit. Like a punch in the gut to have Teddy look at me like that. I felt ashamed.

And that sucked.

Teddy disappeared. Gavin was nowhere to be found. I searched for anyone I recognized, finding Cameron in a corner with Zoe and Erica, I headed over. "Hey guys!"

Erica asked, "Did you see Teddy? He was here . . ." She stood on tiptoes scanning the room.

"I saw him for a second." I took a drink from a water bottle.

Zoe asked, "So you're dating that guy from Broken Blasters?"

All three of them were waiting for my response. Heat rushed up my cheeks. How could I answer that — yes? Gavin and I had never talked about it. I had spent a lot of time at his house, but also a lot of my time not at his house wondering where he was. I said, "I'm here with him." Then I stood on tiptoes, searching, wondering where he was.

Zoe, clueless and unfiltered as always, said, "Wow, Teddy must be pissed." A look passed between Cameron and Erica.

That heat, up my cheeks, had bloomed into bright red splotches. I didn't need a mirror to see it, I just knew.

Suddenly an arm was around my stomach. Gavin pulled tight behind me and buried his face in my neck. He whispered, loud enough for everyone to hear, "Hey beautiful. I was looking for you." He released me, stepped to my right, and took my hand. "Cameron, you put on a great show tonight."

Cameron said, "Thanks, you too, and thank you for the opportunity."

"No worries Mate." Gavin glanced around the circle without noticing or acknowledging Zoe and Erica. Then he took a drink from his beer, scanned the room, pulled my hand up to his lips and kissed my knuckle. "Will you excuse me? I have to work the room, my father is gesturing." He wandered away again.

Erica said, "He is so hot, you're so lucky."

Zoe laughed and said, "I'll say it again, Teddy must be really pissed."

I nodded and excused myself to go — anywhere else.

SEVENTY
TEDDY

I showed the doorman my hand stamp for the second time and walked back into the club. I crept along the edge of the crowd, found a back staircase, and returned to the second level. I stood along the wall, away from the railing.

Down on the floor Sid was alone for a while, then she was talking to Cameron and Zoe and Erica, and then out of nowhere that guy walked up behind her with his fucking swagger, grabbed her around the waist, and — I looked away and watched the roadies set up for the next band.

The rockstar guy swaggered away. Sid wandered off to stand alone near the stage. I didn't want to take my eyes off her, but I couldn't help noticing Gavin bump from group to group talking, smiling, laughing. Then the lights went down and the third band took to the stage and I couldn't see anything anymore.

SEVENTY-ONE

SID

The next band was amazing. Gavin nuzzled into my ear whenever he saw me, calling me beautiful and telling me how glad he was that I came. Then he disappeared into the crowd to go charm someone else. People stared at me. Girls whispered. I was the one who had the sexy British rockstar's attention, sometimes. Occasionally.

I went to the bar for a drink, and Erica joined me in the line and asked, "So where's Teddy now?"

"He left a while ago."

Her brow knit together, "No he didn't. I saw him a couple of minutes ago."

I quickly scanned the bar area. "Where?"

"I don't know. I assumed he was with you, but then again, with that hot guy kissing all over you, he probably isn't too into it."

She ordered a Coke and I ordered another water.

I returned to my spot in front of the stage during the last song. And then the concert was over. The lights went up. My eyes swept the room. Gavin was speaking with his father. I went over to say hello.

I walked up. Gavin cut his eyes at me and continued talking. He was an almost exact replica of his father. (Except his dad was wrinkled, that kind of old that rockers get, where it's impossible to tell their age.) His dad wore his hair in a faux-hawk, his t-shirt and jeans cut tight and formfitting. He wore loads of bracelets. This wasn't the normal collection of random cheap bracelets though, there was some serious money spent on that wrist. Cash. Rock-and-roll meets old rich guy.

Gavin was saying, "I know, we had a problem in the second set, but it won't happen again."

His father said, "Make sure of it, you're too old to be making rookie mistakes like that. And Taylor won't want to share the stage with you if you behave like a rookie."

Gavin's jaw clenched and he took a swig of a beer.

His father said, "Who's this then?"

Gavin pointed at me, "Sid Dalton," He pointed at his father, "Alistair Shift. Allie Shift, Sid of the Southbay."

His father said, "Ah, Sid, the girl named after Sid Vicious who's been distracting you from your music? Well, she's a beauty. Does she write well?"

"She is a writer."

"Maybe she can write those five tweets for tonight you owe me."

His father turned away and left for backstage.

Gavin frowned down at his beer, "I'm sorry about him, I wish I could say he's not usually like that, but . . ."

I said, "It's okay."

We stood awkwardly for a minute facing each other. He said, "I have to go backstage, finish up, be the prince of my father's kingdom. I'll be back."

He followed his father off the floor.

My gaze went up to the balcony where Teddy was in conversation with Erica. I tried not to watch him. Tried to look busy, uninterested, but it was difficult standing all by myself in a crowded room.

———————————————

Twenty minutes later Gavin rushed up, beer in hand, and swept me into his arms. He pulled me up close tight and kissed me on my neck. "God Sid, I feel like I haven't even seen you tonight." He kissed me on the lips. "I missed you. Ready to go home? I mean, not your home,

144

my home, I mean — that doesn't sound as smooshed as I hoped."

I laughed, "How much have you had to drink?"

"Too much to drive, poss-bly too much to work my phone. We might have to walk." He kissed my ear, hot and wet.

I said, "I'll call Uber and get you home."

"Only if you stay, stay, you have to stay." He kissed me all over my cheeks, my neck, my lips. "Have I told you, Sid of the Southbay, how much I adore you?" He smelled of beer which wasn't the greatest, but also sweat from the show. He was the sexy guy who had been up on the stage, that everyone, literally everyone, in the room wanted to go home with. But he was kissing me.

The house lights turned on and a bouncer said, "Time to end the fun, kids — end of the night, grab your stuff, out you go!"

Gavin laughed, "Grab my stuff!" He picked me up by my thighs and carried me, my legs wrapped around his waist, to the door.

I laughed in his ear. "Hilarious Gavin."

"Oh that's right, we don't have to go out the front door with the rest of the rabble, I'm a backdoor man." He turned us around, my legs still wrapped around his waist, to go backstage and suddenly, Teddy was there, walking past us, leaving the bar. We brushed him in the doorway, and his eyes met mine with a small nod.

SEVENTY-TWO

TEDDY

I watched her all night. Like a stalker, like a creep, but I had to, or else it wouldn't sink in. Gavin was so impossibly absolutely wrong, yet Sid kept looking at him so adoringly, waiting so patiently, smiling so happily, that the whole thing seemed like a bad joke. But Cameron said they were together.

It was — I couldn't breathe.

I sat on a stool, my head getting lower and lower. Slinking around, trying not to be seen. He kept leaving her alone, on her own, but in the end swaggered up and wouldn't stop kissing her. Erica walked up and followed my eyes, "Ouch," she said, and it was true. But also a serious understatement. She and Zoe and Cameron left to go home and I stayed, planted, I didn't want to watch but — his hand pushed up under the back of her shirt. He gripped under her ass and picked her up, her legs wrapping around his waist. God.

They disappeared. Sid was being carried out through the front door. I stumbled down the stairs and pushed to the door to follow them to the street. But instead, there they were, turning around. Sid's arms wrapped around the back of his head, a smile — her fucking bedroom smile. Then she looked up and her eyes met mine.

I nodded and looked away. Because that was it. The end.

———————

I picked up my car from the valet and drove back to Santa Barbara that night.

SEVENTY-THREE

SID

On the way home Gavin kept trying to put his hand up my shirt, kissing me, flirting, and being too wild and carefree for the back of a stranger's car, but funny and sweet too. I batted his hand away and luckily the ride was only about eight minutes. We could have walked, but there was some serious drunkenness going on.

I let us in the front door and Gavin said, "So that's me father, Allie Shit, I mean, Shift, whatcha think?" He went to the refrigerator and pulled out another beer and popped it open.

"I think you've had too much to drink."

"Probably." He gave me a half smile. He took a swig of the beer and then slouched down on the couch. "What am I going to do?"

"What do you mean?"

"I've got this career and this father and — and you don't want to hear this stuff."

I came and sat beside him on the couch. I put my arm around him. "I do, I want to hear it."

He said, "He could make my career, with a snap." He attempted to snap his fingers but couldn't get them to make a noise. Sidetracked, he tried three more times. "Instead he helps everyone else and — Fuck."

I said, "That must suck. What's your mom like?"

"My mom was his second wife, of four. He was her first husband, of three. My family's complicated. That's why I live here. To enjoy their infrequent visits. I'm sorry. Let's do something else." He pushed me back, kissing me, hand up my shirt for real.

He pulled my bra up instead of off and kissed my chest and then nuzzled in and said, "I love you Sid of the Southbay." And then his body grew still and heavy and in about four seconds he was snoring asleep.

I waited about five minutes before I shoved him over and climbed out from under. I yanked my bra back down. Gavin slept soundly through all of that.

I checked my phone.

There were texts from Teddy from earlier at the concert:

I need to talk to you.

Can we talk please?
Somewhere private?

Then about an hour later:

Never mind.

Tears welled up. Was Teddy okay? Definitely not. Would he be okay? I tried to imagine seeing him with someone else, but couldn't bear the thought. He had been so present in my life for so long — my Teddy. And now he was gone. It was like I was waking up to the fact that he was gone and wondering why I hadn't noticed before. It was like I had put him on a shelf and just assumed he would be there when I came back.

But he was a living breathing feeling person and that was a dick move.

And then I didn't get him down from the shelf. I got distracted by gorgeous boy the musician and forgot that I was breaking Teddy's heart, and now it was —

I leaned on Gavin's kitchen counter, rereading texts, worrying about Teddy and feeling such despair — again.

Always the sadness. I was a disappointment to Teddy. I made him so sad, that I disappointed myself.

Not Gavin though. I looked into the living room. Gavin was sound asleep, his arm, covered in bracelets, swung out, boots still on. Gavin — he needed me. He took me home at the end of the night. I was the bright spot in his tough days. He adored me, and he had just told me he loved me.

I left Gavin a note and called Uber to take me home.

SEVENTY-FOUR
NOTES AND TEXTS

Gavin,
   Your show was great, I'm headed home for some sleep. I'll see you tomorrow.
xox,
Sid

   The next night, late, I got these texts from Gavin:

Sid you there?

                                                        Yes.

I woke up and you were gone.

                                          Just now?
                        Because a whole day happened.
                                                        ;o)

No, I had to do dinner
and meetings
with dad

something cool happened.

Can you come over?
I want to celebrate.

                                        It's really late.

Please.
You could Uber.
You need to learn how to drive.

                                        True that.
                                Dad's off work tomorrow
                            I was thinking about going
                                        to the beach.

I can't get you
I've been drinking.
Please Uber.
I can't live without my Sid.

                                you make it sound
                                    so desperate.

It will be worth it.

SEVENTY-FIVE

SID

I got to Gavin's about 11:45 p.m. He met me at the door and wrapped me in his arms. "I missed you."

"I missed you too." He pulled me into his front entrance hall and pulled my shirt over my head. I laughed and said, "You missed me or my body?"

"Body, guilty. But in my defense, I was with my father and all these musicians and some radio execs, and I had to be rockstar all day. It's exhausting being my father's son. I need some Sid-time to relax."

He tugged my bra off, tossed it away, and walked backwards pulling me toward the couch.

"You said you had good news?"

"Steve, my dad's head guy, negotiated a radio contract. Two of my singles will be released over the next two months. And played, on the radio."

I threw my arms around his head, "That's awesome! Which songs?"

He pulled back to say, "If Inhaled and Astrobrights —"

"My favorites! When do they play them? I can't wait to hear them on the radio!"

He groaned and bent and wrapped around my chest, "I can't concentrate. You took your shirt off earlier and —"

I laughed, "You are such a smooth operator."

He pulled back, serious, "I'm not. I'm a mess, and you're the only thing I have that makes sense. The only thing." He kissed up my neck and carried me into the bedroom to the bed.

We woke up the next morning. Gavin wrapped around me, spooning, holding on. I nestled in and said, "Good morning," He kissed the back of my head, and we lay there, half in and out of sleep for a long long time. I nestled my hands inside of his and kissed his fingertips.

He asked, "What's that guy's deal, from the concert?"

I said, "Who? Teddy?"

"Yeah, what does he mean to you?"

"I told you. He and I grew up together."

"So you're just friends."

"Yeah, or no, we aren't friends anymore. Why?"

"Because he looked like he wanted to be more. Promise me nothing is going on?"

I blinked. "Nothing is going on."

He pulled me flat on my back and rolled on top.

"Promise me again." He looked in my eyes.

"I promise and stop that. Don't be like that."

"I just . . ." He rolled off me and threw an arm over his eyes. "I'm leaving, I have to go back to London."

"What?"

"Just for a while. Now that this deal has been signed, we go back. There's a tour, an album release, interviews. Besides that, my visa is out."

"How long?"

"Six months."

"Oh." I searched for something to say. There had been no clues, no hints that this was happening. My brain couldn't keep up. Gavin was leaving? It had been a month. "You never mentioned it."

"Well, I didn't know you'd still be around. Plus, it depended on the contract we signed last night. I didn't want to tell you until I knew for sure."

I looked up at the ceiling, "Is that why you were so worried about Teddy, you wanted to be sure you could leave me and I'd —"

"I don't know what I'd do if I lost you."

"You want me to be exclusive? We never even talked about it before. Will you be?"

He pulled his head up, "Are you seeing someone else?"

I sat up and swung my feet off the bed. "No, of course not. I'm here whenever you want." I turned to look at him and smiled trying to cut the tension.

Gavin grabbed my hand. "Sid, I need you. I'm sorry I'm going to London, I wish I didn't have to go, but please, I'll come back. Wait for me."

I watched my toes wiggling on the carpet. "You won't become a big rockstar over there and forget to come back?"

"No way, forget my Sid? When I have the most beautiful California Girl looking up at me from the front row of my concert? There's no way."

I nodded, though six months would be a long time for someone who needed Sid time after a grueling day of meetings. And it sounded like there would be a lot of meetings in London. "When do you leave?"

"Three days, but the good news is that my father leaves right," he looked at his watch. "Already left. That's why I feel better. I can spend them all with you. I just have to get someone to watch over the apartment while I'm gone. Do you want to?"

"Nah, I ought to stay with Dad. He needs me. Plus it's closer to my class."

SEVENTY-SIX
TEDDY

I had a new reality. The campus, walking to class, waking up in my apartment, it was like I was doing it all for the first time, instead of two months after the start of the year. For two months I had been living in a haze, pining, longing, missing Sid, and now I was either clear-eyed, or just heartbroken. I couldn't decide. Either way I was without Sid for the first time in my life. Truly without, and I couldn't figure out how to make sense of it or how to carry on. Everything was changed.

So I went surfing. I surfed for hours in the morning and then ate lunch and then surfed in the afternoon and fell asleep for a late afternoon nap and then watched tv until way past midnight.

I had forgotten to attend my classes, and when I remembered that I ought to go, assumed I was far gone, anyway. No sense walking into the building this far behind.

The Thursday after I returned from the concert, my friends invited me to go out. I didn't worry about what might happen if I let one of the girls sit beside me and fling her hair and accidentally brush my hand. I just didn't want to go to sleep alone. So I didn't.

Then I didn't again and again. For two weeks I peeled girls off me in the middle of the night and woke them up and told them my roommate was weird about guests sleeping over. He wasn't, but I asked him to be, and he agreed to pretend to care.

I sent the girls home with a lie and acted indifferent the next day, either ignoring them or giving them the That

Was Fun But I'll See You If I See You speech. I managed to keep from getting entangled by anyone.

You might think this was the ultimate dick way to behave, and you'd be right, but here's the thing. I wasn't being nice to begin with. I didn't act charming or give them any special attention at all, and still they would come home with me if I asked. All I had to do was ask.

Contrast that with the love of my life. I had worked up the nerve for years and all I got to do was kiss her on the stomach. Once.

So excuse me for taking advantage, I was dealing with a lot of not dealing well with things. Until about a week and a half before Thanksgiving when Samantha appeared.

Samantha was beautiful in all different ways from Sid. Small and petite. Brown hair, perfect makeup, jewelry, everything just so. She dressed like a surfer girl, but never surfed because she had other stuff to do. And she didn't bounce excitedly like Sid, so that was good.

She sized me up and chose me at Trader Joes. I was wearing baggies and flip-flops though it was 11:30 a.m. I was skipping my Marine Biology class. I was staring down at the salad selection picking out lunch. She said, "You're dripping."

I looked down. There was a puddle and enough sand to amount to a tiny dune by my flops. I joked, "Clean up on aisle seven."

She laughed. "The best salad is the broccoli kale chicken one." She grabbed one for herself and then we stood for a second before she said, "What's your name, surfer boy?"

I said, "Teddy."

She giggled, "Teddy, well you do look like someone fun to cuddle up to."

I laughed, startled by her directness. "I've been known to cuddle."

"I have class until four, but if you wanted to prove it you could pick me up for dinner at six. I'm a picky eater, so you need to get creative, but I bet you can impress me. Then we could see what happens."

I patted my pocket for my phone, which I had left charging in the car.

She pulled her phone out of her purse and punched in the number I gave her. "I'm texting you my address. I look forward to our date."

"Okay, I'll see you tonight."

SEVENTY-SEVEN

SID

The day before Gavin planned to leave he asked me out to dinner.

We hadn't 'dated' in any traditional way, I had just started spending the night, and we bought groceries together at the corner store or just grabbed something to eat out.

But this was an official date. There was an Indian restaurant a few doors down and Gavin wanted to take me. I dressed up, Gavin looked handsome. We walked hand in hand from his house and it was November, dark and cool and romantic.

Gavin did that thing again, where he bows down, leans across the table with his hand out and then concentrates on holding and caressing my hand.

He said, "So I'm leaving you Sid, across the big pond."

"You are."

He sat up in his chair and opened a menu. He got something out of his pocket, placed it inside and passed it.

There were two papers inside. I studied one for a minute. "Gavin, is this a plane ticket to London?" I dropped the menu to the table.

"Yes."

"For me?"

"Yes."

"You got me a plane ticket for London?" I tried to read the papers, but my mind was racing ahead of the letters.

He explained, "I got the ticket for the 1st of January. You're supposed to give the passport agency six weeks to process. And since Sid of the Southbay is the only Millennial without a passport, I had to research the process."

"You researched for me and bought me a plane ticket?"

He opened his eyes wide. "Yes, Brainiac, I bought you a plane ticket so you can come visit me in London."

I squealed and ran around the table and slung my arms around his neck.

He laughed and said, "If you expedite the passport somehow, I'll move your ticket up. You could come for Christmas."

I returned to my chair. "No, I think January will be perfect. This is our first Christmas without my mom, and so I need to be here with Dad. But then I'll come." I flipped the pages. "It's one way?"

"We need to talk about how long you can stay. I'll buy the return ticket, we just have to figure it out."

"Okay, yeah, that makes sense. Gavin, this is so great, thank you. I've always wanted to go to London."

"You'll love it, but you'll need some winter gear."

"We have winter in LA."

He shook his head, "Ah, Sid of the Southbay, there is nothing sadder than a California Girl insisting that her weather is the same as everywhere else."

"We have weather, it's just subtle." I looked at the tickets again, unable to believe it.

"Okay, so that's one thing to look forward to. The rest of the time will be drudgery. Just my father bossing me around endlessly."

I said, "What if you talked to him, explained that you want to be a musician, but you want to do it on your own terms."

Gavin looked incredulous. "What nonsense is this? You want me to talk to him? The man that sent me to hospital with a broken cheekbone because I told him I was tired of taking violin lessons. I was five, by the way."

"Oh shit, Gavin, I didn't know."

"Of course you didn't know, you Californians with your blue-sky thinking. If everyone will just communicate, hold hands, wish on a star, you think it will all be all right. Well, it won't be. London is covered with grey clouds all the time. Magical wishes don't work there."

I said, "I don't know why you have to be so mean."

"Because you're being ridiculous Sid, you grew up with a loving family. Your parents want to spend time with you. Did anyone ever make you do anything you didn't want to do?" He waited for an answer and said, "No, never. So I'm thinking you might not know what you're talking about when it comes to dealing with the former heroin addict who can make or break my career and who also happens to be my father."

"I might not know what it's like to deal with parents like that, but I know about sadness, and I know you, and I care about you." My voice wavered and tears welled up in my eyes.

Gavin said, "Fuck." And threw his napkin on the table. "I made you cry? You're crying? I'm so sorry Sid, I'm so sorry. I didn't mean to make you cry." He reached out for both my hands and held them in the middle of the table. "I'm so sorry. I don't know why I said that. Why I do those things." Our food came and he stared at the plates as if he was confused at their appearance. Then he dropped his head to his hands. "I don't know why I said that Sid, please, please tell me it will be okay. That you forgive me."

He looked up with so much anguish that I said yes.

And you know what echoed in my brain through dinner? What he had texted the first night we met: You're beautiful when you say yes.

SEVENTY-EIGHT

SID

Teddy's mom texted, inviting me to lunch. This was a new thing. I assumed she wanted to discuss my relationship with Teddy, which would be awkward, or she wanted to check in, make sure I was okay. Possibly she was looking around to be sure my dad was treating me well enough. No matter the reason I took it as meddling and was uncomfortable with the idea. We had never spent much time just the two of us, and I didn't want to begin now, but she was insistent.

So I was bracing myself for the possibility I would cry the entire lunch date. Either because she disapproved of my life or because of guilt about Teddy, but I relented anyway. As Dad had said, I needed to do things for other people. Plus if I showed her I was fine, maybe this would be the last time.

But that thought made me uncomfortable too.

She picked me up and said brightly, "Wahoo's? I'm guessing you haven't been there in a while?"

"Last time I went was with Dad, when mom was still in the hospital."

"Will it bother you?"

"No, I miss it."

We lucked out with a parking spot right out front, went in, ordered, and picked a table. Televisions in the corner blared surf contests. The music was too loud. Teddy's mom fit in perfectly; she had grown up at the beach, a surf chick, long curly blonde hair. She still looked good in a bathing suit though she was an ancient forty-eight years old. Whether she was going to the beach or not, she always wore beach-style dresses with bathing suit straps showing. Sunglasses on her head.

"So, Sid, first, I'm so sorry this is the first time we've done this. The other day I realized that it's been well over three months since Alicia died and . . . I'm just so sorry."

Great, a lump rose in my throat. I knew it. Once the crying started the whole lunch would be a wet-cheeked disaster. I looked down and said, "It's okay, I've been busy."

She took her sunglasses off her head. "I heard you have a boyfriend."

"Did Teddy tell you?"

"Oh, no, your dad. Does Teddy know?"

"Teddy met him at the concert last week."

She stared vaguely out the window. "That would explain why he didn't come home after, why he went straight to school." She fiddled with her soda cup. "Can I ask you what happened between you and Teddy? He won't tell me anything."

"I . . ."

"Here's what I need to know — did Teddy do something to you? Is there something I should be concerned about?"

"Oh no, not at all. Never. No, it was me, I . . ."

I struggled to find the right words. I finished, "I felt like such a disaster, so sad. Teddy deserves someone happier." I faltered and looked away.

"Well, I'm relieved, but also I wish Alicia was here to advise you, but . . ." She rubbed her brow and down her face. A waitress delivered our food. We both picked up our forks and ate. Then Lori said, "I was hoping you could help me, with Teddy. He's . . ." She finished chewing a bite and said, "He's not going to classes, he'll fail the semester —"

"Teddy's failing?"

She nodded and a tear slid down her cheek. "Alicia and I made so many mistakes. We thought we were giving you guys a long-term friendship, but now you're not even speaking. You were supposed to be there for each other, but now he has nobody. I feel like we failed you both."

"Oh," I put down my fork. "But he wanted it so badly, he's been planning to study Marine Biology since he was seven."

Lori wiped her eyes. "He won't talk. He won't tell me anything. It's like he's lost. And if you have any influence . . ."

"I don't think I do anymore. The last time we saw each other it wasn't good."

She nodded again. "He'll be home next week for Thanksgiving. Maybe you could come to Thanksgiving at my house, you and your dad, like old times. I was hoping maybe you and Teddy could talk. If you don't have plans with your boyfriend?"

"No, I don't have plans. He had to go to London. Have you talked to Dad about it?"

"He said he would like to, if you would be okay with it. We're all a little confused about how to navigate a world where Teddy and Sid don't talk to each other."

I nodded. Teddy was failing? He had been so motivated, so driven. It hurt in my chest to think about him floundering, being a failure.

"Dad and I will come, thank you for inviting us."

She clapped her hands together. "I'm so glad. Though without Alicia's expertise, my skills are such that I can't promise much dinner-wise. Do you have her recipe for her special potatoes?"

"Dad and I can make them if you want."

"That would be great Sid." She took a big bite of her beans and rice. "So tell me about your boyfriend, is he hot?"

"Boiling."

"Would your mom like him?"

I sized her up, what had Dad told her about Gavin? Was she getting information for Teddy? It felt weird to talk about Gavin to Teddy's mom. I couldn't tell if she was my friend or the coach for the other team.

I said, "On my birthday he gave me an Oasis poster from 1994. Signed."

Her eyes grew big. "Seriously? Alicia would have loved that!"

"I know. It felt like a sign."

Lori said, "Maybe she sent him for you. He's British, Alicia adored a British accent. And a musician? He sounds awesome. Your dad liked him too. Do you have any photos?"

"Online." I pulled out my phone and googled Gavin's band. I handed it to her.

"He's gorgeous Sid, wow!"

"Yeah, he's cool. Is Teddy seeing someone?"

"He doesn't tell me anything. Ask him yourself at Thanksgiving, maybe in front of us so we can hear what he says."

SEVENTY-NINE

TEDDY

Samantha spent the night. She spent the next three nights, then begged off for classes, but returned the following weekend. It was thanksgiving break. We were in bed and she was laying in the crook of my shoulder and then she raised up and said, "Are you going to invite me to Thanksgiving or not? My family is wondering if I can come home to San Diego, but it's all so boring, no one cooks, they watch sports the whole time. I'd love to try a real Thanksgiving kind of meal."

I said, "My mom does real Thanksgiving — about as real it comes. She's not a great cook though, but yeah." My mind reeled for a moment, did inviting a girl you've been sleeping with for a week to Thanksgiving constitute a Big Step?

I decided not to worry about it. That was the best part about Samantha, spending time with her, sleeping with her, required very little thinking on my part. None at all. I was just doing what Samantha told me to do, mostly. Not deciding for myself at all.

It was comfortable, like being allowed to go on vacation from my life, but with lots of sex. Plus she didn't mind if I surfed all the time, and best of all she didn't want to come with me. I could keep that part of my life to myself. "Yeah, I'll tell Mom you're coming."

EIGHTY

TEDDY

I walked in with Samantha and apparently had forgotten to mention to Mom that she was coming.

Mom stood at the door with a blank smile and a confused stutter. "Um, Hello Samantha, welcome. I'm Lori. I'll put your sweater here. Um, come to the family room, and Teddy can you come to the kitchen real quick?"

"Mom?"

"I invited Sid and Mike to eat with us! They're coming in thirty minutes. You didn't tell me you were bringing someone. Who is that even?"

"You invited Sid? Who told you to invite Sid? We have nothing more to say to each other."

"God, you sound so callous, this is Sid, your best friend. My best friend's daughter. Her mother died, and I want her to spend Thanksgiving with us. Like every year."

"This year is different, she wants nothing to do with me. Are you sure she's even coming? I can't imagine her agreeing."

"She's coming, and now it's — Who is this Samantha?"

"She's the girl I'm seeing."

"How long? You never mentioned her."

"Two weeks. Maybe less. It's not that big a deal."

Mom ran her hands down her face. "It is a big deal, Thanksgiving is a family holiday, not to share with the girl you happened to wake up with this week."

"Mom, that was rude! Also Sid and I aren't family anymore."

Mom was acting like I had done something terrible, like killed a pet. Her voice was low and measured, "Alicia and I were like sisters. You better be nice to Sid. She has had enough to deal with."

"Yeah, yeah, Sid's been through a lot. But, you know what Mom, she didn't want my help. She didn't want me. She told me to go away. So now you invited her to Thanksgiving. Great. Maybe I should go eat with Samantha's family."

"Oh no, she didn't tell me that's what —"

"Did she also tell you that her boyfriend is a total ass?"

"No she —"

Down the hall the front door opened and Mike called in, "Happy Thanksgiving, Sid and I brought potatoes!"

By the time I made it down the hall to intercede, Samantha was standing on one side of the room and Sid was on the other, both with confused looks on their faces. I stopped being able to think, incapable of running the introduction. Sid's face attested to her dismay; she had been surprise attacked finding an unexpected girl inside my house.

Maybe I should have anticipated this moment, enjoyed her tragic expression, but no, it kind of freaked me out. She looked upset. Her cheeks splotched. Her eyes misted. Mike shook hands with Samantha and then hugged my parents. My mom introduced Samantha to Sid, and Samantha gravitated to my side and grasped my hand. I gave Sid a quick hello, she nodded in reply.

Mom asked Sid to follow her to the kitchen. I was sure she was explaining that she had no idea I was bringing Samantha, that she would have called, warned her, but there wasn't time. Poor Sid.

Mike was oblivious. He asked, "So Samantha, you're a friend of Teddy's from school?"

Her answer was, "Yes, we're dating." Sid returned and slouched into a chair.

168

Mike said, "Wonderful, Sid is dating someone too. It's great to see you guys starting out in the world."

Sid met my eyes and looked away. I was torn between wanting to make everything okay for Sid, I had been doing it for so long, and getting myself out of there. The hell out of there. Fast.

I jumped up. "Samantha want a tour?"

She rose, "Yes!" and we left the room.

As we went up to my room Samantha asked, "Who's that girl?"

"Sid. Just an old friend. We barely know each other anymore," and then we waited for someone to call us to dinner.

EIGHTY-ONE

SID

Teddy just went to his room with that girl.

Don't get me wrong, she seemed fine, nice, pretty, polite. I mean, boring, but I guess it's not up to me to pick Teddy's girls. She dressed like a surf chick, but also like she never surfed a day in her life. Also fine by me. If he likes that kind of thing.

I excused myself to sit on the back porch. I stared out at Teddy's backyard, where I had spent so much time. The swing set had been in the far corner. The picnic table had been covered with brightly colored, patterned oilcloth to protect it from our many messy projects. The wide expanse of lawn had seen so many big games, full-costumed plays, including swords and kings and sometimes Viking battles that ended with Teddy yelling, "To Valhalla!"

I sent a message to Gavin that said:

Happy Thanksgiving!

And then:

(That's an American holiday)

No response, so I sat and stared out over the yard remembering Mom, sitting at the picnic table, smiling, animatedly telling Lori about something crazy, ignoring us kids, while we played our big games, oblivious to them in return, unless we needed them. Mom was always there when I needed her.

Until she wasn't.

I waited for dinner to start.

About thirty minutes later, Lori appeared, squeezed my shoulder, and told me it was time to come in.

EIGHTY-TWO

SID

The table settings were beautiful. Lori sat at one end. I sat to her left, Dad to my left. Then Teddy's dad, Scott, sat on the other end with Samantha on his other side. Which left Teddy directly across from me. It was like a movie: Teddy and his Date. She put her hand on his and met his eyes when he leaned in. (What kind of movie would this be? Rom-Com? Horror?) Whatever — I had a front row seat. I decided to look down at my plate the entire meal.

There was a buffet table at the other end of the room, to keep the table clear, but by tradition everyone sat first in front of their empty plates, to talk about what we were grateful for. I couldn't think of one single thing. And I couldn't imagine anything more horrific than being put on the spot to say, I'm grateful for . . . what? My mom died this year. I trashed my friendship with Teddy. I had forgotten how to laugh. These weren't the normal fare of a good gratitude circle. These were the things you talked over with a therapist. With a confidentiality agreement. Not in front of some girl named Samantha. While she held hands with Teddy.

Lori said, "Because this is our first Thanksgiving without our dear Alicia, and because she was the one who would organize our yearly gratitude circle, I would like us to go around the table and say something we admired, that we were grateful for, that we miss about her."

Fine, gratitude about my mom. I could come up with something nice to say about Mom.

"And I'll begin —" Lori's voice broke. "Alicia was my dearest friend. I counted on her help, her support, her advice."

Lori wiped her nose and seemed about too sad to continue, but then she took a deep breath and said, "She loved to do things. To create things. Every good idea I had in the last nineteen years, began with her. I go for the phone at least once a day to tell her something. I miss her so much." She sobbed and then laughed. "I'm a mess, I'm sorry, I wanted to be a more sophisticated hostess. Sid, would you like to say a few words?"

EIGHTY-THREE

TEDDY

As soon as Mom began talking I realized I had made a huge mistake. An epic mistake. This was Sid's first Thanksgiving without her mom and I had brought a date. What the hell had I been thinking? This was like the funeral all over again. I had wanted a do-over, had begged the universe for a do-over, but here I was, sitting beside a stranger, while people I loved mourned.

Sid's face was drawn and splotchy. She was collapsed in on herself, but it was her turn to speak. She gulped in air. Her mouth pulled down, eyes glassy from tears. "My mother was the kind of woman who could take ten pipe cleaners, two sharpie pens, glitter, and a glue gun, and create something that would keep me and Teddy happy for hours."

She glanced across at me, I gave her a half smile and looked down at my plate.

"She was the easiest person to talk to, ready to laugh, to sing, to dance. She always put me first, in everything." Sid sobbed and rolled into Mike's arm.

He asked her, "My turn?"

She nodded, her face hidden in his shirt.

Mike said, "I have a lot, but I'll go simple. I was thinking today about how much Alicia loved movies, a really good story. I miss her exuberance, but I'm so grateful that she passed it down to this one." He squeezed Sid and kissed her on her forehead. "Scott, your turn?"

I wondered if my dad might pass, but he said, "Alicia brightened every room, plus she was a great cook. When we camped together, her cooking kept my family alive."

Mom sighed deeply. "Baked fish, kabobs, grilled veggies, hot chocolate — now I suppose we can never camp again."

That was probably true. Mom loved to camp, but she hated to cook while camping. Alicia had been the only way she could do the one without the other.

Then everyone turned to me.

I said, "Alicia was like a second mom. When I was a total screwup, which was all the time, she would just talk to me about it. That was it, no judgment, no bringing it up later. And she always let me dig through her cooler. She packed way better snacks. No offense, Mom."

"None taken. I'll let you in on a secret: she packed her cooler with things she knew you loved. She always had bandaids for you too, as many as you needed after a wild day at the park."

I nodded. "That explains a lot."

My mother said, "She also always had chocolate to share with me."

I said, "It's hard to believe someone so wonderful could be gone."

We all cheered with our glasses, "Here, here!"

Mom put her hand on mine and gave it a squeeze.

Sid watched me, chewing on her lips, tears sliding down her face.

Mom said, "So we're a mess. My apologies Samantha for the tears, but it it's time to eat." Everyone got up at once to go to the buffet table and serve their food.

Dad, standing in line, said, "I wish she was here to add to our feast today, she had a flair with gravy."

Samantha took all my focus, asking what the dishes were and checking against her extensive mental list of 'sensitive' foods, and when we returned to our seats Sid had excused herself from the room. I placed my plate on the table and said, "Start, I need to use the bathroom," and went to find her.

She was standing in the living room, in the dark, the only light a street lamp streaming through a window. She was holding a framed photo. It was of the two of us, on the beach, when we were about four years old. She looked up when I entered, almost like she expected me, and said, "My mom took this I think."

"Yep, and you painted the frame. I think it might be my mom's most prized possession."

Sid nodded, replaced it on the table, and wiped her eyes with a wad of tissue.

"Sid, I'm so sorry about tonight, about Samantha. I didn't know you were coming, or I don't know, I wasn't thinking. It's like I can't think these days . . ."

"I probably deserved it, after the concert."

"No, you don't deserve this. Not at all."

"I should go back, or your mom will come looking for us next, and then my dad . . ."

"True." We stood for a second staring at each other, and then she walked by me out of the room.

EIGHTY-FOUR

SID

If all women are eventually, dramatically, and tragically killed by the Ache of the build up tears. If the Ache will kill them — all of them, or rather all of us — from inside that place right behind the eyes. If that is true. And it is. Then I am about to succumb at this point. I have so many tears built up that I can't cry them out for relief. I can cry and cry but more keep coming.

And this freaking Thanksgiving dinner is not helping. My tears are built up and about to burst through, and there's a girl I never met before sitting across the table, holding hands with my Teddy. If this doesn't make the Ache spontaneously and immediately deadly, I think it might be, at the very least, the moment when the Ache becomes incurable. Shit I'm sad.

Hanging out with Teddy and his family was a huge mistake.

EIGHTY-FIVE

SID

About halfway through dinner Lori smiled and said, "I miss Alicia's advice."

My dad said, "She prided herself on giving really terrible advice."

Lori nodded. "But underneath it was really wise, like the time I had the meeting with the CEO of that hip soap company. I was terrified. Teddy was little, so I had to take him with me, had to drive into the city, and had to pitch my idea. There were too many things to worry about. Alicia came over in the morning, hugged me, and solemnly said, 'Lori, just remember, never talk to strangers.'"

I chuckled, "Mom said that? That's funny because she talked to everyone."

"Yep, it was bad advice, but it made me laugh. I always felt better when Alicia made me laugh. Also, I think her point was, walk in and be friendly. Make them your friends, and the pitch will be easier. Which is actually great advice."

I said, "She once told me it was better to ask forgiveness than permission. I said, 'Mom, you're sure that's advice you want to give your daughter?'" Lori patted my hand, and we smiled at each other.

Lori asked, "You have one, Mike?"

"During cold season she would remind me, 'Don't lick any door handles!'"

Teddy's father chuckled and said, "She also talked you into homeschooling, Lori. I thought it was terrible advice, but it meant Teddy could surf with me whenever I wanted. So best advice ever."

Lori asked, "Teddy do you have one?"

"Once when I was ten and deep in my Harry Potter phase, she told me that, and I quote, 'One thing will always be true Teddy, girls will always fall for someone in a wizard cloak.'"

The whole table laughed.

Teddy added, "It's not true." His eyes met mine.

Scott said, "So tomorrow is our traditional Black Friday surf. Everyone's going, right? 7:00 am?"

Teddy said, "I don't know if I can . . . I was driving Samantha to San Diego tomorrow morning."

Scott said, "Oh," a look passed between him and Lori. He turned to me, "You win the award for best kid if you go, Sid. I don't play favorites, but also, don't make me surf alone, not on a holiday."

All the attention was on me, and I was not happy about being on the spot. But hell, I wasn't happy about much anyway, the laughs a second ago notwithstanding. But here's the thing. I couldn't blame Scott for putting me on the spot. We had been doing this for a decade. Going to the beach together the Friday after Thanksgiving. This was one of his favorite days, favorite surfs with his son, favorite things of all time. "Um, I don't know —" I glanced at Teddy wondering what he was thinking, how could he put his girlfriend before the surf with his dad? It didn't seem like him and also made it crystal-clear how in deep he was with this girl.

Scott said, "Come on Sid, this is our tradition." He turned to my dad, "Mike, will you come?"

"I have to work, and no one wants me sitting in front of my laptop on the beach, so I'm begging away. But you, Sid, you should go."

I gave Dad a grim look for using the 'should' and he shrugged. "Everyone needs a nudge sometime."

I nodded. "I'll go, best kid and all."

Scott turned to Teddy and Samantha again. "What if Samantha went with us? It will be fun. We surf all morning, drink coffee and eat muffins, then go home and nap. Anything to stay away from the shopping madness."

Samantha said, "Oh I couldn't, I promised my family I would be home on Friday to go to the mall."

Scott nodded awkwardly.

Then Teddy half-turned in his chair and spoke directly to her, "I could drive you home tonight, after dinner."

Her eyes narrowed. "My family isn't expecting me until tomorrow."

"Yeah, but if I took you home tonight you'd be able to go with them super early. You said they were disappointed you wouldn't be there. You heard my dad, I can't miss the surf tradition."

Samantha looked in Teddy's eyes and then around the table and said, "Okay. You can drive me to San Diego tonight."

Another look passed between Lori and Scott.

After dinner I helped clear the table to the kitchen and noticed a photo of me on the refrigerator. It had been there for years but I had forgotten it existed. I was costumed like Mary Queen of Scots in a neck ruff created from an old tutu, a bodice and blouse from Salvation Army, and skirts I had sewn myself. I had sculpted a crown out of clay and cardboard, painted and glittered. My grin was huge. At the time I thought it was all so perfect, but now it looked so handmade. "You kept this up there? God, I was such a nerd."

Lori said, "I see someone with a single-minded devotion to something."

I said, "Yeah, a nerd, that's the definition."

Teddy walked in just then. "What?"

I said, "I was looking at this photo of myself being a total nerd."

He took the photo and studied it. "Better than a nerd, Queen of the nerds."

Lori said, "You have to be kind to your past self, Sid. What you know now and what you knew then are two different things."

She took the photo and clipped it on the fridge. "I keep it because I remember watching you work on that costume every day for three weeks. You made drawings, lists, you watched tutorials, you left the park early to work on it. And when it was finished Alicia was so blown away with pride. Me too. Look at your smile, have you ever seen such happiness?"

Teddy stared at the photo, nodding. Then he said, "Mom, if there's nothing else, I'm hitting the road, who knows what traffic will be like tonight."

She asked, "Where's Samantha?"

"She's already in the car."

"Oh, What time you think?"

"Midnight? I'll call when I'm turning around. Sid, I think Dad is planning to pick you up in the morning. We're taking two cars. I'll see you on the beach."

EIGHTY-SIX

TEDDY

This is what I thought about while I drove Samantha home to San Diego — I was stuck. Powerless. I hadn't moved from that first day in the waiting room outside of Sid's mom's hospital room. While she lay dying, I sat staring at my hands. Consigned to a chair. The only thing I could do that day that came even close to heroism was refusing to leave if it came to that. It didn't. Sid came out and told me to go home.

Here I was four months later stuck in that same kind of place, wanting to help, but not able to be helpful at all. Sid was being crushed, right in front of me, smaller and smaller and more broken. What was I doing, walking around her, as she died under this giant weight, wondering, would a pulley system work? Or what about a tool of some kind? Do they have tools for this kind of thing? When what I needed to do was just get all superhero and lift that weight. The bigger part of the problem though was this: I didn't know if it was up to me help anymore. I had been circling, trying to figure out the best tool, when I got sent from the room.

That was the thing. What do you do when the girl you love is suffering a brutal compression from this impossible weight, but she doesn't love you back? You could help, you're sure of it, with some time on the problem, you could fix it, you'd like to, but it's not your problem to solve.

I was her best friend though. Now it looked like her only friend. Isn't that person — her best friend, only friend, guy who loved her — supposed to help her? Somehow?

I went around and around trying to decide what to do, but all I could come up with was this: Go surfing tomorrow. Listen. Take it from there.

EIGHTY-SEVEN

SID

We were early enough that we found parking spots right next to each other. Me and Scott in the truck with all the boards. Teddy and Lori in Teddy's car. I assumed Lori had given Teddy a talking to about Samantha and school, because he was quiet when they drove up and stepped from the car, but as we unloaded the boards, he and his dad warmed up and started talking. This was one of my favorite times on these surf trips — Teddy and his dad, pulling on wetsuits, waxing boards, watching the water, talking about the waves and surf reports and wind directions. Scott's hair was greying and clipped short, but they both had the same faces, wide shoulders and intense focus on surfing. Scott turned to me, "Ready?" He kissed Lori on the cheek, "Back soon. Don't miss us too much."

"I have my coffee and a camera, I'll take photos."

The three of us grabbed our boards and ran, plunging into the water.

EIGHTY-EIGHTY
TEDDY

It was so good having Sid go surfing with us. Like fantastic. I didn't want to screw anything up, or upset her, so I had put myself into a timeout, no talking, just letting Mom and Dad run the show.

The waves were big, so we had to work to stay in position. We didn't talk, just paddled and duckdove and caught the occasional wave. Sid didn't take as many waves as she usually did, and Dad mentioned it. She answered, "I'm choosing my waves, it's all about patience."

Dad teased, "Teddy, you hear that, Sid is schooling us on patience —"

Sid spun her board toward the beach and paddled. Dad called, "Sure you want to take that one?"

Sid paddled hard catching a big one. She flew down the line, ejecting with a flying kick-out at the end. We both cheered for her as she flopped to her board and returned to us. "And that fellas is how you do it." Sid even laughed, not in the Through-Her-Tears way of last night, but carefree, like before she lost her mom.

After two hours of surfing, we each caught a wave to the beach.

Mom poured us mugs of coffee from a big thermos and we had choices of three different kinds of muffins. We watched the surf and the surfers riding the waves and drank coffee. Mom asked, "Sid, how's your screenwriting class?"

I turned to see Sid answer. "Good, I mean, different. Okay."

My dad chuckled and said, "That's vague."

Sid said, "Yeah, I guess that's how I feel about it, vague."

Mom said, "Oh. You don't like your professor?"

Sid said, "I like him okay. It's just not very . . ." Her voice trailed off. She stared out over the ocean and said, "I just don't . . ." Her voice caught, like she would cry, and then she said, "I don't want to talk about it if that's okay."

Mom said, "Maybe it's not the right time for you, you know your own heart best."

Sid nodded and blinked a lot.

I swigged from my mug and tried to keep from blurting out, you've been writing this screenplay for years, how can it be vague, heartbreaking, cry-inducing? What good would that do though? It wasn't my place to blurt things.

We all went out and surfed for another couple of hours, and returned to the beach exhausted, spent, done.

Sid stripped out of her wetsuit and put on her traditional winter After-Surf gear, sweatpants and a hoodie. She collapsed to the towels and sprawled. "I'm tired."

I pulled my wetsuit down past my shoulders my eyes on the ocean, the wind had changed direction, trashing the waves. I leaned to my right and started to flick my wet hair on Sid but stopped mid-shake. I looked down and from her sprawl she was watching me through lidded eyes.

EIGHTY-NINE

SID

Teddy stopped himself from flicking water on me.

I missed him, that, everything, so much that I felt heartsick thinking about the sunny days gone by. He pulled his wetsuit down past his waist to his hips and dried his hair with a towel showing off every plane and angle in his shoulders and arms and the curve of his lower back to his — I turned away.

I wished I could have this again — our surf sessions, his family's adoration, him. Especially him. But he was so cold and quiet, and he had a girlfriend now. I had blown it royally. I sighed and threw my arm over my eyes.

Lori said, "So Sid, Scott and I were thinking about going out to lunch, like a date, would it be okay if Teddy drives you home?"

"It's okay with me if it's okay with Teddy."

He said, "Of course," and began wrapping the leash around my board.

NINETY
TEDDY

On the way home we were quiet. Sid punched buttons on the radio until she found The Killers, Mr Brightside, a song we usually sang along to, together, loud, but now she sat singing quietly, staring out the window, as melancholy as anything I ever had to deal with. I couldn't take it. At the next red light, I turned the volume down, and said, "You have to explain that earlier — vague. You've never been vague about Mary Queen of Scots in your life. You have a vivid idea. How did your screenplay become vague?"

She looked shocked. I expected that though, I was barging in unwanted and unasked. "It's not like that, it's not that I'm giving up . . ." Her voice trailed off.

Then she said, "I haven't said this out loud, yet, to anyone, so let me work out the way to say it." She twisted to face the front. "I'm not giving up, the screenplay, it's more formed than ever, but the class sucked. I've always thought I needed a class, and maybe I did or do, I don't know. I needed to know formats and conventions, but I could have bought a book, you know? Watched a Youtube video. I can't say that to most people, without sounding idiotic, but you — I took this class and the professor wanted us to write from screenplay exercises. He chose them. The final project was to take our idea and he would tweak what we wrote. I didn't want him to touch my screenplay. I didn't want to churn it out while they all discussed and critiqued. The screenplay is more important than that. So I'm not quitting, I will write it — maybe I'll hire an editor or someone to help me polish it."

I nodded.

Sid turned to me, "I mean, that sounds good right? It doesn't sound like I'm quitting? I'm not, I just think my idea is —"

I said, "Your writing, your ideas, are great — yes, that sounds good. I was worried for a second, but that sounds good." I turned the music volume up, then turned it down again. "Thank you for coming surfing, it meant a lot to my dad. And me."

She paused, I could feel her gaze on the side of my face. Then she said, "I'm glad I did, I really missed you."

I turned to look at her and missed the light turning green; the car behind me honked. I waved and said, "I'm going, sheesh," and drove through the intersection, taking a left onto her street, "Do you mean that?"

She nodded as we pulled up in front of her house.

I fiddled with the keys overly long and said, "Me too."

She said, "Yeah," pushed open her door and unstrapped her board from the roof. I sat in my seat for a second and then climbed out of the car to help.

NINETY-ONE

SID

When I got home from the Black Friday Surf, I did nap just like always. Something about the chilly air and the post-feast early morning exercise conspired to make me sleepy. No amount of coffee helped. I crashed hard, sprawled sideways across my bed, but it wasn't deep and senseless. Nope, I had an all hot and bothered fantasy dream:

In it Teddy was dropping me off at my house, twisted in his seat saying, "Bye, Sid," when I lunged, grabbed him by both sides of the face, and pressed my lips against his.

His arms went around me and up inside my shirt and we kissed like that, me above, him below, his hands in my wet hair. My Uggs flipped off onto the floorboards, my whole body in his lap.

He asked, "Is your dad home?"

"No, he went to the office. Want to come upstairs?"

Somehow we effortlessly got out of the car, even though I was on top, and he was carrying me up to the front door. (I was weightless because: Dream.) And somehow as he climbed the steps, arms wrapped around me, he was kissing me — on my lips, my cheeks, to my ear, and down my neck.

Suddenly we were in my bedroom. My arms wrapped around his head, kissing him, deeply. Teddy's hands were up inside my hoodie, rubbing all over while we kissed, and I was so hot for him — I wrapped both my legs around his waist.

Okay, that was a mistake, fantasy-wise. For a second Teddy turned into Gavin and we were at the concert, but

I was able, in my half-sleep, to imagine him into Teddy again. Climbing on me saying something like, "You're going to have so much sand on your bed."

I pushed down the back of his board shorts. He said, breathlessly, "Sid, do you have a condom? I don't carry them in my shorts."

"Um . . ."

And then I woke up. Seriously. As my mom would have said, "I always did have terrible timing."

I wiped the drool off my mouth and tried to wrap my head around the time. I was starving. I had been sleeping for hours. Dad would be home soon and the dim light almost looked like sunset.

I looked around thinking about the dream. The truth was I didn't have a condom here. Four years ago the Moms had sent a whole bunch of us to a Sex Ed 101 class and then enlightened and encouraged the Moms had bought small boxes of condoms for each of us. Teddy had one under his bathroom sink. I had one under mine. But guess what? I had used them up during my relationship with Cameron, and Mom wasn't here anymore to restock them. Sucked to be me. Glad I hadn't truly dragged Teddy up to my room. I doubted he carried condoms in his board shorts and imagine explaining, Oh no Teddy, I ran out of all those condoms.

Note to self: Buy more condoms.

Why had I been dreaming about Teddy? I was supposed to be in London with Gavin in a week, my departure date moved earlier because the US Passport Agency returned my passport in a tenth of the time. I wanted to go, right?

I was just confused because I spent Thanksgiving sitting across from Teddy and his new girlfriend. Also, the morning with Teddy in a wetsuit.

And my boyfriend was out of town, equaling: horny.

That was probably what it was.

Except Teddy.

I thought about his wide shoulders huddled against the cool air that morning. His smile when I caught that perfect wave in front of him and his dad. And then last night when he sat at a dinner table and talked about how much he missed my mom.

NINETY-TWO
TEXTS

You got the ticket?

Yes.
Only a little over a week away
;o)

I can't wait to see you.
I have a lot of meetings
and a rehearsal the day you arrive
I'll send a car.

Oh okay.
Really?

Where will it meet me?

No biggie, it will find you.
I got to run.
Super busy.
I'll see you soon.

NINETY-THREE
SID

My mother used to always say, "When in doubt, make a list."

So here goes:

- Teddy was hot
- Gorgeous
- My best friend
- He grew up with me and Mom
- Shared history
- He loved my mom
- He loves me
- He listens to me
- I broke his heart
- He has a girlfriend

- Gavin
- Hot
- Sexy
- New
- Exciting
- I get to go to London
- Said he loved me (drunk)
- Acts like he adores me
- Troubled
- Kind of an ass sometimes.

Trouble was, I couldn't parse out my feelings, I loved Teddy, but enough to love, love him? What if I blew our friendship by loving him? And didn't I already blow it and this was all moot, anyway? He was with someone else.

And here was the thing, if Teddy knew I was making lists trying to decide between him and Gavin, he would be so angry. He deserves better.

NINETY-FOUR

SID

I needed to focus on Gavin; I was flying halfway around the world to see him. I should be excited, not making a list comparing him to other guys. What was I a player? Or was Gavin just very, very confusing? I got to go to London though — Mom's favorite city. I worried about Gavin but Mom would have approved. Oasis poster, seriously.

Mom.

I sat up on the edge of the bed and looked down at my sand-covered toes. I stood and walked down the hall to my parents's room and opened the concert t-shirt drawer in mom's dresser. Like the weeks just after she died, I stared down into it with no plan, nothing, just staring into one of her drawers. It smelled of her oil — sandalwood rose. A year ago she read a book about simplifying and folded her shirts so they stood on end, vertical, as if they were at attention. In color-coordinated rows (but these were concert tees, so basically black and just a few whites). Mom had touched these, each one, so I hadn't touched them, not wanting to disrupt the aura. But today I did, I pulled up a white, and checked it to see what it was — U2, from the War tour, 1983. I clutched it to my chest. Mom had mentioned once that she went to see U2 a billion years ago in a small auditorium. I considered that information fairly boring at the time. But now . . .

Who did she go with? What did she wear? Did she go straight home afterward, or hang out after with friends rehashing the night? I would never know and never thought to ask. The millions of memories that made up her entire life, the loves and fears and laughs were all gone. No one would ever know what that night was like for her.

I fell on their bed and curled up around that t-shirt and cried for a long, long time. I don't know why — this shirt? Any shirt? Or oh my god, every shirt? I was such a mess.

I heard Dad putting bags down on the kitchen counter. He called, "Sid?"

I sat up and hastily wiped my eyes. He appeared in the doorway. "Hey."

I tried to smile, but red-splotched and smeared was how I'm sure I looked.

He said, "You got brave enough to go in the drawer?"

"I don't know if I'd call it bravery, more like stupidity."

He stepped into the room and looked into the drawer. "I'd call it bravery, I haven't been able to open it. Which one did you pull up?"

"U2, War."

"Ah, before my time." He sat beside me on the bed. "She was so lucky to get to go to that show. Did she tell you her seats were about twenty rows from the stage?"

"No, that's awesome." He handed me a Kleenex from the nightstand. I blew my nose and said, "I don't feel like I even knew her."

Dad nodded. He put his arm around my shoulders, and we both stared down at the t-shirt in my lap. "I feel that way too. We're all just travelers and for part of our time we're walking with other people. We meet up, know them as much as we can, as much as they'll tell, and then our paths part. That is, sadly, life. Regretting all that we didn't know, didn't say, that's sadly a big part of death."

"How'd you become so smart about this?"

"I'm living it."

I opened the shirt and looked at the boy on the front, war, written in red down the side. "Do you mind if I wear it?"

"Nope, those shirts are yours now. Though I do like them standing in rows still, is that wrong?"

"Maybe, but also I agree completely."

He smacked his hand down on my knee, the way he had since I was little, to announce a Big Talk was over. He stood, went to the drawer, looked down, jokingly gulped, and dove his hand inside. He pulled up a black shirt and opened it to show me. "Wear this one, it's from the Green Day concert she took you to three years ago. She told me it was the best concert she ever saw because you were there." He tossed the shirt to my lap and said, "I brought takeout, come down for dinner?"

I nodded, went to my room, switched into the shirt, and went downstairs to the kitchen.

The counter was piled with Chinese food. We served and sat across from each other at barstools pulled up to the kitchen island. We ate a little and then Dad said, punctuating the air with his chopsticks, "Speaking of wrong, I was super jealous that Our Teddy had the audacity to show up with a girl to Thanksgiving yesterday. Who does she think she is?"

"I think she thinks she's his girlfriend." I chewed my bottom lip.

He said, "If your mother was here she would've thrown the potatoes in outrage, or overturned the table."

"You can take the girl from the punk rock, but you can't take the punk rock out of the girl."

Dad said, "True that. She had terrible taste in music."

"Coming from someone who listened to Guns and Roses too loud, again last night."

He smiled and dipped his egg roll in the sweet and sour sauce. "When I'm brokenhearted, I like familiar, comforting. I'm thinking I should write a book, Grieving with Guns and Roses."

I chuckled and ate a steamed dumpling. "Do you think mom would've liked Gavin?"

"Well, let's see, first day he gave you the Oasis poster. And he does have the British accent. Plus he's taking her daughter to London. I think she would have liked him. Probably. Perhaps grudgingly, because he's no 'Our Teddy.'" Dad picked up rice with chopsticks and flourished with them, dropping rice all over the counter. "The question though is do you like Gavin. Does he make you happy? That's all your mom would have cared about."

"He doesn't make me unhappy. When I'm with him I'm not crying all the time. All the rest of the time I'm a wreck. Like mom was." A tear slid down my face, proving my point.

"Sid, you're a wreck right now because of your mom, not like your mom." He put his chopsticks down and peered at me. "You know that right — you understand the difference? Your mom did everything she could think of to give you a happy childhood until she couldn't anymore."

"But why couldn't she? Grandma Wilma said she died of a broken heart because I grew up and was going to leave her."

Dad looked shocked. "When did she say that to you?"

"At Hospice."

Dad said, "It's exactly that kind of toxic bullshit which is why Grandma Wilma doesn't get to see you anymore."

I gave a half-smile through my tears. "That sounded like something Mom would have said."

"Well, if she heard it, she might be so mad she's channeling through me." He gave me a sad grin. "Your mother's childhood was awful, brutal and bleak. She was abused, terribly. That's why you never met your grandfather. Wilma did nothing to protect your mom and mostly blamed her."

"Oh, I didn't know. Oh poor Mom."

He shook his head. "You might imagine someone who grew up like that would be a complete mess, but when I met your mom, she wasn't at all. She was the most positive person I ever met. She didn't want to live a life out of fear, or anger, but out of hope for the future. When you were born she read every book she could find on parenting, trying to undo the way she had been raised. Everything from breastfeeding to those baby slings, she would ask herself, 'Is this because I'm afraid of the world or because it will make Sid's life better?' She did that until she couldn't do it anymore, because she hadn't dealt with the pain, she was ignoring it. She had built her happiness on a broken foundation."

"Couldn't she have gotten help? Stopped drinking? Gone to therapy?"

"Yes, yes and yes. She could have. But instead she's gone. We have to take a deep breath and keep living. Her gift to you was a mostly happy childhood, it's up to you to build on top of that."

"I don't feel very happy." I pointed at my red swollen eyes.

"And you look like hell."

"Thanks."

"And you can't say Gavin makes you happy, but he doesn't make you unhappy."

"Something like that, the sex is good."

Dad's eyes went wide. He clutched his heart smearing fried rice on his shirt. "Sid, that was your mom's style, I don't know if I can go there."

"I was just testing if she is channeling through you — it's kind of hard to tell."

"I think she would want me to say that the absence of unhappiness is not necessarily happiness. Sometimes you can be happy with someone even though you feel really, really sad. This shit is complicated."

"That's why I'm just going with the flow."

"That's one strategy. Maybe you don't have to work as hard as your mom did to make things good. Maybe you can sit back and let stuff happen, but strive to be happy, for her."

Tears streamed down my face. He added, "So you're headed to London."

"Yep. The ticket's bought."

"What do you need for your trip?"

NINETY-FIVE
LORI CALLS SID

"Sid, I was thinking about Christmas, and I wanted to see if you and your father were going east, or if you would be here in LA. We'd like to have you over for Christmas dinner. I wanted to ask before you made other plans."

"Oh um, I'm not sure . . . Will Teddy, um — does Teddy know you invited us?"

"Teddy suggested it. I wanted to, but I was worried it might be out of bounds, but he seems to think it would be okay. It's okay right? You guys are good?"

Were we okay? I had no idea. "Will his girlfriend be there, because I don't know . . ."

"No, apparently he broke it off with her on the drive down to San Diego right after Thanksgiving dinner. Also, I'm not sure what you said to him, but he's trying to turn school around. He's negotiated with his professors and is cramming for exams."

"I'm so glad. I didn't have anything to do with it, but that's really great."

"Oh, I just assumed. Something forced him to focus over the break, I assumed it was you. Because with Teddy it's always been about you."

"Oh."

"I'm sorry I said that Sid, I — I'm having a hard time navigating this. That's something I would have said to your mom and without her, I'm a little lost."

"Me too."

"Can you come to Christmas? We'll cry, but I promise we'll laugh too."

202

"Um, here's the thing — I'm leaving for London tomorrow morning. I mean, I'll be home for Christmas, but I don't know if it's fair to make plans . . ."

"London! That's Alicia's favorite place in the world! How are you — oh, you're going to meet the hot singer?"

"Yes. I . . ."

"I didn't realize it was so serious."

"It's not, but I don't know, I'm confused."

"We could all use your mom right about now, huh? I wish I could help. I dated a lot of men in my lifetime before I met Scott. I was boy crazy and, woo hoo, did I learn a lot, but I don't know if my advice will have much merit because I love Teddy and think he's the greatest guy in the world, but if you'd hear me out, I can try."

"Okay."

"The thing is, there are so many kinds of men, but there are only two types of people — the ones that bring out your best, and the ones that bring out your worst. When you're in the midst of a good love affair, it can be hard to bring your head up from the stew of chemistry and look around at which you truly have. Is he good in the sack?"

I chuckled, "Spoken like a true friend of my mom, yes, he's good."

"When you've got orgasms clouding your brain, it's particularly hard to tell which one you're dealing with. Pull your head up, look around, force yourself to. Love is love, but also, if someone isn't bringing out your best, don't settle."

"I was just telling Dad I was going with the flow."

"That might be settling under another name, but what do I know? I had a year long relationship with the drummer of a rock band you've heard on the radio, and he was an amazing lover, but you know what I became when I was around him? Little more than a groupie. He didn't make me that way, it's what I did, but I figured it out, moved on, tried out, oh, four other guys, and then I met Scott."

I laughed. "So a lot of trying out."

"Maybe some day I'll tell you about your mother's list too, she was a big fan of holding auditions."

I laughed again. "I'd like to hear that, definitely."

"The point is, nobody is a mistake, it's all about learning. Pay attention and see what the lesson is. Also it's never too late to move on."

"Well, I do have a plane ticket to London."

"Don't get me wrong, you have to go to London. It's London. But take this trip as a chance to decide which kind of person he is. And still, come to Christmas. I'll make sure Teddy understands about your trip."

"Teddy is the last person in the world I want to hurt."

"Yeah, I know. Love is complicated. So you'll come, right, to Christmas?"

"Yes, I'll talk to Dad, but we can come."

NINETY-SIX
TEDDY TEXTED

Just Skyped mom.
Can we talk, I mean Skype?
Liam says hi.

Yes.

Sid's face appeared on my laptop. "Hi."

"Hi."

"Look, I talked to mom, she said you'll come to Christmas. I'm glad."

"Yeah, I think it will be good. Important for my dad. I don't want him to be sad." Sid looked down.

I said, "Sure. Me neither." Then I said, "I heard about your trip to London tomorrow, that's great."

"I'm exci —"

I interrupted, because I had planned Things-To-Say that I had to get through, "I just wanted you to know I'm happy for you, and what I'm trying to say is, I know I asked if we could still be friends, and you didn't want to, but I need to ask you again."

"If we can be friends?"

"Yes. I'm asking, um," I glanced up and she was looking directly at me. "I mean — yeah."

"Okay. That would be good."

I said, "Good, thanks." We sat awkwardly for a minute, then I asked, "Your dad is driving you to the airport?"

"Yes, my flight is at 6:00."

"You're up late."

"My theory is I shouldn't sleep until tomorrow on the plane. I don't know if it's a good theory, but I've never done this before."

"Are you flying into Heathrow? Because it's easy to get into the city from there."

"How do you know that?"

"I did a lot of research a while ago."

"Oh." Sid looked away. More awkwardness. Skype had a way of taking the worst parts of a face to face and the worst parts of a voice call and combining them. She asked, "So you're at school? Are you in your apartment?"

I looked around. "I am. I'm supposed to be studying. I've taken three exams this week, next I have to write two papers." I rubbed my hands up and down my face. "I haven't surfed since we went out, that might be a record for me."

"A week and a half, that's crazy."

"I'm acting heroically because it was a literal disaster here, but I'm fixing it. I won't have straight As, but I'll get to come back in January. Then I'll surf every day."

Sid laughed, "I don't know if that's the lesson to be learned here."

I stuck my fingers in my ears. "Lalalalala, no reality, please. I've barely slept. All I do is cram information into my brain. I have to dream of constant surfing as my reward."

Sid yawned, the big kind, the wide-open-jaw-and-a-moan kind.

I said, "You better get some sleep, or you might miss your flight."

"Thanks Teddy, I'm glad you called."

"Will you call me, if you need anything, to talk or . . ."

"Yes I will. But I'll see you at Christmas."

"Okay —" One of us accidentally hit the hang up button. Sid was gone.

I stared at my laptop for a long time. I had done it, called Sid. Asked her to be friends. And she had said, yes.

NINETY-SEVEN

SID

My alarm went off and I had barely slept. 4:00 a.m. I put on a simple pair of black leggings, my boots, and a comfy dark grey shirt. I came downstairs and met Dad, already in the kitchen, with the coffee on. "You excited?"

"Yeah, but it doesn't seem real." My backpack was stuffed, leaned up against the counter. I wrapped my hair up into a bun, took a sip of coffee, and went through my carryon bag for the last time — pencils, pens, my 'ideas' journal, two Luna bars, a knit hat, my iPad, my phone, passport, bank card, health insurance card. And a list of contact numbers.

Dad put a hard-boiled egg and a muffin in front of me. "Eat something. Your next meal is in London, terrible food I hear."

NINETY-EIGHT
MARY

The walls were cold stone, and though covered in tapestries, there was a chill that blew through them direct for my bones. I had asked for a fire, and it was roaring, but only warmed a foot in front of the flames. The only tiny window's pane was streaked with shimmering sleeting rain.

As long as I had been here in Scotland, I couldn't get used to how cold it was. I stood and gestured and my maid shoved my chair closer to the fire. I dropped down to the seat and tried to relax my clenched jaw. Also my clothes were constricting, itchy, and heavy. I sighed. And why was it so dark?

I said to Riccio, "There's never enough light."

He nodded. No help at all.

The table in front of me was set with pewter, piles of food — but then I blinked and a vision flashed of a table from France — Francis sat across from me, light streamed through the windows, the whole place glowed gold and warm.

I blinked again, and the vision was gone. The surrounding faces were stark in the candlelight. I felt dizzy.

I blinked to return the vision. My plate was covered in pears, dripping with honey. I'm laughing, the carefree laugh of light and love and happiness.

I sighed, returning to the present and said, "Riccio, it's time for the poetry."

Riccio, who was always agreeable, said, "Of course, your poem first."

He was the closest thing I had to a friend and yet he deferred to me in everything. Sometimes I liked that. Not every time.

I pulled at my bodice, leaned back in my chair, irritated, but if anything interesting would happen, I supposed it would have to be me that began. "I wrote this when Francis died:

> In my sad, quiet song,
> A melancholy air,
> I shall look deep and long,
> At loss beyond compare,
> And with bitter tears,
> I'll pass my best years —"

Riccio interrupted, "Queen, this is your saddest poem, perhaps this cold evening needs a livelier one. We could play a game. You love games."

I waved his idea away with a hand. "I can't argue with my mood, dear Riccio. When it is your turn, your poem can lift our spirits. Mine will toss them low." I continued:

> "Have the harsh fates ere now,
> Let such a grief be felt,
> Has a more cruel blow —

What is that sound Riccio?"

"Just the wind."

"It sounds like heartbreak, but where was I? Oh, the final lines:

> Been by Dame Fortune Dealt,
> Than, O my heart and my eyes —"

The door to my chamber was shoved open and a group of men rushed into the room. I jumped up. A man grabbed my shoulders and held me forcibly. I struggled. I yelled, "I am your Queen! Unhand me!" And yet I was captive. Before me men fought. I tried to make out their hidden faces. A chair tipped over. Riccio clutched at my skirts but was wrestled to the ground and dragged to the door.

I tried to break away from the men, to get to Riccio, to help him as he fought against his captors, but the men who were holding me were too strong. And then a knife was raised and Riccio was stabbed, again and again and again. His screams were loud and long and brutal. I would hear them forever. If I lived past this night.

NINETY-NINE

SID

I landed in England. Outside of customs a man in a suit, with a hat, held a sign that said: Sid Vicious.

Oh. A man for me.

I approached him wishing I had dressed better. He took my backpack, seemed surprised that I didn't check any other luggage, led me to the car, and tossed it unceremoniously into the trunk. He asked if I was cold.

Um, yeah. It was freaking freezing outside. In the twenty feet from the airport to the car I was shivering. It was the kind of cold that pierces through the weaving of your coat and freezes your internal water.

I chattered, "Yes, um, excuse me, just a minute," and retrieved my backpack from the trunk, unzipped it, yanked out my hoodie, and pulled it on. I layered another coat over it. While he waited, a bemused look on his face.

The car wasn't a limo, just a sedan, but the driver held the door open for me. The whole thing was a nice touch. Definitely a close-second to my boyfriend actually meeting me at the airport.

London was dark. Lights twinkling, very Christmasy, sparkling decorations everywhere. And the driver's accent was amazing. Everybody sounded so freaking smart. He asked if I was from California, and I said, yes, and he nodded, happily, as if California Girls were a happy thing.

Gavin texted:

Landed?

Yes.

I'm headed home
see you there.

I sat in the back of the car, holding my phone in my lap, watching a strange city slide by.

Gavin waited for me on the sidewalk. He was dressed in a black thick coat, over pencil-thin pants and boots. He had a knit cap on his head, his cheeks were red contrasting with his pale skin. I had missed that jawbone. He ripped open the car door, pulled me out, and swept me into a hug, "Hi Sid." He kissed me on my neck and my check and, with his gloved hands steadying my cheeks, sweetly on my lips. He said with a big smile, "I missed you!" and hugged me again until I shivered in his arms. It was crazy cold out here. No amount of hot boyfriend would cut through this chill. I would need to add a sweater to my wardrobe, and Gavin would find that hilarious.

He led me up the steps to his apartment, arm around my shoulder, foggy breaths on my cheek, kisses on my temple. This was going to be a fun visit.

His apartment was upscale. Small, but well decorated, not at all like how I imagined a bachelor-rocker's apartment. The style was modern and spare — dark gray, chrome and steel, with a low-slung, sprawling couch. He asked, "What do you think so far?"

I said, "It's a great apartment."

"Silly, I meant London?"

I grinned, "Oh, yeah. So far I only met the chauffeur, and the city was dark . . ."

"We'll sightsee tomorrow, I'm thinking Tower of London. I haven't been in about fifteen years."

"That sounds good." My stomach growled.

He asked, "Flight food? You need real food?" I nodded and he said, "We'll walk to a restaurant around the corner. Do you have another coat?"

"No, actually, I thought this would be enough."

He screwed his face up incredulously. "You don't have The Weather Channel? I told you it would be cold."

"I know, I read the temperature, but seriously, I had a hard time imagining it."

He shook his head sadly, mockingly, "Okay, coat." He disappeared into a hall closet and returned with a dark grey thick wool overcoat and slung it around my shoulders. As I pushed my arms into the sleeves, he pulled a knit hat onto my head, and kissed me on the tip of my nose. We stepped out to the street and Gavin said, "I had hoped that bringing you here would bring some California sun too."

"I can't believe it's so dark!"

He pointed out places while we walked arm in arm, "That's a stationer, there's a flower shop, youth hostel, Chinese food, and here's my favorite restaurant, steps away from my front door."

We ate delicious Indian food. And he was charming and sweet, but I yawned through the last twenty minutes of our meal. Then I stumbled home close to falling asleep in his arms.

Somehow I managed to play around with Gavin before I passed out. Sleeping for eleven hours, waking up at 6:00 a.m.

ONE HUNDRED

SID

It was dark and gloomy outside of the windows. Everything inside was difficult, from finding the light switches, to getting my toiletries bag from my backpack, quietly. I spent forty-five minutes trying to work Gavin's coffee machine. Then tried to decide whether to make breakfast or not. I located a frying pan and eggs, but the kitchen was sparkling clean, and my heart wasn't in it. What if he planned to take me out for pancakes, my favorite? I poured a bowl of Frosted Flakes and ate it while watching the clock. I took a shower. I read a few pages of my book.

Around 8:30 I heard Gavin's voice in his bedroom. I went to check and found him holding his head talking on the phone.

When he hung up he noticed me in the doorway. Staring at his feet he said, "Change of plans, I have to attend a function with Dad today."

"Oh."

"I'm sorry, Sid, I wanted to spend the day with you at the Tower." He ran his hands through his hair. "Man." He shook his head, but then he smiled his most charming smile, put his hand on his heart before extending it toward me. I gave him my hand and he dropped back pulling me down to the bed beside him. He raised up on an elbow, kissed me, and looked down into my eyes. "What I want is to spend the day with you in bed. You're already up though?" He pushed his hand up my shirt.

"I ate cereal."

He kissed across my cheek, down my neck, to my shoulder, and then my chest. "My favorite." He stopped, groaned, kissed me, groaned again, and said, "I have to get dressed, I can't stay here," he pulled my shirt back down, "and you have sights to see."

He jumped up and left for the shower.

An hour later I stood outside his apartment while he explained how to use public transportation to travel around, which station was closest to his apartment, and what time he would be done. He gave me a stack of money and a card for riding the Tube, and then he left, on foot, the opposite direction.

I was on my own in London for the day. I looked up and down the street. Whoa, this was all new.

The Tower of London was amazing. I walked around with my mouth hanging open. I followed tour guides, and asked lots of questions, causing other tourists to furrow their brows. Everyone knows the appropriate response to, "Any questions?" was, "No." But not me, I was on fire to know more. And sometimes their explanations just led to more questions.

I think part of it was I was just so freaking proud of myself. I had walked numerous blocks to a Tube station, figured out which train to take, rode it, got out, walked to the Tower, and paid. I did that all by myself. In a foreign country.

Sure they spoke English, but barely.

I kid.

Their accents were awesome.

I had to stop myself from repeating everyone in a pretend, not good, British accent. It was like I was bubbling over.

And you know what else? Mom did this, before I was born. Backpacked around England. Maybe she was a big part of my bubbling enthusiasm.

But could you blame me? There was literally a stone that marked the spot where Henry the Eighth's second and fifth wives were beheaded. Oh I had a lot of questions about that place.

Also, the Crown Jewels were there. And a tiny armor suit.

And then the sun went down and I had to figure out how to retrace my steps to Gavin's apartment. By myself in the dark. But I did it, yay me!

———————————

When I knocked, he answered with a beer in his hand. "How was your day?"

"It was amazing, so cool. Did you know there are crows that . . ."

His brow furrowed. He looked irritated.

I faltered. "You okay?"

He rubbed his face, "My dad was on one of his tirades. I have to go to a Thing tonight, at six. Do you have something to wear?"

I looked down at my jeans and boots. Most of the clothes I brought were casual. "I have a black shirt I think would look good."

He nodded, seeming uninterested. "I have to get dressed. I'll be out in a bit." He disappeared into his bedroom while I sat awkwardly on the couch, trying to keep from falling asleep.

A while later he came out looking so great — black dress pants, shiny shoes, a black collared shirt. His hair brushed. His face clean shaven. Uh oh. I had a lot of work to do to get anywhere close to that level of good-looking.

He said, "We've only got twenty minutes."

"Oh." I scurried to the bathroom to make myself presentable, though I looked and felt like I had crashed with that train I rode earlier. It might have dragged me a ways too. I was exhausted. I had walked a long, long way, and no matter how ridiculous it sounds, there really wasn't a reason to walk in Los Angeles. Unless you owned a dog. I didn't.

I put my hair up in a messy bun and left tendrils down, aiming for casual confidence. I changed my earrings to large hoops, put on some eyeliner and mascara and made my eyebrows zing. The black shirt had a low ballet collar, which accentuated my collarbones and fit well, so my boobs looked great. It was sexy on me and almost made my jeans passable as going-out clothes. But still I looked like an American who hadn't packed well.

When I emerged Gavin looked at me blankly and said, "Ready? Okay, we better get it," and we left for the street.

ONE HUNDRED ONE

SID

The Thing was at an art gallery. It was crowded and loud. For me. Gavin seemed not to notice the heat and noise and press because the swarm of fabulous London art-lovers parted for him. People stared. They whispered and stood on tiptoes trying to see him. And he wasn't the only gawk-worthy celebrity. There was a lot of aura in that room.

Gavin was profusely welcomed, kissed on his cheeks, called Darling. He called fabulous people by their first names. I was super impressed. He steered me through the crowds, then planted in the middle of the room, and a circle formed around him. I stood at the outer edge, my fingers hooked through my belt loops. I tried to blend in.

Gavin introduced me to two people, Janice and Tony, but then seemed to forget I was in the room, which was just as well. I was too tired to smile anymore. My face pulled into a frown. I wandered away to look at the paintings, finding instead a blank space along a wall to lean on and people watch. It sucked though, I didn't know enough about British music or culture to pick any of them out. I wanted to take pictures, but that seemed like a tourist move, and guess who I needed to identify those photos — my mom.

After a long time of being alone and looking at the same art over and over, I thought, maybe I'll curl up to sleep over there in the corner. Like a little puppy. Gavin could nudge me with his foot when he was ready to go. And that was why I figured I better tell him it was time to take me home. Before I fell down on the floor in a heap.

He was talking to five people I hadn't met. Beautiful people. But not the kind of beautiful that made you want to talk to them or touch them. These people had that kind of beauty that had crossed over into Don't-Approach and Give-Them-Space. Like they were a little dangerous. Like anyone who would go through that many procedures, tightenings and pullings and twistings and scrapings, was probably not a friendly person. Or kind. But I had to go, so I sauntered up to the circle, and when no one made space for me, I stood just behind.

Gavin didn't turn.

After a moment a man in the circle said, "I believe this young lady wants a word?"

Gavin slowly turned. "Oh, Sid, you sidled up." The frightening beautiful people in his circle chuckled.

I kind of felt like crying. Scratch that. I a lot felt like crying. "Gavin I think I need to go home, I'm exhausted. It's been a long day."

He took a long swig of a drink, his brow knit, watching me over the rim of his glass. He lowered it and said, "It's early yet."

I tried to laugh and said, "Jet lag," in a casual, joking tone, but my voice broke, tears were definitely coming.

He scowled. "Looks like I have to go."

One of the older women in his circle said, "Don't go Gavvy, stay. She can get herself home, no?"

I looked away, blinking, please don't cry, please don't cry.

Gavin placed his beer onto a passing waiter's empty tray and led me by the elbow away.

ONE HUNDRED TWO

SID

In the car Gavin didn't speak. I tried not to cry, and was successful for a few minutes, but finally my sad tiredness won and tears slid down my cheeks. I turned to the window and tried not to sniffle or wipe at my eyes, but Gavin noticed anyway. He asked, his voice flat, "Why are you crying?"

"Because I'm really tired, and that was awful . . ."

"What was awful, that art gallery? Those people that are friends of mine? London? What part of this is awful because I think from where you're sitting you should be grateful that you get to be a part of it."

The car slid in front of his house and Gavin stepped out to the street. He held the door for me and then stalked up his steps to his front door with me following a step behind. I was freaking out; what the hell was going on with Gavin?

As he unlocked his door, I said, "I didn't mean it that way, I meant I'm exhausted, that's all I meant. I don't know why you're taking it like this."

He let us in through the front door, tossed his keys to the counter, and ran his fingers through this hair. He put his hands on his head and said, "Aargh."

I blinked away the second round of tears. I dropped my purse to the counter and took my coat off and put it on the back of a chair. "I just had a really long day and I haven't slept well and I walked a lot and I just need some sleep."

"Yeah, well isn't that great? Sid's had a long day. Sid needs to leave early. Sid, Sid, Sid."

I said, "I don't know why you think you get to talk to me like that."

He stared at me through squinted eyes, his hands still on his head, then he dropped them and came around the counter, fast, his chest bowed out. "I get to talk to you however I want to."

"No you don't."

He jerked at me with his shoulder.

I took a step back, my heart racing. "Stop it Gavin."

He jerked his other shoulder forward. "Stop what? You're in my house, last I checked I bought your plane ticket —" His head was cocked, chin up, leaning into my space.

I took another step back. "You're scaring me, stop it!"

His fists clenched — his chest bowed out. "What, you bitch, stop what?" And then his right arm hooked, swung, and connected on my cheekbone with a blinding pain.

I screamed as my head slammed to the side crashing hard into the wall. I dropped to the floor, holding the back of my head, tucked under my arms.

He lunged, grabbed my shirt, yanked me closer, and swung again, this time hitting me really, really, really hard on my nose. The weird part was the sound of the crack was inside my head. Loud.

I threw my arms across my face, dug in my heels, and shoved away, my shirt stretching from his clutch. I scrambled into a corner and sat there for a second, arms up, breathing heavy, eyes closed, taking stock of the searing pain that was bursting up the bridge of my nose, and the ache that was spreading on the back of my head. Warm blood rolled down my chest and there were stars all around. I was going to pass out. Shit, I was going to pass out, here on the floor, in Gavin's apartment — he hit me, and I was bleeding, and I was sliding away. But no.

Gavin said, "Fuck," and then louder, "Fuck!" And then "Get up." His voice had that even tone to it again that scared the crap out of me.

I wanted out. I wanted out fast. I stood up, my sight blurred and spinning. I tried to pass him to the left, to the kitchen, to get my things, but he stepped in front and blocked me.

So I went to the right, walked along the edge of the room to the front door. Out. That's all I wanted was out. He grabbed my sleeve, "Where are you going?"

I yanked out of his grasp, flung the front door open, and made it to the stairs as Gavin slammed the door shut behind me. Loud. I stumbled down the stairs and out to the street.

ONE HUNDRED THREE

SID

It was only about 9:00 p.m. I was on the edge of hyperventilating. The streets were crowded and everyone was staring at me. Oh, and it was freezing. My arms clamped across my chest, my hands in my armpits. I said, "Shhhhhhh," trying to calm my mind, my body, but I was seizing up and my blood splashed in droplets to the sidewalk. From my face.

I tried to use the front of my shirt to stopper the flow, but that exposed my stomach to the freezing air.

An older woman rushed me with a wad of napkins. I held them to my nose. She asked, "Do you need help, dear?"

I nodded. My chin trembling, body shivering, face bleeding.

She said, "I'll take you down the street to the hospital."

And that was when it dawned on me that my pockets were empty. My passport, my money and my phone were sitting in the warmth of Gavin's apartment. "I can't, I —" My breath was ragged, not enough, shallow, gasping, bordering on painful. I couldn't think about this woman, the blood, my phone, Gavin, I could only think, Out. Of. Cold.

I turned my attention to the storefronts — closed, closed, an open restaurant full of people, too many people, the fourth door seemed good — I rushed past the woman (who now wanted to call the police) and shoved my way into a lobby of sorts.

The door closed behind me, shutting out the cold. A young man perched on a stool behind a motel-style front desk with piles and displays of brochures all around him. Two young women stood at the desk. Three other people stood in a huddle to the side of what I assumed must be a lobby. Everyone stopped talking and stared at me, eyes wide.

The young man said, "Can I help you? Do you have a reservation? Because without one —"

I burst into tears.

ONE HUNDRED FOUR

SID

This was what I knew:

I had no coat.
No passport.
No money.
No bank card.
No phone.

I would have to go back to Gavin's apartment.

ONE HUNDRED FIVE
CASSIE

This was my fifth day in London and I was going out to a club with my friends, getting directions from Chris at the counter, when the front door of the hostel opened. A burst of freezing wind blew in with a girl, huddled, shivering, her eye swollen almost shut, her cheekbone busted open, disgusting wads of Kleenex clutched in her hand, blood literally everywhere. Down her face and chest, like the movie Carrie, except it looked painful, because this blood was supposed to be on her inside.

I stared at her for a few beats. She was a disaster. A fricking stranger having a catastrophe, slamming into the middle of my good time.

When that happens there's a moment where you're tempted to think, not my problem, but then Chris saved me from saying, It's not my problem, by acting like it wasn't his problem. He said, "Seriously, do you have a reservation or an ID? Without one or the other you can't stand in this lobby."

The young woman shook her head, sobbing, the kind of sobbing that comes from deep inside, and sounds like a Big Crisis of Epic Proportions. She turned to the door which set me in motion, because now I was a party to further catastrophe.

I put my hand on her shoulder, "What's happening? Who did this to you?"

"My boyfriend."

She was American. I put my arm around her shoulder. "Where are you from?"

"Los Angeles, I got here yester —" She sobbed into her bloody hand

I pulled her to the couch along the wall and sat beside her. "Do you need a doctor?"

"I don't — I think so? But I don't have any ID or money or . . ."

"Okay, let me wrap my head around this. Well, first of all, British hospitals are notoriously free, so I could — Chris, where's like an urgent care or something?"

"A hospital? Or a doctor? There's one about two blocks over."

"So I could take you there."

The young woman nodded.

"Chris, are there any lost and found coats around?" Chris handed an armful of hats, a scarf and a big fluffy sweater across the counter. As the young woman pulled the sweater over her head with a wince, I asked, "What's your name?"

"Sid."

I turned to my friends. "I'm going to skip the club. If we're done quickly, I might call and meet you later. Okay, Sid," I opened the door to the front of the hostel, "we'll walk fast. I can imagine this is cold for a California Girl."

On our walk, Sid was quiet and huddled against the cold.

From the corner of my eye I tried to figure out if she was a junkie scamming me for a free meal or a legit train wreck. She might be a junkie. It was hard to tell in Europe sometimes — the junkies walked around with backpacks and unwashed hair, exactly like the young tourists, but there was something about her clothes, the gold hoops in her ears, her very messy falling bun, that made me feel like she was a My Kind of Girl in trouble.

Just covered in blood.

So it was hard to tell, but she was American. Claimed to have only been there for one day. Man, imagine getting beaten up in a foreign country? If this was a legit situation, then she had a serious legal case against the guy that beat her, because this was a serious beating. She might even need stitches on her cheek, that would suck.

These were my thoughts as I walked with her to the British version of urgent care.

I checked her in at the counter, giving them my passport information and the address of the hostel. And then we sat and waited for her turn to be called.

I said, "So is this the first time he hit you?"

She nodded and then said, "Yeah."

I nodded. "My sister had a boyfriend that beat her regularly a few years ago. You know when they start they rarely stop."

"Yeah, I know, there won't be a next time."

"Oh good, I was worried that —"

Her name was called and she went in to see the doctor. I read a magazine about British celebrities I didn't know.

Thirty minutes later Sid returned. Her face, neck and chest were clean. Her right eye was almost swollen shut, the left was completely closed. Both eyes were surrounded by red and deep purple bruises. She sported a big bandage across the bridge of her nose and a smaller bandage on her cheekbone. Her messy bun had been turned from disastrously messy to casually messy.

She gave me a small smile and said, "Good news is they don't have to amputate."

I laughed and asked, "They're just going to let you leave without paying anything?"

"Apparently yes. Plus, aspirin," Sid waved a bottle, "which is kind of necessary right now." Then she said, "Look, I wanted to thank you for waiting. I'm sorry I ruined your plans tonight, and you don't have to keep helping."

"So what's your plan then?"

"I have to go to Gavin's and get my stuff."

I squinted my eyes, "Do you think that's a good idea?"

"It's the only one I've got."

"Was he drinking? Maybe you should let him sleep it off first."

"Probably, but what do I do?" Sid looked around the room, like this British hospital might be a comfortable place to sleep.

I said, "Let's go to the hostel. Come with me, I'll help you figure it out."

"You don't have to, you don't even know me."

"But here's the thing Sid, I never quit anything halfway. I'm in now. How can I walk away and wonder what happened to the California Girl with the broken face? This story needs an ending."

"Okay. But I can't promise it will be a happy ending."

I said, "From the way you looked when I met you there's only up."

Sid followed me out the door to the street and we hurried down the block in the direction we came.

I said, "You could call your parents?"

"It's just me and my dad, and man, I don't want to worry him you know? He'll be frantic. What time is it there?"

I said, "Probably about two in the afternoon?"

"He's at work too. He would be frantic and there wouldn't be anything he could do about it."

"Any friends?"

Sid nodded, her arms wrapped around her body against the cold, head bowed, walking through London, "Yeah, I have a friend."

PART 3

ONE HUNDRED SIX

TEDDY

I had been writing all day, sitting on my couch, laptop, books, papers, food wrappers, and dirty dishes strewn around me on the coffee table.

In the past week I had finished two big final exams, probably with Cs. I was happy about those Cs, because I came close to failing the classes altogether.

Another class let me drop. I would have to retake it next semester. I was fine with that. I'm a big fan of the do-over and I needed it.

Now all that was left — two classes wanted me to turn in papers. One was my Marine Biology class. The entire point of being at this university. The professor told me that if I didn't get at least a B he wouldn't recommend I move up to the next level. So, yeah, I had to get a B or drop out of school.

The other paper was for English. My first draft was done, I was considering hiring an editor, because the other paper needed finishing too, and I only had until the end of the week.

Suddenly my Skype icon started bouncing and then ringing.

I clicked on the icon, the only person who ever called me on Skype was Mom and never at two in the afternoon on a Monday. Maybe she was bored?

It was a strange number.

Up in the corner was a request to contact me from a girl in Colorado: Cassandra123.

Then a message from the girl in Colorado: Teddy answer, it's me, Sid.

Oh.

It rang again and Sid's voice said, "Teddy?"

"Sid, your video isn't on."

"I know, I can't — Teddy, I need help —"

"What? What happened?"

"I — I got into a —" She sobbed, "Teddy I —"

"Please tell me what happened. Where's your phone?"

"I got hurt, and I don't have my phone or my things and I'm —"

"Sid, I'm freaking out over here, how'd you get hurt, are you okay?"

"I'm okay, I went to the hospital, they said —"

"Was it a car wreck? I don't —"

Her voice was tiny. "Gavin hit me."

"Oh jeez Sid, are you okay? Seriously, are you okay?"

She didn't answer.

I could hear her crying.

"Sid?"

There was a muffled conversation, I made out, "— don't tell him how bad . . . I don't want him to —"

The video sputtered on and a girl I had never met appeared on my screen. "Hi, I'm Cassie, I'm with Sid."

"Cassie, can you tell me what happened, is it bad?"

"Yeah, it's bad. I don't know much, just that about an hour and a half ago she showed up at the hostel here. I walked her to the hospital to get her checked out." Cassie pulled the camera close and spoke quietly, "He broke her nose, busted her cheekbone open, she has bandages. There was a lot of blood. She doesn't have a coat or her passport or money or anything."

"Oh my god, oh my god, oh my god. Are they at that guy's house?"

"I think so."

"Don't let her go back for them. Tell her not to go back."

Cassie said, "I will, I have, and on the bright side, I'm glad you're a normal guy. We all thought she might be a junkie scamming us for a free room and a meal."

My jaw clenched. "You thought she was a junkie?"

"She looked terrible."

I ran my hands down my face. "Cassie, I'm blind over here, what can I do that will help? What time is it?"

"It's ten, night. She needs a bed. The hostel can't legit let her in unless she has an ID or something."

"Is there someone I can talk to, a manager or somebody?"

"Yes, Chris." The phone was passed around, video jiggling, to someone else.

A guy appeared on my screen. "This is Chris." His accent was Australian.

"My friend is there and she needs a bed. What can I do to make it happen?"

"I can't let her in without an ID of some kind."

"Here's the thing — she's lost her passport, her money, her phone, her clothes. She's an American. It's night there, right? She can't go to the embassy until the morning. I'll pay you right now for tonight's room, plus tomorrow night, and I promise you'll have an email with her passport photo by morning. Probably earlier."

"If the email isn't here by tomorrow she's out, no refunds."

"Yes. That makes sense."

"Okay, I'll book her a bed, read me your credit card number."

"Look, I have one more request, will you ask her that guy's name? Don't let him in if he comes, okay?"

"I won't, no worries mate."

I read him my credit card number. While I waited for the computers in London to take my payment from my apartment in California, I closed my laptop, looped up my cords, gathered all my writing and a stack of books, and placed them in my messenger bag.

Cassie appeared on my phone again. "She has a bed?"

"Yes. Can I PayPal you some money to give her — so she has food tomorrow?"

"Sure, I'm CassandratheBeatlenut@gmail.com that's Beatle, spelled like the Beatles. Don't ask."

"Thank you Cassie. Will you be around tomorrow, can I call if I need to talk to her?"

"Yes, I'll be here. She wants to talk to you."

The phone was passed again. The video turned off. Sid said, "Teddy?"

"The hostel is giving you a bed. Okay Sid? Do you need anything to eat?"

"No, I'm just so tired. Thank you. And I just, I'm so sorry Teddy, I didn't know. I thought — I'm sorry."

"You don't have to be sorry for one minute, not one. Please take care of yourself, get sleep. Will you call me tomorrow? I'll get you some money and we'll figure out the passport. Okay?"

"Yes, thank you Teddy."

"No problem Sid, good night."

I hung up the phone. I wanted to stay on for longer, milking the goodbye, because I didn't want to say goodbye, but I had things to do.

I grabbed three pairs of jeans, five pairs of socks, and my boots, and stuffed them in my duffel. I picked out three shirts, two sweatshirts, my coat, and a knit hat and shoved them in too. I checked my pocket: wallet, keys, phone, charger. Checked again that I had the cords for the laptop. Pens. I spun around the apartment for anything else and then said goodbye to my roommate and hit the road. Forgetting, of course, my toothbrush.

———————————

Sid had called at 2:05 p.m. I was on the road at 2:45.

ONE HUNDRED SEVEN

TEDDY

As soon as I was on the 101, I called Mom.

"Teddy?"

"Mom, Sid just Skyped me, that fucking asshole beat her."

"Oh God, is she okay?"

"I don't know, I can't tell. I think so, she had to go to the hospital."

"Oh no. Did you tell Mike?"

"Not yet — I'm calling him next — Mom, she doesn't have her passport or her phone or anything and he fucking punched her and she's in London all by herself."

"Oh poor Sid. Oh no."

"Some girl named Cassie called me, they thought Sid was a junkie. She's — god mom, I can't breathe."

"You're driving, please be careful. Okay? We'll figure this out."

"She has a place to stay tonight, but I need you to book me a flight. I'm on my way home."

"Oh okay, yes, that makes sense, um — you're going to go to London . . ." I could tell by her voice she was already Googling flight details. "What time can you realistically be on the flight?"

"If I drive the speed limit and there's no traffic, I can be there at 4:45. My passport is there — can you find it for me?"

"Yes, it's in the folder. What about this flight: Virgin, 7:50 p.m., lands in Heathrow, 1:50 p.m. tomorrow."

"I would have about three hours to come home, go to the airport? Does that sound right Mom? I can't think straight, I'm freaking out."

"Yes, Teddy, I think that works. Drive safely, okay? Being reckless now doesn't help Sid. We'll get you to the airport. I'm calling your dad. I love you. I'm buying the ticket."

"Okay Mom, thanks."

ONE HUNDRED EIGHT
TEDDY

Next I called Sid's dad.

Mike, this is Teddy."

"Teddy?"

"Sid just called me, she's in trouble, and don't worry too much, she's safe now, but —"

"What happened?"

"That guy she was visiting hit her."

"What? He did what?"

"He hit her, and she had to leave. She doesn't have her wallet or her passport or her phone."

"Where is she now?"

"She's at the Camden Backpacking Hostel. I helped her get a bed, but the guy there needs an ID. Do you have a copy of her passport?"

"At home."

"I need you to email it to him, but I forgot to get his email address — Mike, can you call them — the Camden Hostel in London and ask for their email address? Tell them you're sending Sid's ID."

"Definitely Teddy." He was writing that down. "I'll leave work right now."

"Mom just booked me a flight. I'm going to London. I just, I think I can help, so yeah, I'm driving home now, I'll be there at about five, could you meet me at my house, bring some clothes for Sid?"

"Yes, I'll pack a bag and be there. Teddy, thank you. I let my passport lapse, I don't know why I did that, but it will take a few days to get a new one I would think. I'll get on a plane as soon as I can. So thank you, I'm glad you can go."

"She sounded scared."

"There's no way I can call her?"

"I have a contact, but I think she's sleeping right now."

"Thank you Teddy, I'll see you at five.

When I pulled into my house everyone was there sitting at the kitchen counter. Mom had printed my ticket, found my passport, and made me a sandwich for the plane, she kissed me and hugged me and was teary eyed about Sid. Dad had stopped by REI on his way home from work and bought me three pairs of wool socks. He stuffed them in my bag and hugged me and told me how much he loved me.

Mike's hands were shaking as he handed me a copy of Sid's passport, her student ID, her government ID, a copy of her birth certificate, and a bank card. He also had a bag with clothes. He said, "Make sure she knows she doesn't have to go for her things, we can get new things."

I nodded, "Absolutely."

We all loaded into the car and they all drove me to LAX.

ONE HUNDRED NINE

SID

I didn't wake until 11:30 the next day, the last person sleeping in the bunk room. Two people were cleaning and I slept right through their noise. My pillowcase was stained with blood from my face. I would need to pay for it, probably. With no money of course.

My head hurt. In like ten different places.

When I sat up, there was a note beside my pillow:

Sid,

Here's twenty pounds for food today.

I'll be back later, stay put, okay? Seriously. Don't go anywhere.

Cassie

I got up and went to the bathroom and took a look in the mirror.

Ow. I had rings of dried black blood around my nostrils. My left eye was completely shut. The bandage on the bridge of my nose was peeling off. My right eye barely peeked out from under swollen lids, both eyes were ringed, blue, red, deep purple. My cheekbone's bandage was flapping off and under it the skin had a deep cut and the surrounding skin was deep blue. Dried blood speckled my face like a Jackson Pollock painting. Or better yet — a Picasso painting, one of the weird ones, distorted and creepy. Tears welled up. None of that was true, what I really looked like was someone out of a CSI episode. Come to find out, the sight of my battered face was worse than the actual pain.

I gingerly peeled the bandage off my nose, then the smaller one from my cheekbone, washed my face with water and dried with paper towels, and replaced the bandage with some extras the doctor gave me. I took some aspirins washed down with water out of my cupped hand.

Last night Cassie had found me a t-shirt to sleep in, it was bright green, too big, and said in bold letters: Kiss Me I'm Irish. I tugged on my only jeans, the front splattered with my blood, and my boots and went downstairs to find food.

This sucked.

Like really sucked.

I was trying to remain calm, grateful, positive. But this situation was — I was all alone. I closed my eyes and the image of Gavin, big and terrible and bowed out, yelling, his fist.

I walked down the stairs and all eyes were on me. People stared. People whispered. They stepped aside, curious, but also cautious. I was a catastrophe and whatever damage had happened, no one wanted it on their London vacation.

Poor Cassie. She was dealing with me. On her vacation.

I would do everyone a favor if I would just leave. Go to Gavin's. Get my stuff. Deal with him. If I had my phone, I could call Dad and ask for a plane ticket home. But it was too early to call. And frankly I was scared to go to Gavin's for my stuff. What would he say — do?

Downstairs, off the large lounge, was a snack shop. I ordered a burger and fries with a Coke. And sat at a table wishing I had a phone to — I don't know — check Instagram, look at a map, anything — know what the date was.

Did I mention how badly this sucked?

I ate by myself and then remembered about the copy of my passport. I went to the lobby and waited in a queue of three travelers who stared and whispered.

A young woman with long dreadlocks was working the counter. Her brows furrowed when it was my turn. "Honey, you are a terrible mess," she said in a thick French accent, emphasizing every word as if I hadn't known. "A boy did this to you?"

"Um yeah, I'm a guest and —"

"It couldn't have been a French boy, they would never. It was what kind of boy?"

"British."

She said, "Of course." She shook her head sadly, a little knowingly.

"I wanted to make sure that a copy of my passport was emailed last night?"

The girl held up a piece of paper, studied it and then me. "I can not believe it, this is you?"

I nodded.

She raised her brows and exhaled slowly. "A nice boy will not make your face this way." She squinted, as if that was Wise and Important and I needed to Let it Sink In. Sunk, thank you. She added, "This note came with it."

It was a hand-scratched in Dad's familiar scrawl:

Sid,

We're working on a solution, hold tight.

Love you, Dad

I read it again and again. Tears rolling down my cheek.

ONE HUNDRED TEN

SID

I tried to sit tight. The lounge was bustling with activity. Plenty of distractions, but the more I thought about it the more I knew — I had to go get my stuff. I knew it. But I was scared.

So instead I read a magazine article about the pros and cons of the UK leaving the EU and then stared into space. The day was almost done, the windows were darkening. Sunset. I had let the day go by without coming up with a solution, but that was because there wasn't one.

Except going to Gavin's.

He would probably apologize. I could get my things and bring them here. That was the only thing that made sense. What else was I waiting for, because what could Teddy do, what could my dad do? I was halfway around the world, by myself, and I had to fix this mess I was in.

I had to go to Gavin's. Deal with —

My attention was drawn to the lobby.

I listened, there was a voice that —

I cocked my head. That voice sounded just like Teddy. Weird.

I stood up and picked my way around the furniture and pillows and suitcases and sprawled people to the doorway of the lobby. It was full. Travelers stood and milled and queued, but through the crowd, across the room, there was someone at the counter — pulling his wallet from his pocket — from the back he looked just like Teddy and —

"Teddy?"

He tossed his passport to the counter and turned, "Sid! Oh God."

He pushed through the crowd to get to me. "Oh no, Sid." He put hands on both sides of my face, "Oh no."

I fell to his chest and his arms went around. I cried. I cried hard. In the middle of the lobby, surrounded by strangers, with absolutely no dignity, I sobbed into the front of Teddy's shirt.

He ran his hand down the back of my hair. "God, I didn't know it was so bad Sid, I didn't know." He peeled my head off his chest and studied my wounds. "Shit Sid, that's bad, I'm so sorry. What did the doctors say?"

I sniffled. "They said I would get better, so that's good."

His arms tightened around me. "Yeah, that's good. Yeah, it's going to be okay." He nodded, his jaw rubbing up and down in my hair and for the first time in hours and hours I thought maybe it was going to be okay. Using the bottom hem of my giant green shirt I wiped my tears and then my nose.

Teddy asked, "Um, can you tell this room full of glaring strangers I wasn't the one who did this to you?"

I laughed a tearful laugh, nodded and said loudly, "Everybody, this is not the guy who kicked my ass, this is my friend from home."

That seemed to suffice, the glares stopped, a few people looked relieved. Most everyone pretended like I wasn't the biggest train wreck they'd seen today.

Teddy said, "Look I need to finish checking in, give me a second, okay?"

"Yes." I stood at the edge of the lobby while Teddy checked into my hostel in London, England, trying to understand how he was here and why, but also, knowing and understanding and being so overwhelmingly grateful. My arms hugged around my middle and for the first time in days I felt warm.

Teddy finished finally and followed me into the lounge. "Home sweet home?"

"Yep, I've been 'staying put' waiting for further instructions. I didn't know I was waiting for you."

"I didn't know what to do. I couldn't even figure out the steps. I just packed my bag, drove to LA, and told Mom to buy me a plane ticket. She did, without hesitation, so I guess I wasn't wrong." He sat down on the only empty couch and leafed through his bag. "Here's a copy of your passport, a stack of IDs, a bank card, and here's my phone, call your dad."

So I did, I called Dad, while Teddy dropped his head back on the cushions and closed his eyes for a nap.

ONE HUNDRED ELEVEN
HOW FAR TEDDY TRAVELED

Santa Barbara to Teddy's house- 117.5 miles 2 hours 35 minutes with traffic

Teddy's house to LAX- 2.75 miles 14 minutes through security checkpoints

LAX to LHR, London- 5449 miles 10 hours 49 minutes

LHR to Camden Backpacking Hostel- 15 miles 57 minutes

_____

5584.25 miles 16 hours 25 minutes

ONE HUNDRED TWELVE
TEDDY

I woke up to Sid whispering, "Teddy?"

I opened one eye and looked at her. Blue skin, swollen eye, bloody cuts, bandages, tear stains — she looked like hell. Like I wanted to kill the guy who did it. Kill. Him.

I had been sleeping on a couch in front of lots of people, like an old man at a bus stop. I ran my hands briskly up and down on my face. "Your dad cool?"

"He said to tell you thank you, and he owes you, and me too Teddy. Thank you. I would have talked you out of it —"

"No, you wouldn't have. You might have tried, but you wouldn't have."

She nodded, "Well I'm glad you're here."

"It's dark, what time is it?"

"Five."

"I have clothes for you. I'm sure you want to change out of that, whatever that is."

She smiled and said, "Ow," her hand reflexively going to her cheekbone. Then she said, "This shirt? My nightshirt, bandage, snot rag? Yeah, I probably need a cleaner one. Got any deodorant?"

I nodded and passed her the bag her dad had packed for her. Then she carried a small stack of fresh clothes to the shower to get cleaned up. Forty-five minutes later she returned — clean bandages, the caked and dried blood gone, her hair clean. A huge improvement, because she looked less like someone in the middle of an emergency, but also worse, the vivid blue and red and purple bruises contrasted with her cleanness. Now she was somebody who had lived through some kind of extreme violence. She had lived through it, but ouch, those wounds were real. Fresh. Jarring.

Sid was hard to look at. I averted my eyes. It must be painful because it was painful to see. I sat at one end of the couch, she sat on the other, and tucked up her feet into a curl.

Cassie walked up and introduced herself and dropped into a chair across from us. She said, "So right off the bat Teddy, you never hit Sid, right?"

"God no."

Sid looked at me, "What about at Park Day that time? Remember the playground with the rocket-ship slide? You totally hit me!"

"Yeah, but I was seven, and you were being a total ass."

Sid started to smile, but grabbed her cheek with a wince. "I was and then remember Mom came over and got all NVC on us?"

Cassie looked confused, so I explained, "It stands for Non-Violent Communication. Sid's mom was a True Believer. She talked to me about hitting for so long I swore I would be a pacifist until the day I died."

Sid said. "She knew how to talk a problem to death."

"She was a master."

Cassie squinted her eyes. "So I guess she'd be freaking about your present circumstances. Being nonviolent and all."

"Yeah definitely." Sid gazed off into space.

Cassie turned to me, "You going to go out, see anything, do anything this evening? There's a pub up the street for food and a club that gets super fun later."

My attention was on Sid, blinking, color rising, on the edge of tears. "I think I'll stay here. I'm tired from the trip. Where can I get food to bring in? Also, another coat, this is not warm enough. Are there surf shops in London?"

"Probably, but you're on your own there. Sid, I suppose you're staying in?"

"What? Oh um, yeah, I need to get dinner I guess . . ."

Cassie said, "You're not paying attention. Your friend Teddy just said he would bring food in. The answer you're looking for is 'hell yeah' like a true American. Also he needs a coat, you should go help him pick out a coat."

Sid turned her swollen, misty eyes to me, "You need a coat?"

I nodded and leaned forward pulling my phone out of my pocket to Google a surf shop, "I read the weather, but I did not compute that it would be this cold."

Sid chewed her lip and quietly said, "It's one of the reasons Gavin was so mad at me."

I stopped mid-type.

Cassie said, "He hit you because — what?"

"It all started when I didn't have the right coat."

Cassie said, "Oh no you don't. It wasn't because you didn't pack right. It was because he is an asshole. A You-Aren't-Ever-Going-Over-There-Again Asshole. Am I right Teddy?"

I nodded, "Yep," but glanced over to see a tear rolling down Sid's cheek. Crap, that had been too harsh. Way too harsh for someone with a battered face, but it had also been totally true. I couldn't think of how to walk it back — thankfully Cassie's friends came giggling into the lounge. Sid quickly wiped her cheeks while I was introduced to everyone. I explained again why I couldn't go clubbing with them, then Cassie waved goodbye, calling over her shoulder, "Don't wait up!"

Sid and I sat quietly for a second. Then I returned to my phone and the surf shop search. "It doesn't look like a surf shop is open now, but there is one. In the morning I can go buy another coat. Right now we need food though — I saw a shawarma place a few doors down, want some? If I hustle I won't get too cold."

Sid nodded and so I went out in the streets of London and located and paid for dinner on my own. I was proud of that, and very cold. Even though I hustled.

I spread our food out on the coffee table in front of the couch and while we ate Sid told me about the Tower of London.

I asked, "You went by yourself? Like the metro, the money, the tours, the whole thing? I was just giving myself mental high-fives for walking two doors down and buying middle eastern food. From a guy with perfect English."

She looked down. "Yeah. I was by myself. First day in London and I was by myself."

She wrapped her trash up into a ball and said, "I'm exhausted. Thank you Teddy. For coming. For dinner, for everything. I just, I'm so sorry, and I'm tired and . . ."

"Of course Sid, get rest. I'll see you in the morning."

I cleaned up our dinner trash, and then slid into one of the lounge's corner booths, opened my laptop on the table, and stacked my books all around, hopeful that work would happen. A lot of people were in the lounge, but it was quiet, people spoke in hushed tones — I was exhausted. I needed to write, but I didn't even get one sentence out. I jerked awake, who knows how much time had passed, with a zipper mark pressed into my cheek.

I packed my books and laptop and dragged myself up to the dark bunk room. There were already about ten people asleep. Sid was on the bunk above me. I passed her as I went to the bathrooms, her body curled into a ball, her head down, almost inside her covers.

I had forgotten to buy a toothbrush, so I used my finger.

When I lay down on the bottom bunk, I listened to the soft shifts and turns of so many strangers — how odd to sleep in a communal space. When did someone come up with this, twenty people all sleeping piled up in rooms? I decided that it would be impossible to sleep and then jet lag forced me to reconsider.

I woke up later to a sound — whimpering, a moan, another whimper.

I felt disoriented as my eyes adjusted to the total blackness and shapes. I had to remind myself this was a bunk room. Someone shifted at the other end and through the darkness someone said, "Shhhh."

Another whimper, from right above me. Sid.

I slid out of my bag. My feet hit the floor, ice cold. I stepped onto the bottom rung of her steps and raised myself to her level. Was she awake? Her shoulder heaved in a sob. I groped around, found her hand, and gripped it, wrapping my other arm around her head. Quietly I asked, "Sid?"

She seemed startled, her body tensed, awake, scared.

I whispered, "You're okay."

Two people from different parts of the room said, "Shhhh."

"I'm here, you're going to be okay."

I felt her nod. She gripped my hand tighter and then released it and curled into a ball on her other side.

I stepped to the floor, cold, cold, cold, and climbed into my bag, and stared up at her bunk, alert and not able to sleep at all.

ONE HUNDRED THIRTEEN

SID

The next morning it was drizzling and promised to get worse. I padded downstairs in stupid clothes that Dad had packed, because somehow he had picked all the wrong stuff, too big t-shirts, a pair of yoga pants with a hole in the inseam, an ugly pair of sneakers I didn't wear anymore. The coat was from last year.

Teddy was in the snack shop and brightened when I entered before his expression changed to dismayed and concerned. I understood. I had looked in the mirror. My face still looked terrible, but like a whole 'nother level, not fresh anymore, settling into old, tired, blue-swollen damaged. I wouldn't look at it again, except to change the bandages. He had to look at it all the time. He deserved better.

I kind of felt like I deserved worse.

What kind of girl goes to London to meet an asshole that beats her the first day? I kind of felt like I should stare at myself. Get used to the idea that this was it. Beaten. Deserved it for stupid. I should cry, like all day.

I figured I should also tell Teddy he could go home now. This was too much for him to do, and I couldn't stand the indebtedness.

I sat across him at the table. He said, "They have cereal and milk, want one, coffee?

I nodded and he jumped up and returned with two cups of coffee. Then jumped up again for two bowls with Frosted Flakes and a pitcher of milk. Then left again for a small plate of toast.

"Thanks Teddy."

He poured milk in his cereal and dug in.

I asked, "When do you go home? I mean, now that you rescued me, are you planning to go home?"

He looked up from his cereal, "Yeah, my ticket returns in a couple days. We'll get your passport situation fixed this afternoon, and then you should get your return flight booked, maybe the same time as mine."

I poured milk in my cereal and ate a spoonful.

He continued, "I'd love to see some sights though —" The window darkened and rain poured. It was so loud it was hard to hear each other. He joked, "What is that stuff coming out of the sky over there?"

I said, "I'm choosing to ignore it. If I don't notice it, it can't be real."

He said, "I need a coat, there's a surf shop near the Covent Garden Tube stop. Will you go with me? We'll run between the raindrops. Then we can lie around here all day drying off."

I said, "Sure." I wasn't sure I wanted to — going would interfere with my cry-all-day-feel-ashamed-of-myself schedule, but Teddy did rescue me. And he brought the wrong coat. It was the least I could do.

After lunch we took off into the streets of London without the right coats, freezing wet, and by the time we entered the surf shop, completely bedraggled. There was a bench near the front door for visitors to leave their umbrellas. We dropped our coats because by this time they were soggy. I stamped my feet trying to get heat to them, trying to ignore that everyone was staring at me nervously. Then we fanned out through the store looking for coats.

I found a rack of wool sweaters, stylish and thick and rifled through the hangers when someone cleared her throat behind me and quietly asked, "Do you need help — I mean, are you okay?"

Her peer was intense and made it clear she wasn't asking if I needed help shopping. Here was another stranger, other side of the world, asking if I was okay.

No, not, but better, thank you.

I said, "Yeah, I'm good," and, "this isn't the guy who did this." I thought about adding, "Not that it's any business of yours," but then again — wasn't it kind of awesome that women were offering help, because if this was the guy, wouldn't I need it?

But what I really needed right now was a sign that read:

This is Teddy.
He didn't do this to my face.

Teddy was across the store smiling and holding up a coat. He gestured a question: thumb up, thumb down, or a shrug? I mimed that he should put it on. He did and it looked excellent, an indigo blue, he always looked good in blue. He rubbed the interior fleece lining on his cheek to show how soft it was. I thumbed up and his smiled widened and he headed to the counter.

The woman who had asked if I needed help, left to report my answer to the others.

I continued searching through the sweaters. It took Teddy less than ten seconds before he was in a friendly Everything About Surfing conversation with the three young men who worked there. There was an animated looking at charts, a descriptive discussion of surf spots, a bitch-session about the weather, and a respectfully competitive piss-match over which locale had better surfing. I guessed California would win, no contest. But I had stopped listening because Teddy's dark brown hair curled against his neck, his jawline angled, and his back stretched as he ripped the tags off his new coat's sleeves. He put on the coat and it fell in angles across his wide shoulders. I shook my head to clear it as he said, ". . . she charges down the line."

I strode over and asked, "Who does?"

He said, "You. I was telling them about your surfing."

Oh.

Me.

Teddy was talking about me.

See that was the thing about Teddy, he was an amazing surfer and yet he bragged about me. I blushed. One guy asked what kind of board I rode. I answered, "A five-eleven thruster."

He nodded. Then he said, "You know I hope you pressed charges on the bloke that broke your face."

I nodded and turned away toward the windows looking out over the street.

Teddy said, "If you ever get the chance to come to LA, me and Sid could take you out." He had made friends. Ten minutes in and he had friends he hoped to surf with.

He pulled out his wallet and his credit card. "Sid, did you find a coat?"

"No, I couldn't . . ."

"What you're wearing doesn't look warm enough."

"I know I just — I bought a coat, just a few days ago. It feels weird to buy another one. I don't know . . ."

Everyone was looking at me and my face was hot and my nose throbbed, actually my entire head throbbed, and I kind of felt like crying again. Trouble was: penance. I needed to not buy myself a coat because I had already caused so much aggravation. Spent too much of everyone's good will and energy. I needed to make do. Maybe go sit in the corner, near the umbrellas.

Teddy blinked and paused, like he was trying to figure my whole thing out. Then he nodded slightly. "An umbrella though, you need an umbrella." The guy behind the cash register pulled one from a bucket and placed it on the counter. Teddy spun for a second, stepped to a table of knit hats, and picked up one that was a pale gray, fluffy, wool. "Try this." I pulled it over my head; it was crazy soft. He said, "Matches your eyes. Let me buy it. Christmas present."

"Teddy you already flew to London to rescue me."

He squinted his eyes, "You can't argue with Christmas presents, do you like it?"

I looked in a mirror.

I did. I liked it, and if I pulled it way down to shadow my darkened eyes, it helped me not look so obviously tragic. Plus it would probably look pretty on me once I healed.

Teddy bought me the hat and the umbrella. Then I layered his older coat over my coat from home, and we raced to the hostel, through the rain, but not nearly as wet and cold this time.

ONE HUNDRED FOURTEEN
TEDDY

The lounge was full. The rain made it so that no one should go outside unless they were committed to going out. Sid and I stood for a second taking stock. I pointed, "We need chairs, grab that one." She beelined for an easy chair near the bookcase. I walked to the other side of the room, asked a group if we could take one of theirs, and then hoisted it over my head and carried it across the crowded room, the pillow slouched down almost over my eyes. I tried to look cool, but probably looked like an idiot wrestling an easy chair.

I dropped mine right beside Sid's, creating a triangle with the bookcase. "So what do we do now? Spotify is playing . . . what even is this?"

Sid grumbled, "I think it's Justin Bieber. England has so much great music and the hostel's playlist is American pop. She looked around the room. Can't tell who has the remote, I think we're stuck listening to it."

Outside the windows it was rainy and dark. "We'll be stuck here all day, apparently. I should look up passport offices. The US embassy?"

She winced and gingerly rubbed her temple and asked, "Can I have some of your water?" She dug through her bag and unscrewed the lid on what looked like pain meds.

"Head hurt?"

"My whole everything hurts." She swigged down two pills and leaned back in the chair. "I keep wondering what my mom would say, she'd probably be totally disappointed in me." She closed her eyes.

"I don't think she'd be disappointed at all, maybe sad. Maybe worried. This is not your fault."

Sid opened one eye. "What do you know? Nothing. You don't know anything. This is all my fault, I flew to London to be with a guy that did this to my face. So unless you know what you're talking about you —"

I said, "Ouch, Sid, that was rough — I get it, your face hurts, but don't be a dick." I stuffed the water bottle in the bag. "The thing is, the reason I don't know anything is because my closest friend didn't tell me anything. Ever. For years. You can keep secrets, but don't use it against me when I don't know them." I zipped up my bag and when I looked at her, she was watching me quietly.

"I'm sorry."

"You get a headache pass. This time." I tried to cut the sting with a smile.

"No I mean I'm sorry that I never told you about Mom." Her fingers wrapped around the bottom edge of her shirt. "I just . . . at the time it was too hard to talk about. Cameron said —"

I interrupted, "Cameron knew?"

"He would see, when he spent the night. He was my boyfriend, remember?"

"Yeah. I remember, I'm just surprised." I brushed an imaginary speck off my pants. "You could tell me now."

Sid said, "Or I could just keep it all inside and let it erupt later, when I can afford the psychiatrist."

I leaned, elbows on my knees. "How's that working out for you so far?"

She nodded.

I said, "I don't think it's okay to keep it inside. I loved your mom. She was great, possibly the best, and I don't know, I think I can hear the bad and still remember how awesome she was."

Sid chewed her lip. She nodded slowly. "It's hard to explain. It was like life, you know, everyday life, but then

Mom kept getting worse and worse. And she would have these moments — Dad called them her freak outs — and they were . . ." Her eyes went far away and her arms folded across her middle. "I don't know how to describe them — her freak outs sucked. When we were inside them it was like a terrible storm, but then it would pass. It would be Mom. Just Mom. And I could forget that the storm was even there." She looked at me with her brow knit, and I nodded so she would keep going.

She leaned down and yanked at her laces until her feet were freed from her boots. Then she pulled her feet up under her and rested her cheek on her fist studying the threadbare arm of the chair. She said, "This is what it was like — I was treading water in a pool and I was good at treading water. I was proud of it, and she was proud of me, and my head was up, and everything was okay. I'm smiling and everyone is smiling and what I didn't know was that more water was pouring in. It was getting deeper, Teddy. There was no way I could keep treading. And I got tired and there wasn't any way to get to the wall. But that's the thing — I didn't notice until it was too late. That's the worst part. Nothing seems that bad until everything is awful and now you're drowning. And guess what? You know who should pull you out of the water? Your Mom." A tear slid down Sid's face.

I asked, "Do you know why she drank so much?"

"Dad said she was abused as a kid. And she never dealt with it until somehow she stopped wanting to deal with anything." She collapsed down, her arms wrapped around her head.

"Oh Sid. I'm so sorry."

She said, "I'm crying in the middle of everybody."

"It's okay." I pushed the arm of her chair so she was facing the shelves, her back to the room. I turned my chair to face hers, close. "It's okay, no one is even looking." I lied. Lots of people were nervously glancing our direction.

She sniffled and then softly, quietly, from underneath her arms said, "I loved her so much and she was so mean sometimes, and I said some awful things to her and I hurt her feelings and now she's gone —"

"Aw Sid." I didn't know what to say. This was all so big. I put my hand on the arm of her chair, wanting to hold on, keep her from floating away.

"I don't know where to put it. I loved her and sometimes I hated her and when she was slurring, I felt ashamed. I had to hide it from you. I couldn't bear it if you knew —" She stopped talking, her body wracked with quiet sobs. I wanted to hold her, but the best I could do was hold her ankles, her wool-sock-covered feet. It was the closest thing and the least disruptive. I held Sid's feet while she cried.

Again, me and Sid, we never did things the normal way.

ONE HUNDRED FIFTEEN
FOR INSTANCE

My trip to the UK (that I had planned months and months ago) with Sid was going to be different from this.

It would be early spring for the best waves.

We would fly Virgin first class. Together.

We would stay in London for two nights and go see Westminster Abbey, the burial place of Mary Queen of Scots.

Then we would ride the train to Edinburgh and stay four nights and go do all the Mary stuff.

Then to Thurso, Scotland for freezing cold surfing. Three days.

Then we would take the train south to Cornwall, Fistral Beach, to be exact, and stay three nights at the Surf and Stay Lodge, surfing.

Then we would fly out of London home.

ONE HUNDRED SIXTEEN
TEDDY

Sid said weakly, "I don't know what to do with it all."

I said, "I know, I don't either. That's big Sid, and scary and — you have to figure out how to forgive."

She sniffled and said, "I know, but it's hard. I do forgive her, but she's gone, I can't tell her."

I shook my head. "That's not what I meant. I mean you have to forgive yourself. You. Sid. You're a kid, barely grown up, and you have a right to be treated kindly. You're also human, you get to make mistakes, you get to stick up for yourself, and you have to do your best, right? You do. You have to do the best you can, and when the best you can do sucks, you have to forgive yourself and do better next time."

"With my mom there aren't any more next times."

I nodded, "That's true, but that's also the whole point of this life. You have to grow up and forward. Your next times have to be with new people, new relationships. The people who love you who are still here." She nodded again, pulled one arm off her head. Still curled, she looked at me with lidded, saddened, beaten, swollen eyes. "I can't ask her if she forgives me."

"She does, she did, I'm sure of it."

"How can you be?"

"Because I saw your mom forgive you for some really bratty moments. You argued with her about everything yet she always saw the best in you."

Sid smiled through her tears. "Thank you."

She straightened and wiped her eyes with her sleeve, being careful of the bruises. I jumped up and grabbed a box of tissues and handed it to her. "What did she say to you, the last time you talked to her?"

"It was in the hospital. I told her you kissed me right here." Sid tearfully smiled as she pointed below her belly button. "And she said, 'It's about time.'"

I chuckled. "She was my biggest fan, I miss her greatly."

Sid nodded, gingerly wiped her eyes, and gently blew her nose with an, "Ow." Then she settled back in her chair and fiddled with the Kleenex box. "So, I have to forgive myself."

"Yep, for everything shitty that you said, for all the hate that you felt, the shame, the fear, you have to give yourself a fucking break for it. All of it."

Sid gave one of the saddest smiles, a smile that pushed aside a swollen cheek under a broken nose inside of a sob and covered in tears. "I have to forgive myself for letting a rock star beat me up?"

"Especially for that — and heads up, Cassie is headed over."

Sid groaned, "Man, I don't want her to see me crying." She tried to wipe her eyes with her wadded up wet tissue, but then jumped up, overturning the Kleenex box to the ground, and pushed by Cassie, with a quick, hi, and crossed the lounge to the stairs.

ONE HUNDRED SEVENTEEN

SID

As I fled the lounge Cassie said, "What's going on with Sid? I thought you two were planning to keep it light, play games, or something." I sprinted up the stairs, turning away my splotchy-traumatized-beaten-up and crying face as I passed people in the halls. I shoved the door open on the bathroom, checked under the doors of the stalls for feet, and found myself alone. I leaned on the counter and stared at myself in the mirror. I looked like hell. I needed to pull myself together, but there weren't many solutions for this much drama.

Using a paper towel I gingerly wiped warm water on my cheeks, careful not to get the bandages wet, and then cool water compresses on my eyes. Again gingerly — ouch — touching hurt. I looked again. Still awful.

What I needed was makeup. Some coverup. My mascara, scratch that, eyes were too swollen and wounded, but maybe some brow pencil. Some lipstick in deep red, to draw the eye down to my mouth, the only non-wounded place on the whole face.

This is what I needed to do:

Go to the drug store or whatever they had here in London and buy makeup. Also rubber bands for my hair.

Go to the embassy or wherever it is one goes to get a new passport made.

Buy a new phone.

Get Dad to buy me a plane ticket home.

Crap. This all sounded like a lot of work.

Unless . . .

When I returned, Teddy jumped up. "You okay?"

"Yeah. I'm better, thanks Teddy." I sat down in the chair and he perched on the arm.

I chewed my lip. "I decided I want to go get my stuff."

His face darkened. "You don't need to, I was just researching about your passport. We can leave right now, replace it."

"It's not just my passport though. I can call my phone and tell Gavin to put my stuff outside in the hallway. Plus I ought to —"

Cassie sighed.

Teddy said, "Wait, you ought to what?"

I ignored Teddy's question and said, "He'll give it to me, if I ask."

Cassie squinted her eyes, "I know I'm new here, but that's not the issue . . . we should go to the police. File charges. Have them get your things for you."

I shook my head. "No, I don't want him arrested — it's just —"

Cassie said, "Filing charges is the only thing that makes sense, it protects you, ends your relationship, makes it so that this won't happen again."

"He won't hurt me."

Cassie blew out a big gust of air and dropped back in her chair.

I continued, "And it would be so much easier than replacing my passport, my makeup, my phone, my clothes. My backpack belonged to Mom. I want it."

Cassie said, "Here's the thing, when a guy is like that, he's going to be all apologetic. He'll say it's because he's a victim. He might blame you. He might get angry again. He might beg you to give him another chance."

I glanced at Teddy. He was flexing his hands on his knees staring at the bookcase. Listening, not saying a word. But his face said a lot, he was uncomfortable, pissed. I did not want to talk about Gavin in front of Teddy. At all.

I took a deep breath. "It won't work. He can beg me all he wants. I know why he's the way he is, and it's no excuse, because my mom taught me one thing with her whole life, and it's that people don't have to be that hard and mean and scary. I don't want any part of it."

Cassie said, "We ought to go with you then, right Teddy?"

He stared straight ahead, "Absolutely." His easy smile was gone. His eyes were focused and his jaw set.

"I don't think — seriously, I should go on my own, this is my mess."

Teddy was already shoving his arms in his coat.

I said, "I don't want anyone to get hurt."

Teddy shook his head like that stung, "I won't do anything to him if that's what you're worried about."

Cassie said, "You're under control, right Teddy?"

Teddy said, "Yep."

ONE HUNDRED EIGHTEEN
SID TEXTS HER OWN PHONE

Gavin, this is Sid.
I want you to put all of my stuff
in my suitcase
so I can pick it up.

Sid, listen, can we talk?
I need to talk to you.

No. Just put my stuff in my bag.
Put it outside your door.
I have nothing to say.

ONE HUNDRED NINETEEN

SID

We stowed all of our things on our bunks and left to walk down to Gavin's apartment. I was scared, shaky, and couldn't think of anything to say. Like this moment was grave. Cassie didn't speak either, maybe she felt it too. And Teddy was . . . it was hard to describe — he had gone silent, his face impassive. His fists jammed into his pockets; he had turned to stone. It was scaring me that he was gone like this. Going like this. Was he mad at me? Was this a huge mistake?

I guess when someone does this to the face of a girl, a girl they professed to like, maybe they're too unpredictable, too dangerous to be dealt with. Maybe.

And I was going willingly.

And then there was this: What if Gavin was crying? What if he was begging? What if his hand was over his heart with that plead in his eyes? The answer would still be hell no, right?

Of course.

I was 97% sure. But the 3% was freaking me out.

And making me scared for Teddy.

Was bringing Teddy here a good idea? What if Teddy got hurt?

What if Gavin hit him or got so mad that he hit me again, or what if that insane 3% kicked in and I broke down and stayed?

And Cassie, she was coming with me, an almost total stranger — the whole thing was bonkers. And insane.

And if that 3% kicked in, pheromones or chemical hormones or sexy rock and roller overriding my common sense, what then? What then?

———————————

Someone was leaving, so we snuck through the front door and up the three flights of stairs to Gavin's door. There was no suitcase. I knocked, Cassie's arm wrapped in mine.

Gavin opened the door with a rush. He looked surprised at the strangers on his doorstep, but ignored them. "Sid, oh love, please, we need to talk."

Teddy grunted. I glanced at his face, he was glaring at Gavin.

Gavin placed a hand over his heart and stretched the other arm out. Like I might take his hand, follow him inside.

I said, "We don't need to talk, I need my stuff."

Gavin said, "Love, we do, please —"

Teddy stepped up, his shoulder coming around to my front. Making him hard to ignore.

But Gavin continued to ignore him. "Sid, I'm so sorry, come in, please, let's talk. I feel so —"

Teddy, his eyes focused on Gavin's mouth, growled, low and guttural, "She said she doesn't want to talk to you. Get her stuff."

Gavin kept his eyes on me. "I heard her, but she needs to under —"

Teddy shifted closer, his jaw jutting. "She doesn't need anything from you but her stuff — now."

Gavin focused on Teddy. "What the fuck are you even doing here? Sid, why is he here — this is between me and you, love, come in — please, Sid, please." Teddy growled again.

Cassie tightened her hold on my arm.

I said, "Gavin, there's nothing to say, please get my stuff."

"I have it, I just wanted to —"

Teddy stepped closer, "Yeah. You have her stuff. You have her passport and her coat and her phone, and how many hours has she been on the streets without her coat you think? How long before you found her and gave her her things?"

"I didn't —"

Teddy was inches away from Gavin's face, his fists pulled behind, his chest bowed out. "Yes you did, you kept her stuff so she would come for it, because you're a fucking asshole. She's on the streets with no coat, and you're waiting for her to come back to you."

"Shut up, you don't know."

"I don't know? I know I flew here from LA and got to Sid before you even started looking."

Gavin stepped into the hall. "Sid, tell this guy to back off."

"Look at her face. Look at what you did to her face." The look in Teddy's eyes was scaring me, he pressed closer to Gavin, teeth bared.

I said, "Teddy, it's not worth it, Teddy —" I reached for his upper arm clutching it with both hands, tugging. "Please." My heart was racing.

Gavin looked from my face to Teddy's and then he grabbed the front of Teddy's coat, twisting it, eye to eye.

I yelled, "Gavin stop it!"

The air felt full, the only sound their heavy breaths.

He said, "Sid, you tell this bloke to get off my property."

Teddy said, his voice firm and measured, nose to nose with Gavin, "Don't tell her what to do."

Gavin shoved Teddy, then swung, a right hook aimed for his nose.

Teddy ducked in time, Gavin missed.

Teddy's hands were up by his jaw, his eyes focused on Gavin's face.

Gavin threw a wild, angry, left hook.

Teddy arched away, and Gavin missed him again. Teddy bounced on the balls of his feet. "Careful, you don't want to look like a tool in front of the girls."

Gavin swung again. Teddy ducked and weaved. Gavin bellowed, loud and angry, and lunged. His forearm aimed for Teddy's neck.

I screamed.

Gavin slammed Teddy roughly into the waist-high railing of the stairwell, shoving so hard that Teddy almost fell over. Backward. Over the rail and down. Three flights of stairs down.

It happened so fast that my scream was still going, that's all it took and Teddy almost — Oh god, Teddy almost — he gripped the railing, leveled out, his top half defying gravity, pushed out over space, about to fall — I scrambled for Teddy's arm. Yanking up on his sleeve, screaming, "Don't Gavin, don't, let him go, don't push him."

I begged and held on, trying to pull Teddy to safety. Trying to struggle between them, but they were frozen, locked, too strong. Teddy glared into Gavin's eyes. Daring him. And Gavin was past logic. Was about to let go. "Teddy! Oh god, Teddy!"

Suddenly Gavin stopped. He stepped back.

Teddy stumbled off the railing, bent over, hands on his thighs, breathing heavily.

Gavin said, "I knew it, I knew something was going on between you two." He looked at me, "You're a liar."

I said, "I want my stuff."

Gavin turned, stormed into his apartment, and returned thirty seconds later with my pack, and threw it towards me. It landed with a thud on the carpet. Then he slammed the door, hard.

Teddy was head down, heavy breaths. I crouched to look up into his eyes, "Teddy? Oh my god, Teddy?"

"Yeah." He remained like that for another couple of minutes. Then he stood and rubbed his hands up and down on his face. "Brrrrrrrr." He shook out all his limbs. Like he wanted what had just happened — off. Finally, staring at the door, he said, "Seriously? That guy? Fucking A. I can't believe you went for that guy."

He wasn't talking to me, to himself, but still, tears welled up in my eyes.

Cassie said, "Teddy, I can't believe you didn't punch him."

My hands were shaking so hard they were blurry. Was it cold or fear? I worried I would shake loose at my seams.

Teddy said, "I made a promise to Sid's mom."

I clutched my stomach and sobbed into my hand. I needed to get out of here.

Cassie said, "I mean, that was awesome, that you didn't hit him, I thought you would, but it was so much better that you didn't, he didn't know how to handle it."

Teddy kept staring at the door. "The best way to win a fight is not to fight."

Cassie said, "Well, we better get going."

Teddy leaned down and picked up my pack and slung it to his shoulder. I wanted to protest, but I was seriously falling apart. I was unsure if my legs were steady enough to propel me. What if Teddy had to carry me and my pack — like a god dammed super hero again? Too good for me, clear. Too smart for me, too.

Smart enough to know if he hit Gavin — I might feel sorry for Gavin. The heart is a tricky thing. The chemicals and insane stew of What The Hell — Who Knows Why Women Go Back? But everything bad that happens, it's all because of those tears. The ones behind the eyes. The Ache. It's like a cancer and malignant cells build more. It's science.

Teddy was smart.

And that 3% possibility?

Gone.

But me? Possibly gone too. How do you come back from all of this?

I broke apart starting with a fissure down my core. The tears crashed through. More sobs filled my hands. I needed to fall to my knees but not here. Not on Gavin's doorstep. My shaky feet directed and aimed toward the hostel, walking, barely, my broken self dragging behind. I had one thought: roll up in the fetal position and cry for a good long time — about how scary that was and how awful and dangerous and how I had liked that guy, liked him, really, and now my face hurt and my heart, and I was weak, and if Teddy hadn't come to pick up my pieces — what might have happened to me? And as a thank you I almost got him killed. I walked faster, my body wracked by tears of despair and shame.

ONE HUNDRED TWENTY
TEDDY

"Sid!" I jogged behind. It had taken my brain a few minutes to clear, to focus, to see what was happening. This was happening: Cassie, some girl I just met, was congratulating me on a fight well fought, inviting me to dinner, smiling and praising, while Sid, crying, ran away, through a cold bleak London street, toward the hostel, alone.

I couldn't let this happen. "Sid!" I caught up just as she reached the top step, hand on the hostel door. "Sid, I'm sorry about that, what I said." She held the handle, turned away, I talked to her shoulder. "I didn't mean it, it was just the adrenalin or . . . Jeez Sid, you're shaking like crazy. Are you okay?"

She said, "No, I just — I don't feel good. I need to go to bed." She yanked the door open and stumbled inside. I followed her to the lobby and dropped her bag to the ground.

"Let me buy you some food —"

She shook her head and departed up the stairs, taking two at a time.

I followed carrying her bag up the steps and into the bunk room. She was climbing into her top bunk, pulling her blankets over her head. I whispered, "Sid, can we talk, please?"

I stepped on the bottom rung of her ladder, "Sid?"

Her muffled voice said, "I need some sleep, okay, Teddy? I just need sleep." I watched the lump of blankets that covered Sid for a few minutes more, then I stored her bag into a locker and sat on my lower bunk.

I needed to get out my laptop and books and try to get some writing done. I was way behind. Way, way, way behind. I also needed food. But I couldn't leave, not when the last thing was Sid shaking like that.

ONE HUNDRED TWENTY-ONE
TEDDY

More people entered the bunk room and rustled and wrangled their things trying to get quietly into their squeaky beds.

I laid there staring up at her bunk, too hyperaware to sleep, listening to the soft breathing of Sid and the shifts and snores of strangers, and the multitudes of shared breaths.

Suddenly Sid thrashed and cried out.

A shush came from another area of the room.

I climbed out of my covers — Cold!

Sid groaned.

I stepped on the bottom rung of the ladder. "Sid?"

Someone from a different bunk said, "Shhh."

I patted on Sid's bed, searching for her hand and grasped it.

She curled around my hand and pulled it to her wet cheek. Tears or sweat?

I whispered, "You okay?"

The room was distractingly dark. I closed my eyes.

She whispered, "Drowning."

I leaned in close to her ear, "Your surfboard is right there. Around your ankle, pull the leash, see? There it is, your board. It's been there all along." Her cheek nodded against my hand. "Slide it under you — now stroke, Sid, that's all you have to do, stroke."

She grasped tighter, and while I waited, slowly, she fell asleep. Then I waited longer. Until finally I pulled my hand from her grip and returned to my bunk.

ONE HUNDRED TWENTY-TWO

SID

I didn't fall for Teddy in the normal way, and it was different from Gavin too, not a slam and a crash, Teddy welled up in front of me, like surfing; he was a wave that rose, beautiful and shimmering and big and powerful, the wave of the day, and I had been counting. Teddy wouldn't have believed it, but I had been. Watching the patterns. It was familiar and almost expected, but when my feelings reached their full height, I couldn't believe the size. It took my breath away. All I could do was drop in and ride.

ONE HUNDRED TWENTY-THREE

SID

Teddy must have been waiting for me to get up, because as soon as I stepped from the ladder to the floor, he rose and followed me into the hall.

"Sid?"

Trouble was, I didn't want Teddy to see me like this. I had taken stock when my eyes opened — there was blood on the pillow and my arm. Something crusty was caked on my cheek. I had slept under my covers all night, so my hair felt like a ratty, knotted, birds nest. I didn't turn and made him talk to the back of my head.

"Are you okay, I mean, I know you aren't, but Sid, I'm sorry about that. I'm sorry I provoked him. I'm sorry that you were in the middle of that. Please, can we talk?"

I said, "It's not that, I'm not mad, I . . ." I turned my face to his.

He flinched. "Ouch, that looks awful."

"Yeah, I hoped to get cleaned up before you saw."

He smirked. "Now I wish I had given you the chance."

I jerked my head toward the bathroom. "Follow me, I'll get cleaned up."

"Yes, of course." He followed me into the bathroom and leaned on the counter beside the sink. "I was thinking we should go see something today."

He was talking, but I had trouble hearing what he said because memories flashed whenever I blinked:

Gavin shoving Teddy with his forearm on his neck.

Gavin growling.

My white knuckles gripping Teddy's sleeve, trying to keep him from falling over the railing.

I felt incapable of anything as courageous as going outside.

I peeled the bandage off my cheek. "I don't know . . . maybe I need to stay here . . . you should go though."

Teddy pulled a new bandage from the box for me. "Come on, I want to go with you to Westminster Abbey. My plane ticket out of here is tomorrow evening, and I haven't seen anything yet."

I froze, the new clean bandage aimed for my cheekbone, looking at him through the mirror. Teddy was leaving? "Oh. Your flight is tomorrow? I guess you said that, but I didn't realize it was so . . . .."

"I want you to go with me to Westminster Abbey. I came all this way. And you don't have to, I would never play the guilt card, but what are you going to do, stay here all day?"

I pressed the bandage down with a wince. "That was my plan. I don't know, I feel kind of —"

"Okay, that means I'm playing the guilt card. I came all the way here and you should go with me."

I ran the water and leaned over to splash my face.

"You've got nothing else to do but buy a plane ticket home. That's fifteen minutes tops Sid. You'll be mad if you miss Westminster Abbey. And I'll look stupid there by myself because I won't know what I'm looking at."

I patted my face with a towel. "I guess I ought to."

Teddy grinned. "Awesome. Guilt worked."

I said, "Proud of that, huh?"

"If you're out in London, having fun, then yes." He paused for a second. "You're okay, right Sid?"

"I'm okay. I look wrecked, but I'm okay."

He looked relieved.

I said, "Are you sure you want to go to Westminster Abbey? Cassie said it was boring. We could do the Harry Potter sights, you love those books."

Teddy clutched his chest just above the heart. "What madness is this? I loved those books about seven years ago, and Westminster Abbey is — Oh my god, did you really just say you'd rather go to Harry Potter sights than Westminster Abbey? Did the doctor check you for a concussion? Westminster Abbey is full of dead poets and executed queens, I read about it in my guidebook of cool places to go to in London. It even has that —" He snapped his fingers, like he couldn't remember her name, "Queen or something, you know, the one you used to go on and on about?"

I rolled my eyes, "Mary?"

He said, "I'm not sure that's right, but it'll come to me when we're standing in front of her coffin."

"Okay, Westminster Abbey, after breakfast."

ONE HUNDRED TWENTY-FOUR
MARY

I never got to go to London. I begged my cousin, Elizabeth, to allow me to visit, but she refused. Politics, upheavals, possible overthrows, she never decided if I was a threat or not. And the last thing she wanted was for me to take her crown.

You see, I remained Catholic, though England had turned Protestant, and I was heir to the British throne. Some believed I was the only legitimate Queen. So Elizabeth didn't trust me. At all.

When I entered England and asked for Elizabeth's help, she placed me under house arrest in a castle away to the North. For nineteen years. Eventually I was executed there and buried.

But, consider this, when Elizabeth died, the kingdom passed to my son, James, who became the king of Scotland and England — both.

And one of his acts as King was to have my coffin exhumed and brought to Westminster Abbey. Where now I lie just feet away from Elizabeth.

ONE HUNDRED TWENTY-FIVE

SID

I was going to Westminster Abbey. Today. I had kind of forgotten that it existed outside the hostel. That anything existed. I had been thinking about sitting on the couch in the lounge feeling sorry for myself, but here I was walking up to the most beautiful cathedral I had ever seen.

I said, "Whoa."

From the corner of my eye I could see Teddy smile.

ONE HUNDRED TWENTY-SIX
TEDDY

My guidebook said the best way to see Westminster Abbey was to pay extra for the headphone and cassette-tape-player tour. Sid balked because, as she said, it couldn't be that great if the technology was from the 1990s. I Insisted and won, I also paid and handed her one.

She put hers on and asked, "Should I wait for you?"

"You go on ahead, we do this separate, I guess."

I watched her walk away through the crowds. Then I turned on my tour tape. I tried to concentrate. The Abbey was beautiful, wondrous, the inside so chockful of history, monuments, art, and dead people, that it was unbelievable. Literally, if you studied a British person in history class, they were buried in that church. I found it fascinating and I was only mildly curious, not obsessed with British history like Sid. I listened to the tour guide's voice, looking where the voice directed, mostly, but I'd catch glimpses of Sid up ahead, and distracted, I'd watch — Sid looked fascinated and sometimes excited, almost like the good old days.

Then Sid disappeared through an ornate archway and when I entered a few minutes behind, she stood, mouth agape, eyes wide. She turned and pointed at a coffin, covered in a marble sculpture, surrounded by marble columns, in a marble room. The sculpture was of Mary, her hands pressed together in prayer pointing to the sky.

Sid pulled her earphones down. "Teddy, look. Oh god. Look."

I said, "I see."

There were only two or three other people in the room, so she had space to investigate. Sid stood on tiptoes, leaned across, and crouched down to see see the sarcophagus from different angles. Finally, she slid down the wall and sat looking up at it. I slid down the wall beside her.

She asked, "Can we take a moment, so I can just — ?"

"I've got all day."

Sid scrambled through her bag and pulled out a journal and some pencils. I hadn't seen her singular devotion in so long that, if it would have kept her interested, I would have stayed there all day. Night too, though that might have been kind of creepy. Did I mention there were a lot of dead people in this place?

Finally she clutched her journal to her chest and said, "This was excellent Teddy, thank you."

I stood and offered my hand to pull her to standing. Then we both put our headphones on and listened to the rest of the tour.

We took the tube to the hostel, talking the whole time about what we had seen. We declared which were our favorite sculptures, picked the best stained glass window, and debated which was the most exciting grave. Besides Mary's. Sid was smiling and laughing and I got carried away, believing we were together-together, in London. "Let's get cleaned up and go to a restaurant for dinner. Somewhere with sit down tables and menus."

Sid started to protest, but then paused and said, "I'd like that." I didn't even have to guilt her into it.

At the hostel we rifled through our bags for better going-out clothes and agreed to meet in the lounge when we were ready for dinner.

I made it downstairs first and slid into an empty corner booth. And waited. I tried not to think about how much writing I still had to do. A hopeless amount. I made a promise to myself that I would get to it after dinner, but I was feeling the jet lag; that promise was probably a lie.

A minute later Cassie showed up and slid into the opposite end of the booth. "We had so much fun last night, a blast."

I said, "Oh, that's good. We had a fun day too, we went to Westminster Abbey."

Cassie groaned. "That place is so boring, but if that's your thing — look, there's something I need to talk to you about."

I said, "Sure?"

She crossed her arms on the table. "My sister's boyfriend beat the shit out of her more than once. Really bad. Like Sid. My sister is actually a lot like Sid, too, personality-wise. But her boyfriend, he was gross. Nothing about him was worth going back for, but for some reason she did, over and over and . . . My point is, now that you've seen Sid's guy —"

I scowled, twisted the lid off a water bottle, and swigged, trying not to think about how he talked to Sid. He called her love; I wanted to choke him. I tuned in when she said, "— so smooth."

"You think he was smooth? Is that what girls like?"

"God yes, he was hot in that bad guy way that makes some girls all confused and wiggly. And me and my friends, we've heard of him. He's about to be big time. And, you know — girls will get confused around someone that hot. They'll put up with a lot."

I said, "Jeez. You think she'll go back to him?"

She looked me right in the eyes. "I'm sure of it."

I slumped in my seat and blew out a deep breath of air.

Cassie asked, "Nothing's going on with you two right?"

"No, we're just friends, we tried to be more, once . . . It didn't work out. It was awful."

"Good, because after about eight big beatings, when my sister truly left her 'bad boy,' she had a very damaged belief system. So I'm just saying, be ready. Be ready to deal with that. Try not to be too emotionally involved."

I stared into space, trying to get Sid's self to jibe with Cassie's words. "You think she would?"

"Has she pressed charges? Is she talking about it? Has she bought her plane ticket home? I think all the signs are there."

I said, "Uh huh," but all I was thinking was, more than once, and, over and over. I said, "I'm just not sure it's . . ."

"What have her other boyfriends been like?"

"Band guys."

"See, he's her type. She's attracted to a hot mess. It's personality and also weakness and also stupid girl shit and also, and I'm sorry to keep saying it, but he was way hot. It's a good thing you aren't involved, I mean, emotionally." Her stare was intense.

I said, "Yep, good thing."

"It's important for you to know there's nothing you can do. Say goodbye. Girls who get beat up and go back, they aren't what you're looking for, right?"

I nodded, "True. I guess you're right."

"Oh I'm right, I've been there. My guess is she's waiting until you fly home to California and then she'll go make it up with him."

"Oh. I didn't think of that." I tried to remember all the things Sid said in the past day, looking for proof that Cassie was right or hopefully wrong. "You don't think I can talk sense into her?"

"In my experience they don't listen, they have to learn for themselves, but you should try to get her on a plane."

She pulled out her phone and scrolled through something. She added, "I'm glad you had a good day though. You deserve it after your epic rescue."

I pulled out my phone to give me some cover because Cassie had freaked me out. I wanted to argue with her, but what could I say? Sid was weak and sad and had been for a long time. The only time in the past six months she hadn't looked broken was when she had her legs wrapped around that guy in the club. So yeah, I was feeling hopeless. Like Sid was a lost cause.

Because Cassie was right — Sid wasn't doing anything but hanging out, like she was waiting for me to leave. In a hostel that was literally four doors down from that guy's house. He could walk in here any minute, make some grand gesture, beg her forgiveness.

Heat crawled up my cheeks.

I had mounted an epic rescue, and what is the freaking point of a rescue if the princess wants to stay with the dragon?

Waste of time, totally.

Worse, if this was just some back and forth abuser-abused game of sexual conquest, then having me show up and be a part of it made me a total fool — but this was also Sid.

I had been best friends with her since before I learned to walk. I had fallen in love with her when she paddled out with me that first time. I had come to London not because she asked, but because I had to. I couldn't not come.

I dropped my phone to the table, ran my hands down my face and stretched my arms forward, palms out. Cassie was right, and maybe the rescue wasn't over yet; I needed to get Sid on a plane. That was number one.

I took a deep breath just as Sid entered the lounge.

ONE HUNDRED TWENTY-SEVEN

SID

I strode up to their table and slid in beside Cassie. I smiled at Teddy, but faltered, his eyes were brooding. "You guys talking about me?"

Cassie shifted in her seat and paused before saying, "We were discussing the White album."

It had to be pretend, Teddy didn't know shit about the White album. I looked from face to face. Yep, talking about me. Probably saying I was a wreck, a naïve Should-Have-Seen-It-Coming wreck. Also that I was a burden they had to deal with. A wreck and a burden, me, Sid.

Cassie said, "I wish I could say you look better, but . . . You still need the two bandages?"

"The cut on my cheek is still oozing. My nose isn't scabbed over. Yeah, I need them both."

Cassie said, "Well, yesterday was a trip, huh? That guy was wicked hot, emphasis on the wicked. I see what you liked about him, hot, dangerous, but man, that was scary."

I glanced at Teddy, he was watching me intently. I nodded, past being able to talk about it.

Cassie looked from Teddy to me and continued, "Teddy told me about how you guys are just friends, because you tried to be more and that was a disaster. Can't be more of a disaster than this." She gestured to my face, "but better for all the rest of us that Teddy is still available."

She flipped her hair and grinned at Teddy. "I'm following you on Instagram. Maybe if I come to LA you can take me surfing?"

Teddy nodded, "Sure, I have lots of boards."

Cassie turned in her seat toward me. "Sid, my friend, I'm sorry to say goodbye, but I'm headed to Dublin." She kissed me on my undamaged cheek. "Take care of yourself." I slid from the booth and she climbed out.

She put her hand on Teddy's shoulder and said, "If you need anything, you know how to find me. Hey and check my Instagram — I'm hoping for a Bono sighting." Then she was gone.

Silence descended on our table. Teddy kept looking at the door where she had gone, anywhere but at me. Was there something between Teddy and Cassie? Whoa. And how would I feel? Furious. Jealous. Sad. Lost — Teddy interrupted my internal litany by opening his laptop and running his hand down his face. "First thing we need to organize your flight home."

"Oh, um . . ."

Teddy typed. "My flight leaves at 8:00 pm, it would be good if we were on the same flight, if it's got room."

When I was young and frightened of something, like the dark or monsters, my mom would become a superhero. She put on music, massaged my back and feet with essential oils, administered chocolate to keep the 'dementors' away. And then I would wake up the next morning, all better.

A few years later the fears became more specific, an earthquake would flatten Los Angeles or a fire would engulf my house, and my mom became less capable of helping. It was like she didn't have it in her to tell me things would be okay.

And then I grew up and my anxious feelings were more specific, present, and exhausting. I couldn't ask mom for help because she had become the cause.

As my fears grew up my calm mom faded away.

And here I was, halfway around the world, my mom gone, and I was frightened. Tears dammed up on my synapses, malfunctioning my brain; the Ache was growing.

When I blinked, I had these flashes:

Gavin swinging at Teddy's face.

Gavin growling over me, about to swing again.

And maybe the worst of them all, Teddy walking away, because I was too much trouble. It was only a matter of time.

And one of those flashes? Happened right then.

———

I closed my eyes tight and when I opened them Teddy was staring at me, brow furrowed. "What do you think Sid, there is a ticket, it's expensive though . . . We better get it now before —"

I shook my head. "I thought we were going to go get food. I'm starving."

Teddy looked at me over his laptop screen, his expression worried. "Let's buy your flight home Sid. I have it right here."

A flash of Gavin's forearm on Teddy's throat.

I gulped. "I need food first, I'm having trouble thinking straight."

Teddy nodded slowly, his eyes sad. "Sure. Of course Sid." He closed the laptop, dropped it into his pack, and slung it to his shoulder, ready to go.

ONE HUNDRED TWENTY-EIGHT
TEDDY

We asked at the front desk and Chris recommended a restaurant, The Duke's Bucket, two Tube stops away, that served fish and chips. So we stepped into the cold of the street.

I bundled my arms around myself. "It will be good to get home, huh? After this cold?"

Sid fished her gloves out of her pocket and pulled them on, teeth chattering.

I continued, "I can't wait to get in the water. It's been so long. Saltwater is good for healing too, maybe you could go surfing with me the morning after we get back?"

Sid smirked. "It's not enticing to talk about the ice cold Pacific when it's freezing out here. Let's talk about the hot chocolate I'll be drinking when you're surfing."

I said, "Will you be drinking that hot chocolate on the beach? Or here in London, because without a plane ticket —"

"Ooh, London hot chocolate!" She puffed a cool breath. "Let's get some of that after dinner." Not at all the answer I was looking for.

When we were on the train, Sid asked vaguely, "When did you say your flight was?"

"Eight pm. I should get to the airport by 5:30, I mean, we. Why?"

"No reason, just . . . No reason."

A man, bigger than me, rough, shaved head, shifted into Sid's line of vision and asked, "This guy bothering you?"

"Oh, no — this is my friend."

The man glared at me and remained standing beside us, menacing. I decided to look out the window quietly until our stop, which was next.

We left the station, shoved through the crowds, climbed the tall stairs to the street, and walked one more block to the restaurant.

We were quiet as we were shown to our table and handed the menus. I had trouble coming up with any conversation because my mind was full of this — I had to get Sid on a plane. I couldn't show her how upset I was, or demand to know what she was thinking, because any negative drama and she would definitely stay here with that guy. But my head was also full of this — Sid wasn't leaving with me. She never planned to. She already made her decision, and my feelings never even figured into it.

Our waitress asked for our order.

Sid said, "Fish and chips with a Coke."

I said, "The same."

The waitress cut her eyes at me and left with a huff.

Sid asked, "What's with her?"

"Another person who thinks I beat you."

Sid said, "Oh, right, I keep forgetting how I look, I'll say something." She rummaged through her bag, brought up aspirins and swallowed two down with some water.

Sid's face hurt, probably her whole head, and I wanted to help her. To take some of the pain and anguish from her life, but something was becoming clear — Cassie had been right about a lot of things, especially this — I was too emotionally involved. Still. Even though Sid had broken up with me, even though Sid had moved on. Even though. Still.

Sid said, "That was fun this morning, thank you."

"Sure. It was."

I pulled my phone out of my pocket to test her again. "I guess we can order your ticket here as well as anywhere, one perk of a pocket computer, am I right?"

Sid chewed her lip and then failed the test. "It can wait though, I mean, I should check the price with my dad first."

I dropped my phone to the table.

Yeah. Sure.

This was what I wanted to say:

Of course.

Let me gather myself and get out of your way.

So you can make some kind of peace with that guy.

That seems like an excellent idea, hope it goes well for you.

My brain was on sarcasm overload.

I pushed my fists into my thigh until my knuckles cracked. Was there anything I could do? Say? I looked at her, big blue and red bruises wrapped around the orbit of her swollen eye, butterfly bandages on her cheek, a bandaid across her probably broken nose, and shook my head. This morning had been so great, but this was how it would end. This was how my whole relationship with Sid would end. With Sid going back there.

ONE HUNDRED TWENTY-NINE
SID

Our waitress delivered our plates, turned away from Teddy, and looked directly at me. "I have to say something, dear. You're too wee to have this arse treat you like a punching bag. My mother used to get beat like this, and you need to find the strength to walk away."

I shook my head, "Oh no, he didn't do this, he —"

The waitress said, "Dear, you mustn't make excuses for him, but if you need help, ask for it." She stalked off.

I said, "I'm so sorry Teddy."

He shook his head and shoved his plate away.

I wanted to reach out and hold his hand, to tell him not only that I was sorry, but that I would never forgive myself until he forgave me. I felt so weak and wrong and also, still, not at all his equal, not able to make him happy, because here he was again — strong and wonderful, and me — broken and sad, and my broken disaster was spilling over onto him. Just being across the table from me and a stranger called him an ass. That's what I shared with him — my broken face, life, heart, and because of me he was the recipient of people's ire.

I wanted to cry.

I wanted to run from the room.

But mostly I wanted to beg him to forgive me.

But there's this —

I was looking at him through a face covered in another man's bruise.

So I cried.

Tears streamed down my face and Teddy scowled. "This is what I don't get, what are you doing, really?"

I stared at him blankly, chewing my lip. Crying. I was crying because this whole scene sucked, but guess what — escalating.

He continued, "I leave tomorrow."

He pushed his chair away from the table and put his hands on his thighs, "You're what — staying, right? Or just doing nothing and waiting to see what happens? That's probably it, but hey, I want to thank you for not doing it in front of me. Thanks for the morning. That was good." He ran both hands through his hair. "Here's the thing Sid, I can't do it anymore, not this, not watching this, not being a part of it. I can't. I thought we could be friends, that I could be the guy who you confided in and buddies, you know, but I can't. I want taken off your list. Don't call me anymore when things go tragic. It's too hard." He stood up and spun for a second looking for his things. He pushed his arms into his coat and zipped the front.

"Teddy, what —"

He looked down at the table and around and directly at me. "Will you be able to get to the hostel? It's just to Victoria Station. Remember?"

I said, "Um, yes."

He whipped out his wallet and threw thirty pounds on the table. "I have to go, I have papers to write. I'll see you there, but this has to be it. The end, okay Sid, for me? No more." And then he walked out of the door of the restaurant and away.

Teddy broke up with me.

Really broke up, not just the dating kind, but the whole life kind, the end-end kind, and I had no idea why and was so lost and confused by the whole thing that I just stared at the door. Until I realized the wait staff was applauding.

ONE HUNDRED THIRTY

SID

Dad had said Mom would visit me. That she would come sometime and talk and I would just have to be ready for when it happened.

I had believed the Oasis poster or Gavin might have been Mom talking to me, but now I knew that was obvious shit-total hogwash. There was no way in hell that mom wanted me to be with Gavin.

And wasn't it weird that I saw signs for Gavin and had forgotten how much Mom loved Teddy.

Where had my head been? Was this the cloud of grief that Dad had been telling me about?

Mom was straightforward. She called him Our Teddy. She joked that she would ask him to move in with us if I didn't get on with it.

Mom was too upfront to spend her afterlife sending me strange, hard to understand signals. If she wanted to tell me something she would come right out and say it.

I know that now.

But then, at the table staring at the door. I had no idea.

Until . . .

ONE HUNDRED THIRTY-ONE
THIS HAPPENED

The waitress came to the table and said, "Dear, we are so pleased about this, good on you. Here's the thing, you must be strong. He thinks you'll come back to him, that you'll come running. That's the thing about men, they think they can beat you and that you'll come back for more —"

"I don't —"

"Can I sit down for just a minute?"

I nodded and she sat across from me and scooped Teddy's food into a to-go box. "You have to be strong, prove to him you're too strong to go back. And not just him, everybody, for all the little girls that need to be strong, be strong for them."

I looked at the door where Teddy had just left. "He thinks I'll go back to him after he beat me?"

"It's what so many women do, dear. You have to be the one who doesn't. You have to know that you deserve better." The waitress gestured with the spoon, "Hearts can be full of pain and sadness until it seems like that's all they'll hold. Like they're full to the tiptop, hard to carry without spilling all over everything in your life. You're crying in a restaurant, the saddest girl here, but this is the truth — you deserve to be happy. Find the thing, the person, the place, that makes you happy and fill your heart with that. It's up to you, but when you fill your heart with happiness, guess what spills over?"

I nodded. "Happiness . . . Because I deserve it."

"So the staff and I want to pick up your bill, dear, on us."

298

"Oh you don't need to do —"

"Already done, you can pocket that arse's loot. It's time for you to move on."

I pulled the money to my lap and deposited it in my bag. "Thank you, um?"

"My name's Alicia"

"Oh, that was my mother's name."

"Has she been gone long?"

"About six months."

"Well, no wonder you're as sad as this, with your black and blue face. That's the pain in your heart spilling over my dear. Fill it with happiness, for your mom."

I stood and she handed me the bag of fish and chips. "For dinner tonight."

I raced to Victoria Station. I had a hope that I would find Teddy in the station, but the streets were filling, the sky was darkening, and the thing about London was the Tube runs all the time like clockwork. I tore down the steps, shoved through the crowd, and jumped through the doors of the train. It was a crowded car. I pressed my fingers against the pole for balance and counted the minutes until my stop.

Then I ran to the hostel, hoping to reach Teddy before it was too late. My brain thinking with each step, it's too late, is it too late? It's too late, is it too late?

When I rushed through the front door to the lobby, my heart was racing, my breaths gasping, and I had bloomed a full blown sweat.

ONE HUNDRED THIRTY-TWO

SID

In the cacophony of people and chairs it took a second to find him. He was at a corner booth, a laptop in front of him and a small stack of books.

He was concentrating, head in his hand through his hair.

He looked up at me and my heart broke. He was across the distance of the room and it might as well have been the moon. He was gone and I wanted him to return to me. I descended the two steps and crossed the lounge. He slumped onto the cushions behind him, looking down at a post-it note in his hands.

I placed the bag of food on the table and dropped to my knees beside him and grasped his hand, holding his knuckles to my chest.

"Teddy what did you mean? You can't watch, what?"

He looked at my hands clutching his, "If you go back to him, if you stay . . ."

"If I go back to him? That's not what this is, not at all."

"Oh, it seemed like you would. Like he was what you wanted . . ."

I yanked my sweaty, too warm hat off my head, tossed it to the table, and wrapped my hands around his again. "No, he's not what I want."

"You aren't making plans to go home, you're choosing to stay. He's right here. Cassie said . . ."

"What did she say?"

"She said you would go back to that guy, that you would keep going back. And that I needed distance. She was right, Sid. I'm too close. I can't watch this anymore."

I dropped my forehead to his hand. Wondering how to explain what I didn't understand myself. I looked up at him. "I can't make plans to go home, because I don't want to leave London. I want to stay because I don't know if I'll ever get to return. And I came all this way and I guess I'm stuck. But not in the way you think —"

"I thought you wanted to stay with —"

"No, Teddy, this has nothing to do with Gavin. I just — I want to stay longer, and I don't know if I get to — like it's not okay after all I put you through . . ."

"So you plan to stay, but not with him?"

I gripped his hand tighter, holding on, I pressed it to my cheek, closed my eyes and took a deep breath. "I don't know if it's okay for me to ask you, after all that I did, after hurting you like I did, but I want to stay here with you."

Teddy's brows knit together. "You want to stay here with me?"

I nodded. "I don't know if you can even or if you would want to, because so much has happened. You had to come all the way here, and so it's not okay for me to say what I want. But I want you."

"Wait slow down, this isn't —"

"I'm just so sorry, about all of that, this. When Gavin tried to hurt you I was so scared."

"You were scared for me?"

"Yes, I was terrified."

"I thought . . . something different. I've been thinking everything different."

"I'm so sorry about that too."

He said, "You don't have to be sorry. I just . . ." He shook his head. Then he turned the post-it note to show me what it said in his familiar scrawl:

Tell her that you love her, one last time.

"Oh." Tears welled up in my eyes. I kissed his fingers.

He said, "It's okay with me if you tell me what you want."

"You."

"So really, you want me to stay in London with you?"

I did one of those sob laughs that probably made me look bonkers. "I've actually been dreaming of going to Scotland. There's some stuff there I want to see."

Teddy nodded. "And you want me to go with you — as friends."

I shook my head. "No, as more, but Teddy, we have to go slow. I — I don't want to ruin anything, you know? I'm scared, because you're so important to me and —"

"So more than friends, but slow. I can do slow, I'm patient." He reached into the bag of food I brought, fished out a napkin, and handed it to me to wipe my nose. He reclined and offered me his hand again. I climbed up on the bench seat beside him.

"Sid, are you sure this isn't just that I'm right here, the closest person?"

I laughed through my tears. "I ran through London to get to you."

"You know what I mean, our moms have been putting us together since forever, this isn't proximity based?"

"Not for me, no. You?"

"It's not a competition, but I kind of went around the world to get to you." He gave me a sad smile.

"Sure, but that was as a friend, not as more . . ."

"With me it's all been the same thing, Sid, always."

"Except for when you were seven."

Teddy grinned. "That year I was rebelling because I was pissed that people saw how much you meant to me."

I shook my head. "That's bullshit."

Teddy chuckled, "Yeah. I was young. Once it mattered, then it's always been about you."

I clutched his hand tighter. "So this is it, me and you? You want to?"

"Yeah, I want to."

"Even after all this time? Even after I sent you away and got all tragic? You've been cleaning up after me for so long, I don't know how you can stand it."

"You know, this isn't like that at all. You make it sound like you've been doing things to me, but in reality you disappeared. You being gone is so much more of a pain in my ass than you being here and having a crisis. I can deal with crises — I understand them. I can help. I want to, but when you aren't around I'm a tragedy too. I want you. Every day. Messy and all."

I said, "But remember how in Malibu we never talked about what we were doing, I want to be different this time. Talk about it all. And maybe we could check in with each other occasionally. Like I could say, how into me and you are you, scale of one to ten and —"

"Ten."

I smiled. "Ten thousand billion, you get extra points if you make it exaggeratedly."

"I can't exaggerate, it's too important."

I nodded. "So you'll come with me to Scotland?"

"How long?" He glanced at his laptop.

"I was thinking ten days, then we're home in time for Christmas with our families."

"Yeah, Sid, I'd like that, but I think you get to call my parents to ask them to change my ticket, it will be fun to watch."

"You think your mom will be okay with it?"

"My mom, okay with me and you? Yeah. I think it's a safe bet."

I opened his laptop and pressed Skype and then video-call to @MamaLAyers.

Lori appeared on the screen. "Sid!" And then, "Oh no, Sid, your beautiful face, Teddy didn't tell me how bad it was. Oh, I'm so sorry, wait, why are you — is Teddy okay?"

Teddy leaned into the screen with a wave, "Hi, Mom."

"Phew! That was a heart-racing moment. So why is Sid calling me while you're off screen?"

Teddy leaned in again, "Because she has something to ask you."

Lori smiled sweetly, "Yes Sid?"

"Can you change Teddy's ticket to the um . . ." I opened the calendar and counted ten days, "Twenty-second?"

Lori said, "Uh, okay, why?"

"Because I asked him to go with me to Scotland."

Lori's eyes got big and she clamped her teeth down on her lips like she would burst. "You, Sid, asked Teddy to go with you to . . . like together, together?"

I nodded.

"Oh my god!" Teddy's mom squealed.

I giggled and looked over at Teddy who laughed and said, "Told you."

Scott's voice came from off screen, "Is Teddy okay?"

Lori said, "Sid asked Teddy to go with her to Scotland! I'm freaking so excited!"

He said, "Quiet down, you'll blow it." Scott sat down beside Lori and they shifted the laptop so they both fit on the screen.

She clamped her teeth over her lips again. "I'm trying, I'm just so — tell Teddy we'll add money to his account."

"I have money, from Mom, that I want to use for this part of the trip. I think she would have liked that I spent it on me and Teddy going to Scotland."

"Alicia would have been over the moon at this news."

Scott grinned widely. "So you'll be coming with us to Indo in the Spring?"

Teddy leaned in. "Dad, we're taking it slow, keeping it cool."

Scott said, "This is Sid were talking about? I've been around her since she was a baby, and she never takes anything slow, but okay, I won't book her ticket, yet." He smiled and left the screen, joking with Lori, "Play it cool, don't scare her off."

Lori said, "I guess you get that we're happy about this and just, no pressure, have fun. We love you, both of you, be safe and . . ." She wiped the corner of her eye.

I said, "We'll talk to you when we get to Edinburgh."

She blew us a kiss and then she was gone.

Teddy said, "No pressure, huh?"

I smiled.

He said, "How into me are you now, scale of one to . . ."

I said, "Ten."

ONE HUNDRED THIRTY-THREE
SID SKYPED HER DAD

"Hi, I can't get used to seeing you like that."

"You don't have to, it's feeling better and better and will heal in no time."

"True. I miss you."

"I miss you too, Dad."

"So when do you want me to book your home flight — tomorrow? Lori says Teddy is on the evening flight, I think it was —"

"I think Mom visited me today."

"Oh, what happened?"

"I was in a restaurant with Teddy and he left. He was upset and it sucked and this waitress came over and told me a long thing about how I needed to fill my heart with happiness and love. Her name was Alicia."

"That sounds like your mom, did it feel important?"

"It felt so important, and I felt — I don't know how to describe it — warm. And excited. And when it was over my adrenaline was pumping and I was so clear and . . ."

"That's so great, I'm so glad for you." Dad wiped both of his eyes.

I said, "I asked Teddy to go with me to Scotland, until the twenty-second. Is that okay with you?"

"Definitely. Well, well, this is important news, big news, right?"

"Yeah, it's big. I'm really happy about it. He's here too in case you say something, I don't know, negative." I turned the laptop and Teddy waved at the screen.

"Hi Teddy, and I have nothing negative, but you're doing this for you, right? Not because the Moms wanted it so badly?"

"I'm doing it for me, not for the moms. Though it doesn't hurt that it would make Mom happy."

"It makes me happy too. I love you. Call me in a couple of days."

"I love you too Dad."

ONE HUNDRED THIRTY-FOUR
TEDDY

Sid hung up the phone and I held her hand and we sat quietly in that moment after a Big Thing happened. Calming down. Thinking it over. Smiling. She asked, "Can I have the Post-it note?"

I gave it to her and she pressed it to her journal's inside cover. Then she asked, "Maybe you can explain this laptop and stack of books? You have papers to write?"

"Apparently I tried to fail my first semester of school, but then around Thanksgiving I decided that wasn't the best idea I ever had. I spent the last weeks cramming for finals and now writing papers. I have two due," I glanced at my phone, "tomorrow night."

"Which classes?"

"English and Marine Biology. If the second one isn't a passing grade, then I don't advance to the next level and might as well drop out of school." I ran my hand through my hair and sat up straighter in my seat.

"So this is serious? And you've been dealing with my bullshit for days?"

"This is serious."

"Tell me what you have so far?"

"First draft of the English paper, three-quarters of the first draft of the Biology paper."

She jumped up, "Okay, Dropbox me the English paper. I'll edit it while you finish the biology paper. I'm going for my iPad." She ran out of the room and returned a few minutes later and curled up at the end of the bench seat leaned against pillows with her toes tucked under my thigh.

When I wasn't busy writing I put my hand on top of her foot. I was holding her foot again, but had advanced to holding her hand too, if it was available. I marveled that here we were in the land of casual touches, occasional brushes, when an hour before I had been sitting here broken to pieces.

Finally we were too exhausted to write anymore. Sid had finished my English paper for me, I just needed to give it another read-through. My Marine Biology paper was ready to be edited. We would do it tomorrow, then upload the papers to the professors, and then buy our train tickets to Scotland. We had a plan, a responsible, slow, taking it easy plan.

Then it was bedtime and we stood in the coed bathroom together brushing our teeth. Smiling. Spit rolling down from the corner of Sid's mouth. I said, "I feel like we do everything the wrong way, end first instead of the beginning. Am I supposed to brush teeth with you when I haven't even kissed you yet?" I spit in the sink and wiped my mouth on a towel.

She said, "You've kissed me." She spit in the sink and then rinsed and gargled with water.

I said, "Exactly, just not in the usual place."

She said, "Where exactly was that . . . I can't remember. Can you show me?" She lifted her shirt a half-inch exposing her belly button.

I said, "You know it was in Malibu."

She laughed and looked in the mirror. "I need to change my bandage."

I said, "Let me." I pulled up close to her and peeled the edge of the bandage up and off. She winced.

I said, "It's looking better." I fished another bandage out of the box. Then I unwrapped it, placed it, and rubbed my thumbs down the side to adhere it. She lifted her chin, and I leaned in and kissed her.

Then three people walked into the bathroom and interrupted us, because this was a public bathroom in a coed hostel.

I'd like to say that at least now we had kissed.

I'd like to add, it wasn't my best work.

ONE HUNDRED THIRTY-FIVE

SID

Teddy's papers were done. Mailed. Early because of the time difference. That spinning earth thing was very helpful.

We checked the timetable for trains to Edinburgh and found one that left around dinner time. We would get into Edinburgh at about 11:00 p.m.

We booked the best hostel in Edinburgh according to everybody we asked, called the High Street Hostel. We bought pastries and cheese and chocolate and drinks for the road and then we were on the train.

These things were all new. I didn't ride trains generally, I Uber-ed. I didn't walk around London after dark and make plans to ride across countries with Teddy. Yet here I was, doing a ton of all new things, and oh man, it was awesome. We stowed our suitcases and slid into our train seats at a table. We both sat on one side. The train slid away from the station and slowly outside our window grew dark and there was nothing to see.

Teddy turned on Spotify, his The Waves Suck Today playlist: lots of Blink 182 and Weezer, and offered me one side of his earbuds. I pulled out my iPad and returned to reading a book I started before I left home. Teddy raised his arm and wordlessly I nestled in under, leaned against him. Curled up. My heartbeat sped and

I
just
loved
him
so

much.

See that's what I meant, he didn't crash in to me, he welled up in front, all hot and necessary and comfortable, but oh my god, I literally couldn't breathe but in small irregular breaths. And only when I concentrated. Which meant I couldn't read, not really, and so I nestled more, and then I inched and shifted up so that my lips were on his neck and I kissed there, and my hand was inside his jacket, rising up to his cheek pulling his mouth to mine.

But then the door of the train berth opened and three young men came in, Australian, saying, "Pardon me, Mate," and "Resume the position," with a laugh. I straightened up in my seat and Teddy chuckled, because: interrupted, again.

Then one guy really looked at me and said, "But seriously, did this bloke do this to you?"

I said, "No, you should have seen what he did to the bloke who did this to me."

They nodded appreciatively at Teddy. "Congrats Mate, for winning the prize."

Sexist jerks.

But, fine. Teddy had had enough of blame for Gavin's abuse. He deserved some respect. Another guy said, "Yep Mate, and the sad part is the train is packed. We're stuck with each other." They smiled and laughed and we all rode in the now crowded compartment to Edinburgh.

I nestled in under Teddy's arm but it wasn't quite the same as it was moments before.

ONE HUNDRED THIRTY-SIX

TEDDY

The High Street Hostel was a lot like the one in London. Crowded: with energy, stuff, people, excitement, and more people. The front desk booked us into two different dorms: one for girls, one for boys. I supposed we were taking this relationship real slow. Slower than stacked-in-bunkbeds slow, we were crawling along in down-the-hall slow.

We walked up the stairs to the hallway and stopped for a minute, facing each other, packs on our backs. I leaned on the wall and she mirrored me. I grabbed the strap on her shoulder and pulled her toward me. She smiled.

I leaned in to kiss her on the edge of that smile just as a crowd of Japanese girls came giggling down the hall. One girl squealed, "Ooh! Kissing!" They giggled even more until they noticed Sid's injuries and their expressions turned to worried.

Sid offhandedly said, "Not him, another guy. That's why I'm kissing this one. He's a good one."

I kissed Sid on her cheek. "Good night."

Her eyelashes fluttered. I caught a brief glimpse of her sleepy bedroom smile, "Good night Teddy. I'll see you in the morning."

We got up early and met downstairs for breakfast. Sid was buzzing with excitement. She drank a lot of coffee and get this, after all those months and months of sad, broken despair, she was bouncing. In her seat, on her toes, when she went for another cup, holding her day pack, asking if it was time to go yet. I laughed, "The first tour is at 9:00, the walk to the palace is about twenty minutes, it's 7:55."

She said, "I hear you saying this Teddy, but all my brain keeps saying is, don't be late, don't be late, don't be late. What if we're late?"

I slung my daypack to my shoulder and we left through the blustering cold to walk down the Royal Mile to the Palace of Holyroodhouse, the home of Mary Queen of Scots. It was a monumental thing, this moment. I knew it and she was feeling it to her core. She was wide-eyed and so excited, but somehow held my hand while we walked, tethering herself to me, in case she lifted off but also to pull me faster as she raced down the road.

We had to wait in the courtyard for thirty-five minutes. When the tour guide approached to begin, our group was small, me and Sid with four other people. Sid introduced herself to everyone and with a smile said, "Before anyone asks or wonders, this guy did not do this to my face." Then she asked how long the tour would be, introduced herself to the tour guide, asked how long he had been working there and what his credentials were. (He was a volunteer, passionate about the history of the palace.) Sid said, "Awesome, thank you, I'm so excited, thank you, carry on." Basically letting everyone on the tour know she was seriously fangirl-nerding over this whole thing.

The tour began and Sid walked separately from me, near the front, by the guide, asking question upon question wrapped up in more questions.

Then this happened:

The tour guide looked to the left and right and seeing the halls clear, invited us into one of the inner chambers.

We followed him inside, and Sid asked, "Is this where she slept? Where she ate?" The guide nodded and said to Sid, "Since there aren't that many of you . . ." He unclasped the hook on the barrier rope, "Perhaps you'd like to touch a few things and look around."

Sid asked, "Really? Oh my — really?" She turned to me with a full broad smile. A tear brimmed on her lower lid, but it was a happy tear, had to be, because of that smile. "Teddy, I'm on the carpet, oh my god, I'm touching the mantel. Oh my god."

I chuckled, "I see. Touch the chair — hundred percent she sat there."

"Oh my god."

The tour guide said, "This is the place where David Riccio was murdered, fifty-six stab wounds. He was dragged through here to . . ."

Sid was enraptured. She followed the tour guide asking about details and theories and conspiracies and facts.

I stood to the side, enjoying the show.

SID

To say I was excited would be an understatement. Come to find out, even the bad things, the terrible things that happen to us, that cause us to lose our way, can, if we do our best — wait, better yet, here's a surfing analogy:

Life gives you waves.

I'm a firm believer in taking them and seeing where they go, and sometimes those 'goes' can crash you up on the rocks, but this was me paddling back out, catching the next one and what a ride!

But as Teddy would have said — I could have watched the waves, skipped the ones that would crash me on the rocks. I could have been patient and counted and waited and taken this one, without the injury, and the ride would have been just as good.

But would it have been?

Maybe the crash made this ride even better. And that's not to say the crash was necessary, but maybe I should forgive myself for crashing. And for not being better at everything.

Also, waves, the pattern, the roll, the one right after another, building. It all mattered. It all made sense.

Mom died.

Unexpectedly, terribly, knock the knees out from under my body, blow the top off my life.

But she also interrupted me.

Because maybe that day in Malibu was a mistake, because me and Teddy were just going with the flow, riding the first wave that came along.

Maybe that interruption was important.

Maybe Mom had perfect timing, for her awful death, because of what it brought.

Possibly she sent Gavin, to teach me what it was like to crash.

Because Gavin got me to London.

Gavin brought Teddy to London with a heroic hot awesome urgency.

And then I chose Teddy, completely.

And now me and Teddy were in Scotland, at Holyroodhouse, on a cold day in December, and my tour of the home of Mary Queen of Scots was so sparsely attended that the tour guide let me into the inner rooms.

From there to here. Crash bang roll. Survive. Thrive.

At the end of the tour the guide left us near the gift shop, and I asked Teddy, "Can I go around again?"

He said, "Yes, let's."

He was beautiful when he said yes.

We stopped for lunch at a pub and then walked up the Royal Mile to Edinburgh Castle. We explored for a few minutes with a promise that we would come tomorrow. Because, if you can believe it, the sky was growing dark already.

We walked to the hostel and, freezing, rushed in the front door. 4:00 p.m.

The lobby was empty, but in the lounge almost every seat was full, so I grabbed Teddy's hand and yanked him to a stop. "Wait." I pulled him in by his collar and kissed him, quickly, desperately, his arms went around me. Bundled in coats and hats and scarves, he squeezed me closer. We kissed and kissed, pressed together, with freezing cold noses and bright red cheeks. Until we were interrupted by a large group of rambunctious backpackers walking in the door.

I giggled, my mouth still pressed to his. Then pulled away, "We are definitely keeping it slow."

He smiled, "Except no longer taking it easy."

He led me into the lounge and we found two chairs in the corner. Teddy turned them face to face and he dropped into one and I dropped into the other. I untied my boots and pushed my feet in beside Teddy. He wrapped his arm around my calves.

"So a good day?"

I shook my head, "Nope, second best day. First was two days ago."

He smiled, "I'm glad."

"We should come up with some stuff you want to do too."

"Me? Sure. I want to see where Mary ate breakfast, where she was born, where she —"

I laughed, "No seriously, what do you want to see?"

"Loch Ness, I think I'm the guy to get to the bottom of it all." He grinned.

"I'll add it to the list." His head was cocked to the side, resting on the head rest. Dark brown hair curled and long enough to run my fingers through. His neck strong and —"Teddy, thank you, for today, for it all."

"Of course," He looked down at my leg as his fingers traced the back of my calves. Quiet.

After a few minutes I asked, "What are you thinking about?"

He looked at me for a moment and said, "You. This. How great this is, but —"

"There's a but?"

"I'm also thinking that if we were home we would be waking up together."

I teased, "Oh we would, would we? You're awfully sure of yourself, by my calculations we've been together mere days."

"The first time I held your hand, I was eleven months old, it's been forever, we would definitely be waking up in bed together right now." He grinned. "Have you seen me?"

I said, "Is this cocky attitude how you got all those girls —"

My phone vibrated in my pocket. I plucked it out and looked at the notification. Red climbed up my cheeks.

ONE HUNDRED THIRTY-EIGHT
TEXTS

Hey Sid of the Southbay

I'm so sorry
Just so very sorry
I'll be back in LA January 3
Can we get together to talk?

I miss you

Please

ONE HUNDRED THIRTY-NINE
TEDDY

I could see it in her face. The text was from that guy. She wouldn't look up from her phone she just stared at the screen. I wanted to grab the phone, to see it, to pull him through it and . . .

I sat up and forward, elbows on my knees.

"Can I see?"

She said, "Nah."

I said, "Yeah, that's probably best. Can you give me the safe version?"

"He's apologizing. Also wants to see me in LA in January."

Teddy ran his hands through his hair. "How are you going to respond?"

"Not sure." She stared off into space while I twisted my fingers between my knees.

After a minute she said, "Can you put on your Friend Hat for a minute, to advise?"

"Um . . . I can try."

"So, I don't want him to call me, or text me, or anything, but . . . what do I do?"

"Let me renounce my pacifism and punch him in the face and see how he likes it."

"Very funny, and no."

"Well, that was my Friend Hat talking, with my Boyfriend Hat on I have better advice. I think." He looked down at his hands. "You have to tell him no and tell him you're blocking his number."

She looked down at her phone and typed.

ONE HUNDRED FORTY

SID

I said, "So that's it, blocked. He won't bother me again. So don't worry."

He leaned in the chair. "Okay. I mean, I probably will, but that's not your fault."

"Also, I'm sorry about that."

"I told you you don't have to apologize for him —"

"Not for him, for asking you to put on your Friend Hat, I won't do that again. I like the Boyfriend Hat on you better. Also, your Boyfriend Hat is smarter, that friend advice was not good. Clearly my relationship with you makes you a better person."

He nodded. "Yeah. Probably." He stared out in space and then asked, "Are you hungry for dinner? It's still early, but then we can come here and play board games all night."

We didn't. We ended up going with three British guys and two American girls down the road to a pub for dinner, hanging out at a table, talking for hours, though Teddy was quiet through most of it. He held my hand, but seemed distracted. That text from Gavin must have upset him, more than he would admit, and I couldn't blame him. I still had the bruises across my face.

We walked to the hostel in the freezing cold darkness, arms wrapped around ourselves, breath floating away over our shoulders, hunched, focused on walking fast. This was freezing for two Southern California kids.

Just before the door he grabbed my elbow, slowed me down, and turned me around, "Please don't go in yet." He drew in for a kiss, sweet and soft, but then his kiss gained urgency, pulling me closer through our layers of coats. The only warm places our breaths and our mouths and so we kissed and breathed onto each other's cheeks.

"God Sid," he whispered into my ear.

Then he said, "I don't want to go inside, but it is cold as an Eskimo's left nut out here."

He kissed me again, but a giggle started inside that I couldn't suppress and it burst from my lips. "An Eskimo's left nut?" I giggled some more. "What's up with his left nut, is his right nut warm?"

"I don't know, it's just a saying." His face was close beside my cheek, breath in my ear.

I giggled more bordering on too-much-giggling. "What about pants? Why isn't the Eskimo wearing pants?"

He said, "I don't know — forget I said anything about the Eskimo."

I laughed again, "But now I seriously can't get that image of a left nut out of my head."

Teddy moaned.

I said, "You brought it up not me."

He stood straighter and ran his hand through his hair. "Yeah, I know, and we ought to go inside."

I said, "Oh Teddy, it just struck me as funny." I pulled the lapels of his jacket, but he resisted, "What, Teddy?"

"Let's go inside." He opened the door and we stepped to the wall just inside the empty lobby. We leaned, facing each other.

I rose higher on my toes to kiss him, and he pulled his head away.

"What?" I asked.

He said, "We all have images in our heads that won't leave. I just wanted to kiss you."

I asked, "What do you mean?"

He looked at me, sighed, rolled his eyes, and said, "Nothing, forget I said anything about Eskimos or images." He unzipped his coat.

I said, "Nope, can't, tell me. We're doing that thing where we talk about everything, right? One of the conditions of our relationship."

Teddy looked at me for a minute, brows furrowed, cheeks red. Then, looking at the wall beside my head, said, "When I'm thinking about you, being with you, I have an image in my head, that's . . .." He shook his head and looked down.

I raised his chin with my gloved hand. "Tell me."

"It's you, with your legs wrapped around that guy, at the concert, and you're smiling. It's the first time you were smiling in so long, and his hands were —"

My eyes grew wide with horror, "Oh no, oh. I didn't realize you were . . ." But I had seen him that night, passed him, our eyes had met, and somehow I had just forgotten. "Oh. Is that what you've been thinking about?"

"Yeah, you know, can we forget I said anything? In hindsight that comes off as kind of a dick thing to say." He looked everywhere but at me. "It was cold outside, and we've had a lot of interruptions, and I haven't surfed in like forever, and you know," he cut his eyes at me and said, jokingly, "cold left nuts are kind of damn funny."

I shook my head and said, "They are funny, and someday I would like to sit down and work through the logic problem of where in the hell is one half of that Eskimo's pants, but right now, here, we need to talk about this . . ."

"No, no more talking, we've been talking our whole lives, Sid; we've done that. I mean — you want me, don't you Sid?"

"Yes, I do, I — I am so sorry Teddy. I'm sorry I sent you away after my mom died. I'm sorry that I hooked up with Gavin. I'm so sorry about that night in the club."

"You don't have to say you're sorry."

"You know, you keep saying that, like these are all things that just happened to me, but you're being too nice. My mother dying, that was out of my control. But the way I behaved after, the mean things I said, the way I treated you, those things I did. I regret them. I need to apologize to you for them, I'm sorry, I'm so sorry Teddy. And Gavin was such a big mistake, but it was like I wasn't thinking, I was just going along. Swept away."

Teddy's brow furrowed. "But that's the problem, maybe you aren't swept away by me."

I put my hand on his cheek, "But I am Teddy, I just needed to go slow, to make sure, and I am sure, but now we're booked in this hostel, bunkbeds, and we have all the time in the world, right?"

Teddy nodded. "Yeah, we do."

"I have a surf buddy back home who is always telling me, 'Go slow, be patient, wait for the right time.'"

Teddy gave me a half-smile. "He sounds like a total ass."

I leaned up and kissed him.

He said, "Did I mention that it's been a really long time since I surfed?"

I laughed and said, "Yeah, you mentioned it, and I get the tragedy, Teddy Ayers, not in the ocean." I smiled. "We'll get through this, because we're together now. Me and you."

"Of course, me and you." He kissed me and (terrible timing) I checked my phone for the time, it was past eleven.

He sighed, "We have a tour tomorrow, should we head to bed?"

We kissed and headed up to our separate bunk rooms.

ONE HUNDRED FORTY-ONE
TEDDY

When I walked into the kitchen, she was standing at the counter toasting bread. Her large bandage was gone from her nose, replaced by a small bandaid, instead of a big bandage, her cheek had two small butterfly bandages. Her eyes looked like they were closer to a normal color. When I walked in her face lit up, like she had missed me. "Hi, want toast?"

I strode up, placed a hand on her cheek, and kissed her in front of the toaster and the four other people in the kitchen, because I seriously couldn't help myself. This interrupted, never-alone business was hard. But I had given myself a pep-talk, no more sulking or being depressed, Sid and I were together now. Traveling the UK. We might not have any privacy, but deep breaths and long term thinking would be good.

Up close I said, "Your face looks almost perfect again."

She pointed over her shoulder with her thumb at a girl who smiled and waved, "Trudy loaned me some heavy, heavy duty foundation and concealer. I thought it might be an improvement if I didn't have to explain that you aren't an abuser to every single person we meet."

"I appreciate that, thanks Trudy."

We took our toast and coffee to the dining room and sat at a table full of people talking about what adventures they planned that day. A few were headed to Edinburgh Castle, so I warned them that Sid would hog the tour guide asking question after question.

Sid slugged me on the shoulder. "I'm just making sure they know what they're talking about."

After a few minutes, as the crowd at our table thinned out, she cocked her head to the side and asked, "Are we good, after last night?"

I nodded, "Yeah, we're good. I'm sorry about that. Petulant is not usually my style."

Sid said, "I know. If you're upset, it must be big. And it was, and I'm glad you told me. If I could go back in time and tell Sid-Whose-Mom-Just-Died to do everything differently I would. She needed some serious help."

"I tried to help."

"I know, and I thought I was protecting you from my sadness by sending you away."

"We both could have used good advice, huh?"

"Yeah, it was a terrible time for my mom to die."

"True that."

"But here we are —" Four people sat down beside us at the table, talking and laughing and being loud, and Sid finished, "alone together." And we both laughed.

A large group of us went to the castle and they all got to see Sid in action, asking questions, jotting things in her journal. I teased her a little, but not seriously, she was bouncing and so happy. I couldn't take my eyes off her.

After the castle, Sid and I ate a late lunch at a pub right outside the castle gates, and then we went to the Tartan Weaving Mill and watched the looms. So that was cool. After we had seen everything, we stood looking out the doors — almost a whole day had passed. I said, "It's almost dark and it's freezing. This climate is insane."

Sid said, "I know, it's like the weather is saying, 'Stay in bed, stay in your pajamas.'"

I laughed, "It is. And that was my whole point yesterday. We should be in bed together. When we return to LA, the weather will demand we get up and go surfing." I threw my arm around her and she kissed me on the side of my neck and we left the museum to hustle to the hostel, blowing frosty breaths and laughing.

ONE HUNDRED FORTY-TWO

SID

We walked into the lobby and stood shoulder to shoulder facing the doorway to the lounge. It was warm in there, a giant painted rainbow arched over the back wall. It was inviting, but also crowded. We stood there just looking at it, but not moving toward it. Teddy said, "Maybe we could just stand here and kiss for a moment."

"In the lobby again?"

"Yeah," he reached for my gloved hand and pulled me toward the corner, backed me up to the wall, and kissed me. We kissed for a long time. Then his lips left my mouth and travelled up my cheek to my ear, where he asked, all breathy, "Remind me again, why we're going slow?"

He kissed down my neck and somehow I said, "I think it had something to do with being scared, but who can remember . . ."

He pulled his lips away, a teasing centimeter apart, looking into my eyes, and whispered, "Scared of me?"

"Never."

He paused for a second and then trailed kisses down my cheek to my ear and asked, "Scared of blowing apart our relationship? Because you've blown everything apart and guess what, I'm still here."

I said, "Now that you're putting it like this I can't remember what any of the reasons were."

"I feel the same way." He kissed along my forehead, my eyelids.

My arms went up around his head, he pulled me close, pressing against me. "Scared that this is so important? It is by the way, big deep important. You're not usually one to sit and wait it out."

A group of giggling tourists walked by and one said, "Get a room."

I giggled.

He kissed to my ear and whispered, "That stranger has a great idea, I say, let's get a room."

My lips to his ear, I said, "Yes."

He stilled, and looked at me from the side, "Yes?"

"Yes."

"Awesome." He pulled away.

I straightened, grabbed my bag up from the ground, and walked directly for the counter, Teddy following.

There was a young woman sitting there scrolling through her phone. I hadn't noticed her, half-hidden behind brochures and posters and fliers and informational boards. She said, "Let me guess, private room?"

I said, "Yes, um, you have them?"

She said, "We have them, but you don't want one — twin bunks." She grinned. She grabbed a piece of paper to the side and shoved it across the counter. What you want is a room here. That's where we send everyone in your particular predicament. Though I must say, yours might be more particular than most." She raised her eyebrows with a laugh.

The paper read:

The Stuart Bed and Breakfast

It had a phone number and a hand drawn map.

"Tell Mary the hostel sent you, she'll give you a deal. No refunds here though."

I was already dialing my phone.

A woman answered with a deep Scottish accent, like seriously, deep Scottish.

I said, "Hello, I'm calling from the High Street Hostel, I need a room tonight."

The voice said, "Good! (Unintelligible something something) double, but (something unintelligible) sixty."

I made a confused face at Teddy.

I said, "Okay, we can come now?"

The voice said, "Yes (unintelligible something) lassie, hostel (unintelligible) toodly-oo."

I said, "Okay we'll see you in a few minutes."

I hung up. "How fast can you pack?"

"Fast."

ONE HUNDRED FORTY-THREE
TEDDY

It was dark outside. Too cold to be out on the streets, but here we were, Sid and me, packs on our backs, leaving our warm hostel for another place. Together.

She had surprised me with her yes. Not because I didn't think she would want to, eventually, but mostly because I had surprised myself by asking. We had talked this all out. I was going to be patient. We would wait, take our time.

But here we were, the next day, deciding to go to the next level, because we had started kissing and didn't want to stop.

It was a lot like Sid had been swept away.

ONE HUNDRED FORTY-FOUR
SID

That had been amazing. All the logic and reason and excuses I had been making were gone, and this — me and Teddy, racing through the cold dark streets of Edinburgh was really happening. I was two steps ahead, and I reached for his hand and said, "Come on Teddy, faster."

His grin was wide.

ONE HUNDRED FORTY-FIVE
TEDDY

Mary, a short, plump woman with a gray helmet of hair and thick eyeglasses, met us at the front door of the B and B, took a look at Sid, and immediately rushed me with a dish towel, whipping it at my shoulders, yelling, "You're a scoundrel (unintelligible) scamp (something) no good (unintelligible) ninnyswallop!"

I ducked and tried to block her swinging linen.

Sid yelled, "He didn't do it. He didn't hit me. He wouldn't."

The woman slowed down. "(Something something) scallywag (unintelligible)."

Sid said, "It was a boy from London. This is my American friend, here to help me forget the scoundrel in London."

Mary scowled. "Bah, London, all hooligans." She shook her head, then smiled, her face brightening, and put her hands on the side of my shoulders, "(Undecipherable) — the Prince!" She kissed me on the cheek and then she kissed Sid on the cheek and put her arm around Sid and led her to her dining room table to take our information and payment for the room. We figured all this out by watching her body language and lots of guessing. Because she talked fast, thick, and with so much slang that we only understood every fourth word.

After about fifteen minutes she led us up to the room, pointed out the bathroom in the hallway, and then opened our room door, entered, showed us the spring on the mattress, and how to open the drawers. At the end she said a whole thing about something and left, so I threw my arms around Sid and leaned in for a kiss, but Mary reentered without knocking, and said something like, "Common you, find waste want with yourselves." She looked directly at me and gestured to come with her.

I sheepishly followed down the stairs to the kitchen where she handed me a teapot with involved instructions I understood none of and a plate with a dozen chocolate chip cookies on it. They were warm from the oven. She said, "(Something, something,)" and gestured that we were through with the tour.

I climbed the stairs, lost for a few minutes, because in all of that I had been distracted by Sid and did not remember where my room was.

ONE HUNDRED FORTY-SIX

SID

Teddy walked in with a flourish, "I have come with trophies, a teapot with questionable instructions and cookies!"

"Yum!"

I reached for one, but Teddy pulled the plate away, "I know they look all warm and delicious, but I swear I can't watch you eat one without real trauma." He dropped the plate to the dresser and scooped up my whole shirt, sweater, and undershirt and pulled them off over my head.

He grinned. "This is why people live where it's this cold, so when they take off all these layers it's like Pow! Wow! This is why we should move here." He unzipped his coat, slid it off his arms, and then yanked his shirt off over his head. By this time I had started shivering.

He said, "I did not think this through. It's freezing in here." He wrapped me in his arms and pulled me close.

I said, "Under the covers quick," and dove for the bed.

As Teddy climbed in underneath the bottom of the down comforter, he said, "Oh my god, Sid, are you feeling this, it's like a cloud. Wow." It was spread over two blankets and crisp sheets. We spent some time, giggling a lot, trying to keep our top halves under the covers while we untied boots, kicked them off, and yanked off our socks, and undressed.

Then Teddy crawled out from under the covers and kissed me and we made love, under a cloud, at the end of a crash, in the height of our friendship, in a bed-and-breakfast named after Mary Queen of Scots's family, in Scotland.

When we were done, Teddy lying on my whole body, my legs sprawled, my arms flung above my head, he rose up on his elbows and kissed me slowly.

I looked up and deep into his eyes and said, "That was amazing, I don't know if it's because I love you so much or —"

He stilled and his eyes grew wide. "What?"

I said, "That was amazing."

He said, "I heard that, and it was, but you just said you love me."

"I'm sure I've said it before?"

"I would know, I've been waiting."

His thumbs were on my temples. He raised his brows. "Sid loves me?"

I nodded solemnly.

"You're sweaty and your eyes are, God, your eyes, and you have your bedroom smile, and you said you loved me. Say it again."

"I love you so much."

"Now it sounds too scripted, like I made you. Wait," He kissed me on the lips and down my cheek to my ear and back to my lips and looked at me and said, "Now."

I said, "I love you Teddy Ayers."

His head dropped to my pillow. "I love you too Sid Dalton. When did you know?"

I raised my head a little to see his face. "When did you know?"

"I knew when you were twelve and you said, 'Teddy I've been reading a book about Mary Queen of Scots and I said to myself, 'This is the nerd I'll spend my whole life loving.'"

I pretended to push him, "You did not."

"If that wasn't what I said exactly, it was something like that. What about you, just now, when you saw my awesome sex moves?"

He had a curl loose on his forehead. I brushed it back and said, "I think when we went surfing, the day after Thanksgiving."

"It was my amazing surf moves? Man Sid, this just gets better and better."

I laughed. "It was more the way you stood there in your wetsuit, looking out over the waves, like you can't take your eyes off of them, every minute. You're so committed. So true to your nature. So real. I fell in love with you a bit, and then over and over a bit here and there until I was so deep I can barely breathe thinking about you."

He looked down at me and blinked and said, "Whoa, for saying it like that you get a cookie."

He crawled under the cloud and out, gingerly stepped to the cold floor, and hustled to the dresser, grabbed two cookies and ran back and dove in. He handed one to me, laying on his side, eating a cookie, his head resting on his hand. He chewed and watched me chew and then he smiled, a big smile, ear to ear.

"What?"

"That was before you came to London."

"True. I started to love you before I came to London."

"I knew it, I one hundred percent knew I should come. I packed my bags, jumped on a plane, I just knew it." He pulled the covers over his head and burrowed down under the covers, and said, "I'm going to eat mine on your tummy, where we first kissed."

I giggled and ate another bite of cookie.

His muffled voice said, "Crap, now there are crumbs everywhere. I didn't think this through either." His head emerged from the covers and he smiled. "But you have to admit, cookies in bed are epic."

"I completely agree."

He crawled up and sprawled beside me, offering his arm for me to curl under, and so I did, happily — in a pile of crumbs, under a cloud, after saying I love you, truly, the big kind, the kind that changes everything.

A few minutes later he said, "I don't want to move, it's too cold to leave the cloud, and the crumbs are um, crumby, but I want another cookie."

I giggled, "Me too, I'll jump this time, it's only fair." I scampered across the room while Teddy grinned, holding the covers up for me to return to.

Finally, after the plate of cookies and some hot chocolate we convinced Mary to make for us around 8:00 p.m., after she said something that sounded like, "No, the kitchen is closed," but then she made two mugs anyway, we fell asleep wrapped in each other's arms.

In the morning, I lay wakeful, watching, as Teddy still slept, on his side, broad shoulders vertical, cheek pressed into his pillow. I checked to see if my hand fit inside his hand, it did. Then I checked to see if I could kiss his knuckles without waking him, I could. Finally I needed to get up — needed to pee, had to have food — faster than this. I dropped a foot to the floor and Teddy rustled. I stilled to see if he would go back to sleep, and he did, so I climbed out of bed, gathered my clothes from my pack, and then looked up. He was watching me.

"You're up? Any chance you'll come back to bed?"

I grinned, "We have sights to see, plus, there are entirely too many crumbs in that bed, what kind of establishment is this?"

"Sub par, but I definitely want to stay here tonight." Teddy grinned, his cheek resting on his arm, bicep showing.

I said, "That goes without saying," then I had to look away to keep from climbing into bed and kissing him right there, bicep, then cheek, and then — "I'm going to shower. I'll meet you downstairs."

ONE HUNDRED FORTY-SEVEN
TEDDY

The breakfast room was full. There were other tables, with other couples, also a family, about twelve people in all. I had kind of forgotten that this place had other guests, our treatment had seemed so special, so entirely for us alone, like we were the best guests of Mary's B and B.

Mary was sitting across from Sid. They were holding hands, speaking intently, smiling at each other. Mary jumped from her chair, bellowed, "Scottish breakfast (Incomprehensible something) pronto," and gestured for me to sit.

I did. Sid looked beautiful, hair pulled up in a wet bun, cheeks pink, just showered, glowing. She had two butterfly bandages on her cheek, and one small bandaid across her nose. Under her eye was tinged blue but hidden with makeup again. She looked injured, not beaten. I hoped between her fading injuries and my adoring gaze maybe less people would be judgmental today.

A second later Mary delivered plates piled high with toast and eggs and ham and beans in front of us both.

I devoured one big bite after another. The ham was delicious and necessary — cookies and hot chocolate were not the best diet for the past fourteen hours. I smiled to myself and Sid asked, "What?"

"Nothing, just famished."

"Me too. Marathon hungry." She spooned egg to her mouth.

"So what were you and Mary talking about?"

"I was telling her about my screenplay, and how this is research, and she was telling me she was thrilled that her B and B was a part of it, and that I could come write here anytime." Sid spread marmalade on her toast and added, "Unless she said something else, I don't know." She grinned. "I realize now I'm writing for an American audience, because apparently English and Scottish aren't even the same language."

"Whenever I think I have it figured out, she adds the next word, and I realize she's talking about something totally different."

I shoved a few more bites into my mouth watching Sid. I was building my strength and courage because I was building up to a big question. I was so in love with her I didn't want this to end. Not only the big things, but the little things too — the eating breakfast together, the planning our day, the strapping-our-boards-onto-the-roof-of-the-car together moments, the day-to-day Sid, the bouncing, riding in the car to go surfing Sid — I wanted to ask if that was something I could have all the time. Please.

Maybe it was too soon though, too big a question.

I had already rushed headlong into this, impatiently asking for it. I didn't want to push her more. Scare her away.

Maybe, probably, I needed to go slow. Count the waves, but one thing Sid taught me — slow sucked. If I loved her my whole life wasn't that seriously slow enough?

I chewed a piece of ham as she ate her toast, from the diagonal cut towards the corner of the crust, marmalade messily smeared on her cheeks.

She licked her tongue around her mouth trying to get the mess off. "Marmalade, it's no Nutella. Not usually a fan, but here in Scotland I kinda like it."

I nodded, not hearing what she said. "So, speaking of your screenplay, I was thinking — I mean, I know we have a lot to talk about, our future. I know you want to go slow, and that I went against it by asking if we could get a room, and thank you for agreeing by the way."

Sid squinted her eyes as I meandered around my point. I continued, "So I feel bad asking for more, but I want you to reconsider and go with me to Santa Barbara. I have plenty of room in my apartment, you'd like my roommate, we could go surfing every day, if I don't have class, and you could write. There's a breakfast nook in the kitchen that you . . ." I trailed off, not only had she paused, but she wasn't chewing, just watching me talk.

Then she nodded. "Of course." She smeared marmalade on another triangle of bread.

"Of course — you will? Really?"

"Yes, Teddy. I wondered if you still wanted me to — if you want me to come, I'll come, definitely. But I'll need to go home a lot of weekends, for Dad."

I leaned back in my chair. "Absolutely."

"But also, I'll learn to drive when I get home, so if I need to go home to LA and you can't drive me then it won't be that big a deal." She took another big bite of toast, grinned cheekily, and said, "How into me are you now, scale of —"

I said, "Ten."

ONE HUNDRED FORTY-EIGHT

MARY

Mary embroidered her motto, En ma Fin gît mon Commencement, on her cloths of estate. It translated as, In my end is my beginning, a belief in existence beyond her earthly life, a deeply religious, heaven-bound sort of longing.

But perhaps the phrase applies to an earth-remaining sort of hope. Because to crash, to fall, to succumb to deep despair — that could be the end of us, but to survive the crash, to clamor out, to continue and begin anew — that's the ultimate act of hope.

It saddened me, Mary's story. What happened in her life was so devoid of hope — the loss, the heartache, the tragedy of it all, the Never Able To Begin Again. Even though she loved and married and gave birth and battled, continuing on was never a possibility, because the end was going to happen — to be executed. There was no stopping it. No living through. How tragic, how epically wasteful.

But me. I could stop it. Live through. Love.

To fall in love, despite all that had happened, was supremely hopeful.

The kind of hope that would have made my mother proud.

ONE HUNDRED FORTY-NINE

MARY SCREENPLAY. INT. SHOT. B AND B

Teddy leans back in his chair, legs splayed, watchful expression.

Sid leans both elbows on the table, attentive, smiling.

Table spread with food, mismatched china, tableware and coffee cups.

They look into each other's eyes.

Teddy: I love you, Sid.

Sid: I love you too, big love, Teddy, the biggest.

Teddy: So today we go to Linlithgow?

Sid: Yep, the birthplace of Mary. Isn't it funny we started at her coffin, in Westminster Abbey, then the palace where she lived, now the castle where she was born.

Teddy: We like to start at the end and work to the beginning, and this is a good one I think.

Sid raised her coffee cup: The best beginning of my life.

Teddy smiled: Me too Sid, me too.

The camera pans away, taking in their table, the wider room, then out the door and over the road, then up above with an aerial shot of the bed-and-breakfast and finally out and away, beyond the Scottish country side.

The animation of the embroidery begins, Mary's motto: In my end is my beginning, stitching away and off the screen.

345

ONE HUNDRED FIFTY

SID

My mom wanted the best for me. Always. From the moment I was born she fretted over my world, the temperature, the breastmilk, my learning, our environment, my god damned baby pimples, which were terrible. Dad said. Mom never mentioned it.

Because that was the way she was, wanting for me perfection. Her pursuit of perfection came at a cost though, in her robustness, her stamina. She had those tears behind her eyes and though she blinked and smiled and hoped, those tears got her in the end. Like the Ache always does.

But now I knew it wasn't the everyday sadness, the inevitable dramas that killed her, the present people and places and loves, but the past. The tears that built up, that she didn't let go of, that she loved me in spite of.

That spite, that was what did it. Even when I didn't see it, or even know it was there.

I was protected from it. But when that death crashed into her, it crashed into me, and there I was, crashed.

But Mom's perfection, her pursuit, gave me a resiliency, I suppose.

The ability to see the better.

To expect the best, without the 'in spite of.'

That was her gift to me.

Not making the world always perfect, but making me able to crash and live on. And be better.

And to know I deserved it.

The better.

My mom's tragedy, that she gave up on her life and mine, still threatened, sometimes, to drop me to my knees.

But not always. Not anymore.

I was ready when the wave came. I pulled my board underneath me and stroked. I stroked hard, and the next wave was what I hoped it would be: epic.

AFTERWORD

Thank you for reading Sid and Teddy. Please take a moment to sign up for my newsletter. Maybe I'm working on a sequel to a book you love, and you'll want to know. Perhaps you just want a free book occasionally. Better yet, you'd like to know what's next. I'm thinking dragons. But in a friendly way.

I have some other books you might enjoy. There's a fairytale retelling that's dramatic and exciting and sort of funny and very romantic. If you loved Teddy you'll totally fall for Hank:

Fly: The Light Princess Retold

I also wrote a dystopian trilogy (the first book is free so what are you waiting for?) and again, if you loved Teddy, you're going to love William. And Estelle is awesome.

Bright (Book one of The Estelle Series)
Beyond (Book Two of The Estelle Series)
Belief (Book Three of The Estelle Series)

And if you sign up for my newsletter:

hdknightley.com

I give away a lot of free books to my friends.

Thank you,
H.D. Knightley

ACKNOWLEDGMENTS

This story is a work of fiction. Any characters within these pages are completely made up. They might share names, traits, or circumstances with people that I know in real life, but it is not them. I promise.

I did lose my mom. My experiences in the hospital were much like the ones I wrote about here. I was aged 43 through, she was 63, so really it wasn't the same at all. The reason for Sid's mom's death, the loss and sadness and the Ache, that's all made up. The family stuff, the abuse, the love of Oasis, the being a little punk rock — all invented.

Some of the events and places in Los Angeles are my favorite things. Becker's Bakery has the best cakes. Wahoo's Fish Tacos is a fabulous place to eat. El Porto is a great place to surf. And the Independent Shakespeare Company is the best Shakespeare. If you're ever in LA in the summer you should go do all four. Definitely.

I never had a boy punch me. But I saw a boy punch a girl one time and she went back to him and if you're reading this and it has happened to you, please ask for help. You deserve better. You can do better. Live through to the other side and then love again.

To Paige Herring, you left us too young. I didn't know you well as a mom, but you were my best friend growing up, and I wish you could have found the hope to continue on. Life is hard and alcohol sucks for taking you too young.

The Moms, Alicia and Lori, are based on a wide variety of women I have known in my life. Starting with my own mom who I miss every day.

Thank you to Michelle Dupree, the first friend I met as a mother. Once, in the backseat of her car, her baby, Will, held hands with my baby, Isobel. Comforting her while she cried. It was literally the cutest thing we ever saw. And for the first time, not the last, I thought, what if my kid grew up to marry your kid, wouldn't that be awesome? Thank you for being my first mom crush.

Thank you to Maggie Baird for Friday Project Day, our time in your backyard, making crafts, watching our kids play, inspired much of this book. Your desire to make everything great, for your kids and mine, was an inspiration.

Thank you to Mara Donahoe, for being the kind of Mom-friend that dared to dream with me about making alliances and marrying our children together (but only if they wanted to.) For coming to Ean's birth and also for being his godmother. And for feeding my family on camping trips. We would have starved, that part is true. You have always put the best in bestie, even when we don't see each other enough.

Also thank you to Brenna Johnson, we shared a lot of hopes and dreams for a few months there, and it didn't work out, but I think the best parts of our friendship remain. (And maybe our friendship was the whole entire point.)

There are a lot of other moms to thank, and I can't thank them all by name, but if you ever sat on my picnic blanket and talked with me about hopes and dreams for our kids, then this book was written with you in mind. I adore you all. Thank you for being at the park, on the beach, in my life.

And thank you to all the homeschooled teens that I have watched grow up, you lived lives full of wonder and exuberance, even though the Moms were watching. Good on you. I hope your future selves remain awesome.

Thank you to Kevin Dowdee for reading and editing the surf scenes so that I don't sound like a kook and also for giving me the space and time to write. I love you.

And thank you to my kids, Isobel, Fiona, Gwynnie, and Ean, it's true that I dream; hopefully you remain forgiving of me when my dreams get too big. It's a mom thing. You'll understand someday.

And to my dad, who is creative, loving, philosophical, poetical, and humorous. I think my writing style owes an awful lot to you. Maybe it's listening to all those A Frog walks into a Bar jokes.

And to Anna Smith, for taking the photo that inspired this whole thing, thank you.

MY BETA-READERS ROCK!

I wrote this book in July of 2016 in a little over a month. Then I wrote more and tweaked and edited and then I kind of stopped and took my time and then I got too nervous about sharing it. So my beta-readers had to really hold my hand and make their suggestions sound sweet and kind or else I would spin out into despair and worry. They managed to give me notes and keep me from freaking out and helped me turn it into a really good book.

Thank you to Isobel Dowdee for the pages and pages (and pages) of notes. You were right about (almost) everything. I don't know how you got so good at this, but I'm grateful for it.

Thank you to Kristen Schoenmann De Haan for being the first (not in my family) reader and beginning her notes with, "I think this may be your best yet!" And other notes and praises and kindnesses that made finishing the book that much easier.

Thank you to Jessica Fox for your advice and notes and for saying, "Sometimes I would laugh, sometimes I would get mad, and sometimes I came close to crying. It was very enlightening to see the changes and feel a long with them." You made me think, "Maybe it really will be all right."

Thank you to Amie Conrad for finding so many mistakes and missteps and still saying, "You're amazing at channeling boy super heroes, and fragile, yet strong young women. Well done!" I appreciate the kind words.

ABOUT THE AUTHOR

H.D.Knightley lives in Los Angeles. She's the mother of four children and is married to the surfer boy she fell in love with when she was a teenager.

She likes writing stories about people faced with huge issues — light-polluted skies, droughts, piles of hoarded things, encroaching water, abuse — that rise above and carry on anyway. These are insurmountable difficulties, yet her protagonists choose hope and love instead of despair.

Her heroes include, Estelle (The Estelle Series), who becomes a celebrity dissident for starting a farm; the Princess Amelia (Fly: The Light Princess Retold) who discovers gravity and rescues her kingdom from a drought; Edmund who scales heights to rescue Violet (Violet's Mountain); the paddleboarder Luna (the Leveling Series) who finds love, shelter, and possible disaster, at the edge of a rising ocean; and Sid and Teddy who find each other through a fog of grief.

H.D. Knightley can be found writing in parks and on beaches throughout Los Angeles and can be found online at one of these cool and interesting sites:

HDKnightley.com
Twitter.com/hdknightley
Facebook.com/hdknightley
Pinterest: HD Knightley
Goodreads: H.D. Knightley